THE PROFESSOR MURDERS

by

Sheila & Ron Stewart

THE PROFESSOR MURDERS

Published by
Acadia Scale Press

For Craig & Steven

ONE

Prosecuting Attorney, Lorraine Brensley was not particularly interested in the students that were exiting the College of Science building at Westland University. Her attention was focused on the man who appeared to be propositioning them. Lorraine was sure she had seen him somewhere, although she couldn't remember when. Probably one of the cases she had been involved in, she decided.

A short distance away, Private Investigator, Jennifer Brookbaine watched both Lorraine and the activity in front of the building. Her attention was also focused on the man. Since Jennifer had encountered him before and was afraid he might recognize her, she had asked Lorraine to help her keep an eye on him.

Jennifer had seen him earlier that day at the university during an investigation at the College of

Science. A laboratory had been broken into, and although nothing appeared to be missing, she had been asked to investigate. The man had been standing outside the main entrance when she arrived and was still there two hours later when she left. She had attempted to approach him to ask if he was familiar with the campus and the science department, but he quickly walked away.

The next time Jennifer saw him was later that evening as she and Lorraine left a seminar they had attended at a nearby college. He was still watching the science building, although his attention appeared to be as much on the female night school students and women faculty members who were leaving their classes.

"Maybe just a pervert looking for a date," Jennifer remarked to Lorraine, but she asked if they could watch him for a while anyway to discover what he might be up to, and to find out what his interest might be in the College of Science.

After several minutes of not being able to get what he wanted, or perhaps just losing interest, the man turned away and glanced around the campus in search of other action. Apparently seeing nothing that interested him, he crossed a narrow patch of grass and sauntered past the park bench where Lorraine fidgeted in a futile attempt to remain inconspicuous.

A look of puzzlement suddenly crossed his face and he came to a stop. He turned slowly and stared inquisitively at the neatly attired woman in the yellow dress who occupied the bench. He looked around at the other more casually attired students as if to draw some kind of comparison, then returned his attention to Lorraine. After studying her a few more seconds, he approached.

"Come here often?" he inquired, sitting on the bench beside her. "Do I know you?" he added, a touch of puzzlement in his voice.

"No, I don't think so," Lorraine answered. She stared back at him, trying to decide where she had seen him before. Unable to identify him, she looked around to see if Jennifer was nearby. She wasn't anywhere in sight.

"Huh," he grunted. He fidgeted, as if working up the courage to take another step in their conversation, then hesitantly slid across the bench. His knee stopped close to Lorraine's and he looked into her eyes for the invitation he was sure was coming. Seeing none, he nonchalantly lifted his arm and let it come to rest on the bench behind her head. "Where have you been all my life?" he asked.

Lorraine grimaced at the age old line. She glanced up and down the sidewalk, hoping to see Jennifer. Getting no help there, she decided to try to ignore the man and moved away.

He licked his lips, wiped the moisture away with his fingers, and shuffled after her. This time his knee touched hers and his hand brushed her thigh.

"Maybe you and me, you know, we could go some place and share an intimate moment or something," he suggested.

Lorraine scowled at him. Without speaking, she grabbed his wrist, hoisted his hand from her leg, swung it around in front of him, and half dropped and half flung it into his lap. She moved away once more, but he continued the pursuit until she came to a stop at the end of the bench. There, she put up a hand to warn him he had gone far enough.

"Unless you want to spend the night in jail, I would suggest you keep your hands to yourself," she ordered.

There were varying interpretations of exactly what took place after that.

Lorraine said she was about to inform the man that she was a prosecuting attorney for the City of Westland, when the fight started.

The man testified that he thought Lorraine was a lady of the evening who was looking for customers, had solicited his encouragement, and appeared to be offering her services.

Jennifer contradicted his statement, insisting that Lorraine didn't look *all that much* like a lady of the evening, and described him as a degenerate pervert who deserved everything that eventually happened to him.

Other onlookers had varying opinions regarding what happened. Fortunately, most of them agreed with Jennifer.

The man's expression suddenly changed as he exhaled with a contemptuous snort. He no longer had the stupid grin of an ungraceful pervert trying to make a clumsy attempt at a pass, but the determined look of an individual who was sure he could get his own way. He wrapped one hand tightly around Lorraine's shoulder, grabbed her with his other hand, and pulled her against him.

Lorraine's hand, which a moment earlier had been held as a warning for him not to go any farther, was now pushed firmly against his nose as she tried to shove him away. Her other hand gripped his wrist in a futile attempt to escape. The toe of one shoe was making intermittent contact with his shins.

Jennifer, who had been watching the scene with some amusement until she realized Lorraine was in a predicament she might not be able to get out of, ran toward them. She clutched the man by an arm and attempted to pull him away.

He grabbed Jennifer by the front of her dress. "This is none of your business," he growled as he flung her across the small expanse of lawn and returned his attention to Lorraine.

"Do something!" Lorraine yelled frantically after her. "Anything!"

Jennifer was about to reach for him again, then deciding it would just earn her another trip across the lawn, reconsidered and instead drove her fist as hard as she could into his jaw.

This time the man tumbled off the bench, pulling Lorraine with him, kicking and struggling to break free. He cursed in anger, threw her aside and scrambled to his feet. "You'll pay for that," he snarled at Jennifer as he charged after her.

"I don't think so," Jennifer snarled back. She grabbed the straps of her handbag and swung it in small deliberate circles like a member of a street gang would threaten an enemy with a knife.

The man guffawed at the ridiculous sight and continued to advance, but before he could reach her, Lorraine scrambled to her feet. She grabbed the shoulder of his jacket, pulled him around, and drove her fist as hard as she could into the side of his face.

His head jolted sideways from the impact and his eyes opened wide in surprise. He hesitated for an instant, shook his head rapidly from side to side to clear away the confusion, then turned and lunged toward her.

Lorraine backed away until her legs hit the edge of the park bench and doubled under her. She came to an undignified halt as she abruptly sat down.

The man stood menacingly over her, his face twisted into a scarlet sneering rage and his hands extended into frozen vice-like claws. He was about to grab her when Jennifer swung her handbag as hard as she could.

The purse connected with a mixture of leather and metal and bone coming together as his head snapped to the side and his hair stood on end from the impact. He seemed to hang in the air, then his eyes rolled up in their sockets, his chin fell to his chest, his legs buckled under him, and he slumped to the ground.

The two women stared at Jennifer's handbag in astonishment, then turned their attention to the unconscious man on the ground before them. When he didn't move, Jennifer cautiously leaned over and opened his coat to see if he was carrying any identification.

She hesitated for an instant when she uncovered the handle of a thirty-eight revolver that was protruding from a leather holster attached to his belt. She hesitated once again when she saw another glint of metal attached to his belt on the opposite side. Then, as though she had to complete the remainder of an unpleasant task, she folded both sides of the jacket away from his body. Her face grimaced as she stared at the possessions on the limp figure.

Her eyes opened wide and her mouth dropped open as she murmured, "Uh, oh . . . ."

Lorraine closed her eyes for an instant as if hoping the metal would disappear. It didn't. As she stared at the shiny detective's badge that Jennifer had just uncovered, she remembered where she had seen the man before.

"Uh, oh is right," she exclaimed.

They had beaten up a cop.

TWO

Jennifer tapped a finger lightly on her cheek in time to the distant music that was filtering into their jail cell through the police station wall. She smiled as she watched Lorraine pace impatiently back and forth in front of the bars.

This wasn't the first time Jennifer had found herself in trouble with the law, and it wasn't the first time she had found herself locked in a jail cell. As a private investigator, she sometimes went places where regular police officers couldn't go, and she occasionally paid the consequences.

But Lorraine had never been in jail. She was a lawyer, and lawyers didn't go to jail, at least that's what she kept mumbling over and over on the way to the police station.

"In my whole life, I never managed to beat anybody

up," she complained to the empty space in the next cell. "Not in my whole life. And now when I do finally beat somebody up, he has to be a cop. A cop of all people."

"I can't help but wonder if perhaps we might have gone just a little too far," Jennifer offered.

Lorraine stared incredulously at her friend. "A little too far! You call what we did to him, a little too far!"

"He was a dirty rotten low life degenerate pervert who got what he deserved," Jennifer declared.

"But he was a cop," Lorraine lamented. "We beat up a cop. And then we knocked him unconscious and probably gave him a concussion. And I don't care what he is. Look where we are." Her hands swept in a gesture around the cell to remind herself and Jennifer where they were.

Jennifer raised a finger for permission to speak, but before she could, Lorraine continued. "The police department doesn't like it when one of their officers gets beat up and knocked unconscious with a concussion." After a partially agreeable nod and a shrug of the shoulders from Jennifer, she turned away and continued to complain to the empty cell next to them.

"They haven't determined yet that he has a concussion," Jennifer said. "As far as they know, we just beat him up and knocked him out. And how was I supposed to know he was a cop? If the son of a bitch had been a mugger, you would have thanked me for hitting him."

Until her brief discussion with Jennifer, Lorraine had not spoken to anybody, except herself and the adjoining cell since they had been placed in the cell block. She stopped pacing for a moment, ceased her mostly one sided conversation, and squinted her eyes squarely at her best friend.

"If the son of a bitch had been a mugger, he'd be in here instead of me," she exclaimed. "This is a hell of a place for a prosecuting attorney to find herself. I'm supposed to be a servant of the court, a person who is presumed to uphold law and order, not obliterate it by beating up police officers."

Her finger shook accusingly at Jennifer. "And you, you should know that private investigators can't go around hitting people with their guns, and get away with it."

"I did not hit him with my gun," Jennifer proclaimed. "I hit him with my purse." She smiled crookedly. "My gun just happened to be in my purse. Anyway, you didn't have to help me. I was doing all right all by myself."

Lorraine stared at her in disbelief. "What do you mean, I didn't have to help you? You left me alone on a park bench and let a strange man crawl all over me while you hid in the bushes. Then you might have annoyed him just a little when you hit him with your purse, which according to you, just happened to have your gun in it. He would have killed you if I hadn't distracted him."

"That was some distraction," Jennifer said. "You practically laid him out with one punch. By the way, how's your fist?"

Lorraine curled her fingers and rubbed the knuckles with her other hand as she examined her fist for bruises. "It's sore."

"Why do you think he was hanging around the College of Science?" Jennifer asked, attempting to change the subject.

"Night school?" Lorraine answered facetiously.

"He wasn't going to night school. He was watching the science building, at least when he wasn't watching the female students, and you. Do you think he might have had something to do with the break-in at the science laboratory? And why do you think he was trying to pick up nineteen-year-old scantily clad oversexed female college students? Not to say that you look like a nineteen-year-old scantily clad oversexed female college student."

Lorraine turned away and went back to talking to the vacant jail cell next door. "Why oh why do I ever let her get me into these things?" she protested to the emptiness.

Jennifer ignored her friend's discomfort. "Because you enjoy it. Besides, I needed a pigeon to help me find out what that guy was up to."

"A pigeon? A pigeon? Is that what I am? A pigeon?" Lorraine flailed her arms wildly in the air as she spat out the words, like a pigeon desperate to escape.

Jennifer was laughing out loud now. "No, of course not. Well maybe. O.K., you were, but only for this one time. Since I thought he might recognize me, I needed somebody to help me keep an eye on him."

She extended her hand in the direction of Lorraine the way a vaudevillian performer would point to an assistant. "Like a pigeon. When he grabbed you, I thought you were in trouble."

"Well, I wasn't in that much trouble," Lorraine answered.

"Is that why you kept yelling, do something, do something?"

"O.K., I was in trouble, but not so much that we had to practically kill him. He just wanted to know where I'd been all his life."

"I didn't know that."

"He wanted to know if we could go some place and share an intimate moment."

"An intimate moment?"

"That's what he said."

"I didn't think cops were capable of having an intimate moment."

"If they are, it must be brief, because that's all this one had before you hit him."

"It didn't look intimate," Jennifer remarked. "It looked like he was getting ready to mug you, or worse. Anyone with his approach and a line like that must have a hell of a difficult time getting a date."

The scowl that had been engraved on Lorraine's

face since their arrest slowly disappeared and she also began to laugh. "He sure looked surprised when you hit him."

"He sure did. Do you think they believed that story he told when he had us arrested, that he thought we were hookers and he was staking us out? Do we really look like hookers?"

"No," Lorraine exclaimed. "He just said that so they wouldn't know he was trying to pick up women when he was supposed to be working."

She raised her eyebrows at the hint of a plunging neckline on the red dress that Jennifer was wearing. "Well, maybe you do, a little. We should have put you on the park bench."

Jennifer pouted. "I do not look like a hooker!" She glanced down at her clothes. "Do I?"

"No, of course not." Lorraine's expression slowly changed to a crooked smile the way Jennifer's had a moment earlier when she referred to her as a pigeon. She extended her open hands toward her cell mate as though Jennifer were now the vaudevillian assistant.

"Maybe not a hooker. Maybe just a courtesan."

"Gee, thanks. Hey, wait a minute. What's a courtesan?"

"The mistress of a king or nobleman used to be referred to as a courtesan. I heard a lawyer use the expression in court once to describe a client he was defending."

"Really. Who was his client?"

"She was a hooker."

Jennifer screwed up her face. "I think I like courtesan better."

Their conversation was interrupted by a door clanging open at the end of the cell block. A police officer entered and approached their cell.

"A lawyer is here with your bail," he said as he studied the two women through the bars. "He says he's your husband. Which one of you is Lorraine Brensley?"

"I am," Lorraine and Jennifer both replied at once.

The officer raised his eyebrows. He had put the key into the lock, started to turn it, then stopped. "He says he came for two people. He also came for a Jennifer Brookbaine."

Jennifer put an arm around Lorraine and pushed her toward the cell door. "In that case, she is."

The officer swung open the heavy iron door and motioned for them to leave the cell. They followed him along a corridor that led to the main precinct area, and to what they hoped was freedom.

He gazed at them as he held another door open. "You don't look like hookers."

"Thank you," Lorraine replied. "That's because we're not hookers, at least I'm not. I don't know about the madam here."

"In spite of what she might say about me, I'm not a hooker either," Jennifer added. "We thought that cop who had us arrested might be involved in a break-in at Westland University. We didn't know he was on official police business, if that's what you call ogling female night school students and trying to pick up women he doesn't know."

The officer gave a partial nod of understanding. "A lot of people here have mixed feelings about what you did to him, you know. He can be a mean sort, and he's not very popular. He's not very happy right now either. He says you assaulted him with a gun."

Jennifer offered her own version. "I hit him with my purse. Let's see him put that in his report. Besides, he was assaulting my friend here who happens to be a prosecuting attorney."

"Why don't you tell the whole world who I am," Lorraine muttered as she rolled her eyes at the ceiling.

The officer looked at Lorraine as if trying to recognize her. "He says he was questioning her."

"He was trying to pick her up."

"He says he was trying to find out what she was doing there when you hit him with your gun."

"I did not hit him with my gun," Jennifer responded defensively. "I hit him with my handbag. And he wasn't questioning, he was trying to, and I quote, get Lorraine to share an intimate moment with him. Isn't that right Lorraine?"

"That's right."

The officer chuckled. "About the only thing we've ever seen that detective have an intimate moment with is his revolver. You two be careful. I wouldn't be surprised if he tries to get even."

"He already has," Lorraine reminded him as she gestured back toward the cellblock. "Look where we are."

As they approached the front desk, they saw Lorraine's husband, George, talking to the desk sergeant. On the other side of the desk was the police officer they had assaulted at the university. He had a bandage on one side of his head and a black eye that was nearly swollen shut.

"There's your boyfriend," Jennifer said. "He looks a little different now than when you first met him. If it wasn't for the bandage and the black eye, and his personality, and his obnoxious attitude, and the fact that he's a cop, he might be almost acceptable, but only if a woman were extremely desperate."

Jennifer was right in a way. The police officer was fairly tall, appeared to be about thirty-five years old, and except for the bandages on his face, was not bad looking. He had dark wavy hair combed to the side with a deep part, and a wide, almost sinister looking mustache that covered his top lip and curled out over his cheeks.

"We should have known he was a cop," Lorraine replied. "He looks like a cop. I mean he doesn't really look like most cops. He just looks like what we expect a cop to look like."

Whatever the police officer looked like, he did not

appear to be in a very good mood. His bluish lips were drawn tight and pressed firmly against each other. Hard lines etched across his forehead and thick striped veins bulged out on his neck. When he saw the two women, he stiffened in a semi-controlled rage, and his eyes, or at least his one good eye, glared wildly across the room.

The officer who had led them from their cell looked at the injured policeman and then shook his head and shivered. "I'm sure glad I didn't meet you two out there," he said. "You must have hit the poor son of a gun pretty hard."

"Poor son of a gun, my ass," Jennifer exclaimed. "The man is a sex pervert. And what do you mean I hit him? Lorraine gave him the black eye. If anyone deserves credit, she does."

"I know what you're trying to do here," Lorraine complained. "You're trying to have me thrown into jail for twenty years."

"No I'm not," Jennifer replied. "I'm just trying to give credit where credit is due. Besides, they couldn't possibly give us more than five or ten years for a little thing like this."

George Brensley left the front desk and came over to meet them. "Are you all right?" he asked.

"We're fine," Lorraine assured him. "Considering the circumstances." She put her arms around him and held him tightly. "Am I glad to see you."

George nodded toward the policeman who had the

bandage and the black eye. "Did you do that?" he asked in disbelief.

"She did most of it," Lorraine declared, wrinkling her face and pointing a finger at Jennifer. "I was just a pigeon."

"Some pigeon," Jennifer exclaimed. "You should have seen her, George. She gave him the black eye. I gave him the bandage."

"You sure did a number on him," George said. "Everybody's laughing at him. The other officers are saying he was beaten up by two women with a purse. He keeps saying he was hit with a brick and pistol whipped from behind."

"I did not hit him with a brick," Lorraine protested. "I hit him with my fist."

"I believe you," George assured her, "and so does just about everybody else who was standing nearby and witnessed the whole thing. They saw him grab you and they also watched you beat him up. They say he deserved what he got, and they didn't see any bricks or guns either, at least until Jennifer's gun fell out of her purse. Everybody agrees on exactly what happened, except him."

"I did hit him once with my fist," Jennifer agreed, "after he grabbed me and threw me half-way across the university. I wasn't going to wait for him to turn around, but he did anyway. He was coming after me when Lorraine hit him. Then I hit him with my purse." As an afterthought, she added, "Which just happened to have my gun in it. It wasn't until he was unconscious and we went through his pockets that we discovered he was a cop. The man is obnoxious. He's a sex pervert. And he tried to pick up your wife."

"His name is Lieutenant Dickey," Lorraine said. "And we're not absolutely sure yet that he's a sex pervert."

Jennifer looked at her in amazement. "And just what would you call a man who tries to pick up female college students, and then slides from one end of a park bench to the other end and grabs a woman he doesn't know?"

Lorraine thought for a moment. "Maybe a pervert."

"That sleaze," George hissed as he put his arm around Lorraine. "But at least he has good taste. What were you two doing there anyway?"

"Like I said before," Lorraine explained, "I was just a pigeon." She motioned with her thumb toward Jennifer. "At least that's what she calls me. Jennifer thought he might be involved in one of her cases and that he might recognize her, so she asked me if I would watch him while she watched me. Instead, he made a pass at me."

"That's what you get for being so attractive," Jennifer admonished her. "I should have asked George to go with me."

"I wish George had gone with you," Lorraine replied. "Then he could spend an evening in jail and I could be at home reading a book."

"Don't listen to her George," Jennifer continued as she waved her hands for him to ignore Lorraine's protests. "She enjoyed every minute of it. I think she even enjoyed meeting Lieutenant Dickey."

"I thought you were going to a seminar at the university?"

"We did. We were walking past the College of Science afterwards, when we saw Dickey lurking around like he was up to no good. He had been there earlier and I thought he might have had something to do with a break-in at one of the laboratories, so we decided to watch him. We didn't realize he was a cop and that he was on a case, or that he would find your wife so attractive."

The officer who had let them out of the cell block motioned for them to come to the front desk. "I have your belongings," he said as he dumped the contents from two envelopes onto a desk. "And you don't have to worry about being prosecuted. They talked the lieutenant into dropping the assault charges."

Lorraine looked relieved. "I don't know why there were charges in the first place, and I can't say I'm unhappy about them being dropped, but why?"

"I think we're an embarrassment to him," Jennifer said. "He probably doesn't want to listen to us tell a judge that two women beat him up with a purse because we thought he was trying to steal an intimate moment. But what about us? I think at the very least, you should have your day in court."

Lorraine grimaced. "Will you please be quiet, and maybe we can get out of here before someone recognizes me."

"If you are ready, let's go then," George said. He looked at Lorraine. "And I don't want you to get involved in any more investigations with Jennifer, at least for one night."

They finished picking up their belongings and walked away from the desk. They had gone only a few steps when Lieutenant Dickey moved from the other side of the room and blocked their path. His bruised eye was almost closed while his good eye opened wider than normal, like a member of the gestapo preparing to interrogate an enemy.

"I'll be keeping an eye out for you two," he snarled. His gaze stopped at Lorraine for a second. It seemed to soften a little, then he curled up one side of his mouth in a sneer and looked at Jennifer. "You can be sure of that."

Jennifer's one eye closed and the other opened in mockery as she sneered back. "And we'll be looking forward to it. Won't we Lorraine."

"No we won't," Lorraine uttered between clenched teeth and lips that barely moved. She grabbed Jennifer's arm, pulled her away from Dickey, and guided her toward the outside door.

As they neared the doorway, they bumped into George who had stopped to watch an attractive woman pass them going in the opposite direction.

The woman's auburn hair curled around her face and shoulders. Dark eye shadow and liner highlighted her eyes, and rosy red rouge illuminated her cheekbones. Her lips glistened under shimmering red lipstick. She wore a tight blouse that dipped in a deep oval over her breasts. It appeared to be held in place only by two narrow straps that were tied in a bow over her otherwise bare shoulders. Her skirt was just as tight. It hugged her thighs and stopped just above her knees. She wore sheer black stockings and shoes with spiked high heels that stretched her already attractive legs.

"Now that's a hooker," Jennifer remarked.

The woman stopped in the middle of the room and looked around for several seconds as though she were searching for someone. She glanced at Dickey who was still standing where Jennifer and Lorraine had left him. She looked harder at him as though she recognized him, then apparently changing her mind, walked past and approached the main desk.

The desk sergeant looked up from his paperwork. "May I help you?" he asked.

She answered with an English accent. "I want to report a missing person, my husband. His name is Professor Sheridan Winslow. He teaches chemistry at the College of Science at Westland University, and he could be in terrible danger."

THREE

"A professor's wife?" Lorraine whispered to Jennifer in astonishment as she stared at the curvaceous woman standing in front of the desk. "Did she say she was a professor's wife?"

"Professor's courtesan, if you ask me," Jennifer whispered back. "And she did say her husband is a professor at the College of Science."

"Shh," George chided. He held his finger over his lips for them to be quiet. "I think I might know her husband."

Jennifer and Lorraine stopped talking and listened to the conversation between the professor's wife and the desk sergeant.

"What makes you think your husband is missing?" the officer inquired as he prepared to enter the information into his computer.

"He didn't come home from work tonight," she answered.

"Is that unusual?"

"Yes. He always comes home. We've been married for more than twenty years and he's never missed an evening."

The sergeant's eyebrows lifted in amazement and his forehead folded into creases of disbelief. The woman didn't appear old enough to have been married that long. "Twenty years?" he repeated, a question being obvious.

"Yes." Mrs. Winslow answered neither offensively nor defensively, but rather matter-of-factly.

"And he's never missed an evening?"

"No." Again she answered matter-of-factly.

"Not even once?"

"No, not even once."

"Don't you think he might have gone somewhere else, just this one time?"

She looked at him impatiently. "He would have told me if he were going somewhere else."

"Is it possible that he decided to work late and just forgot to phone?"

"No," she said adamantly. "He would have called me, and besides, I checked. I'm afraid something terrible has happened to him."

"Are you saying you suspect foul play?"

She hesitated slightly before she replied. "Yes I am, because it's just so out of the ordinary for Sheridan not to come right home when he's finished at work. It had to be foul play."

"I'm sure I know her husband," George whispered to Lorraine and Jennifer. "He taught chemistry when I was in college. But I didn't know he'd been married for twenty years. I thought he was a bachelor when I attended his classes."

"She must have married him when she was ten years old," Lorraine said. "She doesn't look like she could be more than thirty."

"Is there any other reason why you suspect foul play?" the sergeant asked the woman, "other than the fact that he didn't come home from work tonight?"

"Isn't that enough?"

"I'm afraid not," he sympathized. "Perhaps if he'd been missing a little longer we could do something, but as it stands now, we can't declare your husband missing until he's been gone at least twenty-four hours."

Mrs. Winslow was quiet for a moment. Then as though an idea had suddenly come to her, she shook one finger into the air. "But he has been gone twenty-four hours," she declared. "He didn't come home last night either."

The sergeant looked at her suspiciously. "But you said he wasn't missing until tonight."

"I meant last night," she exclaimed in a tone that suggested he had misunderstood her. "He didn't come home from work last night either."

"She said tonight," Lorraine whispered to George. "She didn't say last night."

George held his finger to his lips once more for Lorraine to be quiet while he strained to hear the conversation at the desk. "Shh," he said, furrowing his brow.

The sergeant rubbed the nape of his neck with his hand and moved his head back and forth against it like a man trying to relax a tightened nerve. He pressed against the back of his chair for a moment while he considered the new information he had just been given. When he finally leaned forward again, his voice was laced with skepticism. "Are you sure you meant last night and not tonight?"

"Of course I'm sure," she retorted.

"And this was the first time in twenty years he didn't come home?"

"That's right."

"May I ask why you didn't report his disappearance last night?"

"Because he hadn't been gone for at least twenty-four hours last night," she said, taking the information the sergeant had just given her and throwing the words back at him.

The police officer took a deep breath, held it for a moment, and then exhaled with a noisy and somewhat helpless sigh. He began to ask routine questions as he tapped the keys.

"You did say your husband is fifty-eight years old?"

he repeated when she told him her husband's age. He emphasized fifty-eight.

"That's right."

He was silent as he looked questioningly at the sexy young woman in the tight clothing, wondering how someone her age could possibly have been married for twenty years. "And you're . . . ?" he inquired, attempting to find out how old she was.

"I'm not missing," she snapped.

He shrugged his shoulders in resignation, satisfied that he had at least given it a try. "Would you happen to have a picture of your husband you could leave with us?" he inquired.

"Not with me."

"You mean to tell me you've been married for twenty years to a man who has never missed an evening coming straight home from work, and you don't even carry a picture of him?" His voice carried a condescending air of arrogance that he usually reserved for disturbed people who walked into the precinct off the street.

"I know what he looks like," she shot back. "I don't need a picture."

"Could you possibly bring us one?" There was a hint of glibness in his voice, but it was lower than it had been and it conveyed the sound of defeat.

"Yes. I suppose so."

The desk sergeant continued to stare at her suspiciously, although with a new appreciation for her sharply barbed tongue. "I suppose in the meantime, we could keep an eye out for him," he offered.

His skepticism was apparent as he finished typing the rest of the information she gave him. Although he continued to inquire as to possible reasons for her husband's disappearance, he did not attempt to probe any further into her age or marriage.

Lorraine leaned her chin against George's shoulder and whispered into his ear. "A woman her age couldn't possibly be married for twenty years. And what man do you know that has never been late coming home from work?"

"What man do we know that has a wife who dresses and looks like that?" Jennifer quipped.

"Shh," George repeated. "I want to hear."

Jennifer and Lorraine remained quiet as they listened to the conclusion of the conversation between the sergeant at the desk and Mrs. Winslow.

The officer promised he would put out a missing person's report on her husband, but cautioned that there probably wasn't very much the police could do until he had been missing a little while longer. He continued to scrutinize her with suspicion.

She returned his stare with a cynical gaze of her own as though she had already decided that not much was going to be done to find the professor. "Thank you," she muttered hollowly.

Mrs. Winslow turned away from the desk and glanced at Lieutenant Dickey again. He had stopped nearby and had been watching and listening to the conversation between her and the desk sergeant.

Suddenly her face became pale and she came to a halt. She scrutinized the bandage on the side of his head and his swollen black eye as though trying to see the man beyond them.

"She knows him," Jennifer whispered. "And she seems to be afraid of him."

Lorraine had also seen Mrs. Winslow's reaction as she looked at Dickey the second time. "Probably one of his dates," she said facetiously.

The professor's wife backed slowly away from Dickey and then quickened her pace as she walked to the exit. When she neared, George held out his hand to get her attention.

"Excuse me, Mrs. Winslow," he said. "I couldn't help but overhear your conversation with the desk sergeant."

She stopped and examined him with a kind of distrustful curiosity. "Yes . . . ?"

"My name is George Brensley," he continued. "I attended some of Professor Winslow's classes in college. This is my wife, Lorraine. She and I are attorneys. And this is Jennifer Brookbaine. She's a private investigator who is doing some work for the College of Science. Maybe we can help you."

Lorraine looked at her husband with surprise. Her lips barely moved as she uttered his name.

"George . . . ?"

Mrs. Winslow's eyes shifted ever so slightly in Lorraine's direction. Then she quickly returned her attention to George.

She gazed at him attentively. "Oh, I would appreciate that so much," she exclaimed. "I have a feeling the police officer didn't believe me."

"Imagine that." Lorraine's voice carried a hint of mock astonishment. She looked up and down Mrs. Winslow's provocative attire. At that moment, all she could see was a very seductively dressed woman who looked like a hooker, lied to the police, and was making eyes at her husband.

She glanced at Jennifer, hoping to get some support. None was forthcoming. It was obvious that her friend could smell another investigation and was waiting for an excuse, any excuse, to get involved.

She looked at her husband again. He appeared to be mesmerized. He and Jennifer were both intrigued by the woman's deceitful story.

"George!"

Lorraine snapped his name as though trying to wake him from a spellbinding state. "Don't you remember, you said you didn't want us to get involved in any more investigations tonight."

George continued to be held under the hypnotic trance of the mysterious woman for several more seconds. Then, as though it had taken that long for the message to reach him, he blinked his eyes and turned to his wife.

"Of course we can get involved," he responded. "And I think we should, especially since Professor Winslow is one of my old college professors and could be in trouble. What do you think Jennifer?"

"Of course we can," Jennifer agreed with a smiling enthusiasm. In response to Lorraine's displeased frown, she pulled a shroud of seriousness over her face. "If George says so," she quickly added, as though he were the only one who wanted to get mixed up with Mrs. Winslow.

Lorraine scowled at them both. It wasn't that she didn't want to get involved in Jennifer's investigations. She just didn't want to get involved with this particular woman. She didn't trust her.

George couldn't help but notice her displeasure. "Mrs. Winslow does need our help," he emphasized.

Lorraine looked at George and Jennifer again, and then at the professor's wife who seemed to be much more pathetic and helpless than she had appeared a moment earlier. She had seen the same look many times before in courtrooms on the faces of the accused as they tried to play on the sympathy of a judge or jury.

"It will only take us a little while," Jennifer encouraged with an expression of optimism.

Lorraine had also encountered that look many times before. Jennifer used it effectively, along with the accompanying words, "It will only take us a little while," whenever she wanted to implicate Lorraine in one of her investigations.

Lorraine knew Jennifer was doing it to her again, along with George's assistance, but she couldn't say no. What if Mrs. Winslow did need help? What if the professor really was missing and possibly in danger? She gave a deep sigh and opened her hands in a gesture of surrender.

"Of course we should help," she relented in the manner of someone who was giving in because she knew what had to be done but still didn't want to do it.

"Oh, thank you so much," Mrs. Winslow responded. She looked at George rather than Lorraine as she spoke.

George smiled at his slighted wife, then reached for her hand and squeezed it lovingly. A silent, "Thank you," formed on his lips.

The same silent, "Thank you," also appeared on Jennifer's appreciative lips. "Well, let's get started then," she suggested. "Probably the best place to begin would be the College of Science."

Mrs. Winslow gazed helplessly at George. "Do you think you could give me a ride? I took a taxi to the police station."

"Of course we'll give you a ride." George glanced at his wife for approval.

"Of course we'll give you a ride." Lorraine repeated. Her voice carried a slight tinge of sarcasm.

Mrs. Winslow ignored Lorraine's generosity and instead looked into George's eyes. "You're so very kind," she said as she wrapped her arms around one of his. "Sheridan will be so grateful to know you're helping me search for him."

"How come every time I offer to do something, he gets thanked for it," Lorraine muttered to Jennifer.

Mrs. Winslow continued to hold onto George's arm until they approached his car. When she finally let go, it was to quickly slide into the front seat before either of the other women could make a move to enter.

"After you," Jennifer gestured as she held the rear door open for a grumbling Lorraine to join her in the back seat.

George walked around to the other side of the car. He shrugged to indicate there was nothing he could do, and then slid in behind the steering wheel.

As he backed out of the parking space, Jennifer and Lorraine noticed another car parked nearby. It was a blue Chevrolet sedan like the ones plain clothed detectives drove when they were on duty.

As the lights from another car shone briefly on the automobile, it was not difficult to make out the wavy black hair, wide curled mustache, and bandaged head of the driver.

It was Lieutenant Dickey, and he was watching them.

FOUR

"Probably going home to nurse his aching head," Jennifer whispered to Lorraine as they pulled out of the police station parking lot and away from the blue Chevrolet and Lieutenant Dickey.

Mrs. Winslow had also observed the Chevrolet, and the driver. Seeing Dickey again appeared to frighten her and she glanced behind several times after they turned onto the street. When there was no sign of him following, she relaxed.

"I'm sure there could be many probable reasons for your husband not coming home tonight," George said as he drove toward the university.

"But he always comes home," Mrs. Winslow insisted. "And he's never late. He always comes home at six o'clock exactly. And if he's going to be late, he calls."

"No exceptions?" Jennifer asked.

"No exceptions."

"In twenty years?" Lorraine asked incredulously.

"In twenty years," Mrs. Winslow answered. "That's why it's so important that we find him right away, tonight. If we don't find him soon, I know something terrible is going to happen to him."

"Like what?"

"Like being murdered."

"What makes you say that?"

"Some strange men were hanging around outside our house."

"And you think these men might want to hurt your husband?"

"Don't you?"

"I don't know your husband, or the men," Lorraine reminded her. "Do you happen to know who these people are?"

"No."

"You don't suppose one of them might have been Lieutenant Dickey, the officer with the bandage on his head you saw at the police station? He was watching you all the time you were inside, and you appeared to recognize him. He might also be carrying out some kind of investigation at the College of Science where your husband works."

"No." Her answer was emphatic and abrupt.

"Do you know Lieutenant Dickey?" Lorraine asked.

"No." Again her answer was emphatic and abrupt.

"Did your husband happen to mention a break-in at one of the laboratories at the college?"

"No."

"Do you have any idea at all why anybody would want to hurt your husband?"

"No."

"Do you even know for sure that he's in danger?"

"No, but why else would he leave home?"

Lorraine held a finger in the air and was poised to offer a suggestion, but before she could, Jennifer nudged her.

Lorraine grumbled to herself as she searched for something else to say. "If he left last night, he could be a long way away, if he wanted to be. Couldn't he?" she said almost cheerfully.

"But he didn't leave last night," Mrs. Winslow replied.

Lorraine's mouth fell open and her finger hung in the air, poised once again as she went over in her mind the statement Mrs. Winslow had given at the police station. "But you told the sergeant down at police headquarters that he didn't come home last night either."

"That's right, but I knew where he was last night. I don't know where he is tonight."

Lorraine's lips moved several more times without making any sound, then she looked inquisitively at Jennifer, silently questioning whether she was really hearing what the woman was saying.

Jennifer also looked bewildered. She opened her hands in an unknowing gesture. "But you just said your husband had never failed to come home at six o'clock."

"In twenty years," Lorraine added.

"Unless he called," Mrs. Winslow replied.

"Did he call last night?"

"Of course he did."

"Why didn't you tell them that down at police headquarters?"

"They didn't ask me."

"Where was he when he called?"

"At his lab at Westland University."

"And what did you do when he called?"

"I met him for dinner."

For a moment there was silence in the car.

"Where?"

"At the university."

"Where did you go after dinner?"

"I went home."

"And where did he go?"

"Back to work. He sometimes does that. He works on his projects in his laboratory."

"Then why on earth did you tell the sergeant at the police station that he was missing last night if you knew where he was?"

"I didn't tell him he was missing last night. I just said he didn't come home. But he is missing tonight."

"How do you know he's missing tonight?"

"Because he didn't call," Mrs. Winslow and George both answered together.

"See, he understands," Mrs. Winslow said as she moved a little closer to George.

"Professor Winslow was one of the most interesting teachers I ever had," George said. "He could make lectures on even math and science seem enjoyable. It's funny, I don't remember him being married when I attended his classes. You did say you'd been married for twenty years, didn't you?"

Mrs. Winslow was quiet.

"You did say twenty years, didn't you?" Lorraine repeated.

"Of course I did," she replied. "I wouldn't say twenty years if I didn't mean twenty years."

"When was the last time you saw your husband?" Jennifer asked.

"Last night at dinner."

"And when was the last time you talked to him?"

"Last night at dinner. He said he'd be working in the laboratory most of the evening."

"You haven't seen or talked to him since?"

"No."

"Are you sure he didn't come home last night?"

"I'm sure."

"How?"

"Because I was asleep."

"How would you know he didn't come home if you were asleep?" Lorraine asked.

"Because he didn't wake me."

"Why would he wake you?"

"He always wakes me." Mrs. Winslow's voice had a musical ring to it. She smiled and turned her body so that she was facing George.

George glanced at her, then returned his attention to the road. Then his eyebrows lifted and he looked at her again. "You mean . . . ?"

She nodded her head and continued to smile at him without speaking.

"For twenty years?"

She nodded again.

"Holy cow."

"Maybe he just wore out," Lorraine whispered out of the side of her mouth to Jennifer.

"Let's go over this one more time," Jennifer said. "You told us your husband didn't come home last night but you knew where he was."

"Yes."

"And he didn't come home tonight and you don't have any idea where he is."

"That's right."

"Maybe we'll find him in his laboratory," Jennifer suggested as they pulled into a parking lot near where the College of Science was located.

"Maybe," Mrs. Winslow agreed. "Sheridan's office is right over there."

They followed the professor's wife to a side entrance in the four story building. It opened into a hallway that was in semidarkness. About halfway down the hall, she stopped at a door that was slightly ajar. She either didn't notice, or chose to ignore the unusual condition. "This is Sheridan's office," she said, opening the door and turning on the lights.

Inside, the desk and floor were littered with books and papers that appeared to have been picked up at random and strewn around. It was obvious that someone had turned the room upside down searching for something.

"Any idea who might have done this, and what they might have been looking for?" Jennifer asked.

Mrs. Winslow shrugged. If she was concerned, she didn't show it. "I don't know," she replied. "Can you tell if Sheridan was here?"

"Not from this," Jennifer answered. She picked up a photograph that had fallen out of its broken frame. It was of Mrs. Winslow and a grey haired man in a lab coat. "Is this Professor Winslow?"

Mrs. Winslow nodded. She took the photo and casually threw it onto the desk.

George also looked at the photo. "That's Professor Winslow," he confirmed. "He hasn't changed much since I was in college."

When Mrs. Winslow turned away, Jennifer picked up the photo and put it in her handbag. In answer to Lorraine's scowl she whispered, "She already knows what he looks like."

They were about to look around when a security

guard poked his head through the doorway. "May I help you?" he asked suspiciously. "Oh, hello Mrs. Winslow."

He stared at the ransacked room. "What happened here?"

"We're not sure," Jennifer answered. "We just got here ourselves. We're helping Mrs. Winslow look for her husband. Have you by any chance seen Professor Winslow?"

"About an hour ago. I saw him leaving the building. He looked like he was in a hurry."

"Do you know where he was headed?"

"I think he was going home. He usually walks since he doesn't live very far away."

"I was home earlier," Mrs. Winslow informed him. "He isn't there."

"We'll check again," Jennifer said. "He could have gone there after you left for the police station. Do you have any idea where he was coming from when you saw him?" she asked the guard.

"Probably one of the labs he works in."

"Could you show us?"

"I don't see why not. It might still be open. But if it isn't, I'll let you in. He's not there though. Like I told you, I saw him leave an hour ago."

Mrs. Winslow took George by the arm. "We can go to my place to see if Sheridan went home," she offered, "while they check the laboratory. I know he would like to meet you again."

George and Jennifer waited for Lorraine to object. She didn't. Instead she offered, "I guess Jennifer and I could check the laboratories for anything out of the ordinary."

Jennifer stared at her. "While George goes with Mrs. Winslow?"

"Yes."

"Are you sure?"

"Of course I'm sure. It's kind of late, so I think Mrs. Winslow should have somebody with her. And I know George would like to see Professor Winslow again."

"I wouldn't mind saying hello to the professor," George said.

"We'll see you in a little while then," Lorraine replied. "We'll meet back here."

"Don't do anything we wouldn't do," Jennifer called after them as George and Mrs. Winslow walked away.

She turned to Lorraine. "Have you gone completely nuts? Sending George off with Mrs. Winslow is like sending a goldfish off with a barracuda."

"I trust George."

"I think you could have found an easier way to show your trust. Maybe you could have fed him to a tribe of sex starved Amazon nymphomaniacs or something."

"Why do you have to show that other guy you trust him?" the security guard asked. "Is he a cop? Are you two cops? Is Mrs. Winslow safe with him? Is Professor Winslow in trouble?"

"We're just helping Mrs. Winslow find him," Lorraine explained. "He didn't go home tonight, and she's worried about him."

"He doesn't go home most nights," the guard said. "He usually works here until at least eleven or twelve o'clock with Professor Reid, and sometimes even later."

"Professor Reid?" Jennifer replied. "Isn't she the one whose laboratory was broken into?"

"That's the one. And if I worked with Professor Reid, I don't think I'd want to go home until eleven or twelve o'clock either. What a knockout."

"I thought the professor went home every night at six o'clock. Mrs. Winslow says he's been doing it for twenty years."

"If he does, it's news to me. Especially since they've only been married six months."

"Six months?"

"Are you sure?"

"I'm sure."

"Six months, twenty years, practically the same thing," Lorraine muttered. "We thought she was using us before, I know she's using us now."

"Doesn't he call his wife if he's going to be late?" Jennifer asked.

"I don't know about that," the guard replied. "But he doesn't go home. He and Professor Reid lock themselves in the lab and study science, or chemistry, or whatever it is they do. For all I know, they're studying each other's chemistry, if you know what I mean. It's common knowledge they've been having an affair." He opened the door of the laboratory and switched on the lights. "Anything in particular you're looking for?"

"Not really," Jennifer replied. "We were just going to have a look around to see if we could find anything that might indicate why Professor Winslow would be missing. He's probably at home by now, but do you mind if we look anyway?"

One wall of the laboratory was lined with glass enclosed shelves that were filled with test tubes and other scientific apparatus. Along another wall were desks of computers and test equipment that hummed continuously. A third wall had a chalkboard that was covered with scientific formulas and equations.

The formulas did not appear all that unusual, except at the top of the chalkboard the lines were straight and neat, but by the time they had reached the bottom they were scrawled and crooked.

As they approached the wall, they saw the reason for the change in neatness. Lying on the floor below the chalkboard, with a piece of chalk still clutched in her fingers, was the semi-nude body of Professor Reid.

Her long reddish hair curled around her face and flowed to the floor. Light makeup on her cheeks and lips continued to provide color to her still features.

Her eyes were closed and her glasses still rested on her nose as though she had just decided to stop writing and take a nap. Except for her lace lined bra and panties, which seemed strangely out of place in the science laboratory, that was all she was wearing.

On a laboratory bench nearby, neatly folded, were her lab coat, and a skirt and blouse. Beside her clothing, not folded quite so neatly, were a man's jacket and pants, and a shirt and lab coat. On the floor beside the bench, a pair of woman's shoes and a pair of men's shoes were placed side by side. One green sock lay across the men's shoes. The other sock was nowhere in sight. Whatever the couple had been doing appeared to have been interrupted.

The guard stared at the nearly naked body. "Didn't I tell you she was beautiful."

The two women glared at him with disapproval. "Is there a phone around here?" Jennifer asked.

"Yes, across the hall." He still did not take his eyes off the professor.

"Would you please go and phone the police?" she half suggested and half ordered.

"Right. I'll be right back." He gawked at Professor Reid for a few more seconds, then turned and left on the run.

Lorraine studied the body as she checked for a pulse. "Do you think she was murdered?"

Jennifer shrugged. "Search me. I don't see any wounds or signs of a struggle. Maybe she was having a little hanky panky with Professor Winslow and had a heart attack."

"I thought the man was supposed to have the heart attack."

"He is. I knew it would come to this if we kept insisting on equality."

"Why does she still have her glasses on?"

"I don't know. Maybe they were fooling around and she wanted to see what they were doing, or maybe she was having trouble finding it. They can be pretty small sometimes."

"How can you have such a warped sense of humor at a time like this."

"Maybe Professor Winslow has a fetish for glasses," Jennifer suggested.

"Men don't have a fetish for glasses," Lorraine informed her. "They have a fetish for underclothes, or breasts, or behinds, or the back of the knees, or toes, or . . . ."

"Toes? Who do we know that has a fetish for toes?" Jennifer's eyebrows lifted. "George. George has a fetish for toes, doesn't he."

"No he doesn't."

"Yes he does. That's where you heard about it, isn't it? I've seen him watching your feet. Remind me to ask him about it, will you?"

"I will not. And don't you either. He'll get embarrassed. And worse than that . . . ."

"Yes?"

"He'll kill me." Lorraine's eyes bowed toward the professor. "Sorry," she apologized. "Can we get back to what killed Professor Reid?"

"Sure. Let's ask that guard some more questions about what Professor Winslow was wearing when he ran out of here. If these clothes were his, he wasn't wearing much. Maybe he was running away from a murder and that's why he was in a hurry."

"That would put me in a hurry, especially if I thought Mrs. Winslow was coming to check up on me."

"But why would Professor Winslow turn his own office upside down?"

"Maybe Professor Reid did it, then they got into a fight over whatever she was looking for, and he killed her."

"Who do you know that takes their clothes off to have a fight?"

"I suppose it would depend on what they were doing when the fight began. What if Mrs. Winslow was involved? What if Professor Winslow and Professor Reid were fooling around. Then the professor's wife walks in. She sees them, kills Professor Reid, and her husband runs for his life. Maybe that's why he was in a hurry when the guard saw him."

Jennifer stared at her skeptically. "And then when Mrs. Winslow couldn't catch him to kill him, she went to the police station to report him missing so they would catch him for her. And all this is supposed to have happened in the past hour? She was at the police station an hour ago, so she couldn't have done it."

"Unless it was done earlier. Professor Reid doesn't look like a person who would die for no apparent reason."

Jennifer bent over the body, looking for signs of foul play. She pointed to a hypodermic needle that was mostly hidden beneath Professor Reid's body. "Maybe she had some help from this."

Without touching the evidence, she examined the professor's arms for needle marks. "I wouldn't be surprised if there was something in it that didn't agree with her, although it doesn't look like she uses drugs."

Just then the security guard returned. "I called the police," he informed them. "I also had a look in Professor Reid's office. Somebody ransacked it the same way they wrecked Professor Winslow's."

"Whatever they were looking for, it looks like both Professor Reid and Professor Winslow had something somebody wanted," Jennifer said.

Lorraine nodded. "Maybe an experiment that she and Professor Winslow were working on?"

"Could be, but that means that someone else is involved. Professor Winslow and Professor Reid wouldn't ransack their own offices. And I'm sure they would know what it is, or where it is, if they were working on something together. But why didn't whoever killed Professor Reid kill him too?"

Lorraine shook her head. "I don't know, but it

looks like there's more here than just an affair between two professors. Maybe Mrs. Winslow can help us, if we can get her to tell the truth. It's obvious she was lying about her relationship with her husband, along with everything else."

Their conversation was interrupted by the sound of an outside door to the science building opening and closing. "Probably the police," the security guard said as he headed into the hall to see who it was. "Right down this way," he called out.

A moment later they heard him exclaim, "What happened to your head?"

FIVE

Lorraine and Jennifer looked at each other, then at the doorway. They waited, hoping that what they feared wasn't going to transpire. It did.

"Oh, oh," Jennifer exclaimed as Lieutenant Dickey entered the room.

"Ohhh, yesss," Dickey exclaimed back in a deep, somewhat threatening growl. He half stared and half glared at the two women with his one good eye. His other eye was barely more than a slit and he was forced to tilt back his head to see out of it.

His attention moved beyond them and around the laboratory. Seeing only lab benches and cupboards, his lopsided gaze kept returning to Jennifer and Lorraine. "To what do I owe this . . . pleasure?" he announced with a rasping hoarseness that rose from his throat in the same threatening growl.

Jennifer rose up in her high heeled shoes as far as she could until they made her almost as tall as the lieutenant. She unconsciously raised one eyebrow while closing the other in an instinctive mimic of the way Dickey appeared.

"Keeping an eye out for us?" she asked as she wrapped her fist around the strap of her handbag and let it swing in small deliberate circles.

Lorraine wedged her shoulder in front of Jennifer's wavering arm and moved her away from the officer. "We were helping Mrs. Winslow . . . the lady . . . the woman who was at the police station tonight, search for her missing husband. He teaches here at the university and we came to look for anything that could help us find out what might have happened to him. Instead, we found another professor who works with him, dead. Although we can't be sure, there's a possibility she could have been murdered."

Dickey licked his lips as he concentrated his stare on Lorraine. She expected him to inquire further about the body they had found. When his bruised face appeared to soften a little, she began to wonder if he was preparing to rekindle their relationship. He wasn't.

"Who's Mrs. Winslow?" he barked as his face hardened again. Although he had asked a question, his words came out as a demand.

"You were present when she came into police headquarters," Lorraine reminded him. "In fact, you were standing right beside her when the desk sergeant took down the information about her missing husband. And you were sitting in your car watching her, or us, when we left the station."

"I don't know any Mrs. Winslow," he snapped. His gaze moved away from Lorraine and around the room again. "Where's the body?"

Lorraine decided not to pursue the matter, even though she was sure Mrs. Winslow had recognized the lieutenant at the station. "Over there behind that lab bench," she said, pointing to the other side of the room.

Dickey made his way between the rows of benches until he came to Professor Reid's body. There was no change in his expression when he saw the beauty of the woman and the way she was clothed. His attention shifted to her face and then methodically moved to different points along her frame. He nodded to himself when he saw the hypodermic needle. He carefully lifted the professor's limp arm, examined the needle without touching it, and then checked her arms for scars that would be present from drug abuse.

When he came to the clothing that had been left on the lab bench, he lifted each article slightly with the tip of his pen and then let it drop. He held the one green sock a little longer as he searched for its mate.

He looked across the floor, following a path the victim's assailant might have taken. His gaze stopped for a brief instant at the doorway where he had entered the room with the security guard and another police officer who had accompanied him. Then it followed the floor again to the area where Professor Reid's body was located.

"Decide anything?" Jennifer asked.

Dickey ignored her question. Instead, he studied the length of the room. His head tilted to one side and he glowered deliberately and suspiciously at Lorraine. "What makes you say it was murder?" he asked in a tone that was filled with accusation.

"We don't know for sure that it was murder," Lorraine shot back. "But she is dead, and there is a hypodermic needle, which I think you will have to agree could be the murder weapon. She doesn't look like she used drugs, although I suppose she could have given herself an overdose of something. But why would she take off all her clothes before doing it? And why are these other clothes here? It's obvious to me that she took off her clothes for someone else, and whoever that other person was, would have called for help, unless he had something to do with her death or has also met with foul play. Also, the security guard told us her office has been ransacked, like something was hidden there and someone tried to find it. My bet is that whoever it was, killed her."

"Umm," Dickey grumbled as though he had no other choice but to agree. He continued to stare at them suspiciously. "What about you two?"

"What about us two?" Lorraine exclaimed. Her voice rose in indignation as she surmised the meaning of his question.

"Where were you when all this took place?"

Lorraine glared at him with a flustered anger. "We were with Mrs. Winslow. You remember her. She's the woman you say you have never seen before even though you were standing right beside her, ogling her body at the police station. We were also with my husband, and the security guard here, and before that we were in jail, thanks to you."

Her face twisted into a crooked smirk and her voice lost its cutting edge as it changed from a defensive inflection to a tone of offensiveness. "And before that we were beating you up outside this building. Why?"

Dickey's own face was twisting in anger. "Because I would like nothing better than to lock you two up again, especially for something as juicy as murder."

Lorraine planted her hands on her hips and pulled herself up as far as she possibly could the way Jennifer had when Dickey first came into the laboratory. In her new position of almost equal height, she leaned toward him. She enunciated each word as she spoke.

"Now see here, Mr. Lieutenant Dickey. I know it must be terribly embarrassing to have two women give you a black eye and lay you out cold with a purse, and we're very sorry about what happened to your head, but we really didn't know you were a policeman when we beat you up."

"We thought you were just a dirty rotten low life degenerate pervert," Jennifer added. "If we had known you were a police officer . . . ."

"Shut up!"

Dickey's face began to twitch and turn red, and even his good eye was closed in rage. When he finally opened it, he didn't say anything. He just cocked his head back further and glared at the two women.

The officer who had accompanied Dickey had been watching and listening quietly while the lieutenant carried out his investigation. But now his body was moving in involuntary spasms as he tried to stifle laughter that was escaping through the hand he was holding over his mouth.

Dickey's scowling glare shot past Jennifer and Lorraine to the other police officer.

"Shut up!" he yelled again.

The officer stood upright, pulled his cheeks inward, and clamped his lips shut to repress the laughter that was still threatening to escape. One more small guffaw spilled out before he managed to compose himself.

"If you don't mind, Sergeant, I'm attempting to carry out an investigation here," Dickey reminded him. "Did you come here to help, or are you just looking for some entertainment?"

"I'm sorry," the other officer responded as he tried to become more serious. "Just let me know what you need."

Jennifer and Lorraine turned away from Dickey to observe the police officer who had come in with him. Lorraine didn't recognize him, although Jennifer knew him from a previous investigation.

"Hello Sergeant Chambers," she said. "What are you doing here? Working the night shift?"

"Hello Brookbaine," he answered, referring to her by her last name. "I'm working homicide now, along with Lieutenant Dickey."

Aside from being police officers, Sergeant Chambers and Lieutenant Dickey were an unusual combination and had very little in common. Dickey was in his thirties, with a full head of wavy black hair and a mustache. Chambers was in his forties, clean shaven, with thinning blonde hair that was quickly receding. Also, where Dickey was mean and abusive, Chambers tended to be outgoing and congenial, even when he was positive the person he was investigating had committed a crime.

"How are you doing?" the sergeant asked.

"Right now, I guess that depends on whose point of view you want to take," Jennifer replied, glancing at Dickey. "I take it you were sent to investigate the death of Professor Reid."

"I came along to help the lieutenant," he answered. "The dispatcher tried to persuade him to go home, but he insisted on taking the call. He must have known you would be here."

"He should be in a hospital for his head," she remarked.

"You mean the injuries you gave him?"

"Yeah, that too," Jennifer said with a wry twisted smile.

Chambers smiled back but wisely chose to ignore the last comment as he shifted his eyes to Dickey's stern face. "What have you gotten yourselves into?" he asked.

"Like Lorraine said to Lieutenant Dickey, we came to look for information that might tell us why Mrs. Winslow's husband disappeared, although it looks like he might have just gone home. The security guard saw him leaving the building. Anyway, we came in here to check and that's when we found Professor Reid. It looks like her death could be foul play, but I guess we won't know for sure until you're finished with your investigation. Will you let us know what you find?"

"Sure will," Sergeant Chambers promised. "Do you have any suspects in mind?"

"Not really suspects," Jennifer informed him, "but you might want to question them. One is Professor Winslow. According to the guard, he was having an affair with Professor Reid and was seen leaving the science building about an hour ago. The other person is Professor Winslow's wife. She's nutty as a fruitcake and has told us some strange stories about her husband's disappearance."

"Mrs. Winslow . . . and George," Lorraine suddenly exclaimed. "We forgot all about them."

"Who's George?" Sergeant Chambers asked.

"Lorraine's husband," Jennifer said. "He went with Mrs. Winslow to her house to see if the professor had gone home."

Lorraine was already heading out the door. "I'm going after them," she shouted over her shoulder. "If the Winslows are involved in this . . . ."

Jennifer and Chambers fell in behind. Dickey looked at the body and then at the people disappearing out through the doorway. "Hold it right there," he ordered. He waved one finger in their direction as he chased after them. "I'm not finished with you yet."

"I'll make sure they come back," Chambers assured him as he followed the two women down the hallway and out of the building.

Lorraine had walked only a short distance in the direction that her husband and Mrs. Winslow had gone earlier, when they appeared around a corner. George moved at a brisk pace and was followed closely by Mrs. Winslow who was struggling to keep up in her tight skirt and high heels.

"George," she called out. "Are you all right?"

"I'm all right," he said. He did not appear to be in a very good mood.

"Did you find Professor Winslow?"

Mrs. Winslow replied before George could answer. "No, he wasn't at home. And we didn't see any sign of him. Did you find him?"

"No," Lorraine answered. "But we found one of his co-workers, Professor Reid. We discovered her in one of the laboratories. I'm afraid she's dead. It appears she might have been murdered." She waited for the professor's wife to respond.

Mrs. Winslow shrugged slightly as though it meant very little to her.

"Professor Reid," Lorraine repeated. "She worked with your husband. You must have known her."

Mrs. Winslow shook her head. "No, except to see her. I suppose she might have occasionally assisted Sheridan on one of his projects."

Lorraine pressed on. "According to the security guard at the College of Science, your husband and Professor Reid worked together all the time. I hate to tell you this, but the guard says they were having an affair."

"Oh no," Mrs. Winslow exclaimed. "Sheridan might have worked with her once in a while, but he didn't see her all that much, and I know he wasn't having an affair with her."

"The security guard told us they worked together practically every night," Lorraine answered, "or did whatever it was they were doing every night. You must have known."

Mrs. Winslow didn't say anything. It was the first time they had seen her without an answer to a question.

"Why did you tell the police department your husband came home every night at six o'clock when he didn't?" Jennifer asked.

The professor's wife was still silent. When the words finally did come, she blurted them out. "Do you really think the police would have helped me if I'd told them my husband didn't come home at night because he was carrying on an affair with another college professor?"

Taken aback by the sudden admission, they stared into Mrs. Winslow's face, searching for anything that would help them understand the latest version of the relationship between her and her husband.

"But why did you say he was missing?" Jennifer asked.

"Because, he was missing. He may not have been faithful, but he was a good husband. For twenty years he . . . ."

Lorraine stopped her. "Mrs. Winslow," she said in exasperation. "The security guard told us that you and Professor Winslow had been married for only six months."

"Oh."

"Why did you feel you had to say you had been married for twenty years when you hadn't?"

Mrs. Winslow hesitated again. "Because if I told the police we had only been married for six months and he was having an affair, they would have thought he just got fed up with me and left."

"Well, did he?"

"Did he what?"

"Did he just get fed up with you and leave?"

"No, no. He was in some kind of trouble. He came home this afternoon, gathered up some clothes, and left without telling me where he was going."

"What kind of trouble?"

"I don't know. I just know he looked scared, and he kept staring out the window like he was expecting someone to be there. The next thing I knew, he was gone, and so were his clothes."

"Do you think he was leaving town?"

"I don't know, but he would have told me if he was. I always knew what he was doing . . . even when he was screwing around with Professor Reid in the science lab."

Mrs. Winslow's listeners looked at each other and then at her. "I don't mean to offend you," Jennifer said, "but if we're ever going to help you, you will have to be more truthful. We just don't know when you're telling the truth and when you're not."

"This is the truth," Mrs. Winslow answered. "My husband is missing and he's in some kind of danger. I also knew he was having an affair with Professor Reid, but that didn't bother me. He was good to me and he supported me. If Professor Reid and Sheridan wanted to fool around a little between experiments, who were they hurting."

"You didn't mind?"

"Of course not. Why should I? We have an open marriage. He has his freedom and I have mine. But we're still close. You know what I mean, don't you?"

"No I don't," Lorraine said indignantly. "If any other husband did that . . . well, I wouldn't want to think about what would happen to him." She looked intently at Mrs. Winslow, waiting again for a reaction.

"I did not kill my husband, or Professor Reid," Mrs. Winslow protested. "And Sheridan didn't kill her either. I know he didn't, but something terrible has happened to him, and I want you to find out where he is. Will you help me?"

A counterfeit frown of sympathy appeared on Lorraine's face. "We would really like to help you, but you won't be needing us anymore, now that the police are involved."

Lorraine pointed a finger at the Sergeant who had accompanied them from the science lab and had been listening patiently from the sidelines. A hint of a satisfied smile began to take over the frown.

"This is Sergeant Chambers of the Westland Police Department," she said. "He and Lieutenant Dickey will be looking after you now."

"Lieutenant Dickey?" There was a slight touch of apprehension in Mrs. Winslow's voice as she spoke the name. She looked toward the science building, then grabbed George's arm and pulled him against her.

"Oh, no," she exclaimed. "I want you to stay and help me. I'll be happy to pay you whatever you want. I just don't think the police believe that something has happened to my husband. They might even try to blame him for Professor Reid's death."

"He is a suspect, you know," Lorraine informed her. "And for that matter, so are you, especially with the different stories you've been telling."

"I don't care. You will help me, won't you?" Mrs.

Winslow was almost pleading as she held George's arm tighter and looked into his eyes.

"We can't." Lorraine also looked into his eyes with a demanding stare that carried a touch of pleading. Her gaze fell on what appeared to be red marks on one of his cheeks. "Are you all right, George?" she asked.

Jennifer interrupted. "Of course we'll help you, Mrs. Winslow. But first you have to talk to Sergeant Chambers and Lieutenant Dickey, and tell them everything you've told us. And tell them the truth. All right?"

Mrs. Winslow gazed at Chambers for a moment. "All right," she promised. With that, she released George's arm, wrapped her arms around the sergeant's arm, and let herself be guided in the direction of the science building where Lieutenant Dickey was standing in the doorway.

"I still think she's afraid of the lieutenant," Jennifer said.

"And I think they're both nuts," Lorraine replied. "Are you actually considering taking Mrs. Winslow on as a client?"

"Yes we are."

"What do you mean, we?"

"You're on vacation for the next two weeks, aren't you? And you know you'd love to do this. I'll give you half."

"Oh no you don't," Lorraine said defensively. "You can't pay me to do this. There isn't enough money in the world to make me get involved with that woman again. Besides, you can't pay me, I work for the prosecutor's office. I could be trying to put her away for fifty years next month. And hasn't it occurred to you that she might just be crazy enough to have killed her husband, and Professor Reid?"

"She's crazy as a loon," George interjected. "And you two are crazy if you get involved in this. In case you haven't noticed, she's taking advantage of us. Why don't you let Lieutenant Dickey have her. He probably deserves her. And it's obvious they know each other, in spite of what she says."

The two women glanced at each other and then looked inquisitively at George. Lorraine's brow folded in an expression of suspicion. "Is this the same man who couldn't resist the temptation to get involved with our Mrs. Winslow, and then insisted that we get involved?"

Jennifer touched the red marks on George's cheek. She had an exaggerated look of puzzlement. "He appears to be the same man. I'm beginning to wonder if perhaps your husband discovered something about the professor's wife he isn't sharing with us."

"Perhaps there is one little thing I did discover about her," George said.

"Yes?"

"The woman is a nymphomaniac."

"We knew that," Jennifer replied. "But how did you find out?"

"I'd like to know that too," Lorraine added. "How did you find out?" She stared at his face. "And how did you get scratches on your cheek?"

"They're not scratches," Jennifer said as she wiped George's cheek with a tissue and showed Lorraine the evidence she held.

Lorraine examined the tissue, then looked more closely at his face in the pale light.

"Lipstick??!!"

Jennifer shook her head in mock disgust. "And to think you trusted him."

"I do trust him," Lorraine declared, her voice softening, then it got stern again.

"Well?"

"She made a pass at me."

"What!"

"She made a pass at me. I thought she just wanted to thank me, but she grabbed me and made a pass at me."

Jennifer laughed. "Boy, she wasn't kidding when she said she had an open marriage. And what did you do?"

George's face twisted into a sarcastic smirk. "What do you think I did? I told her I couldn't tonight because I was out with you two."

Lorraine frowned at him. "What about Professor Winslow? Weren't you looking for him?"

"I was, but I don't think she was. He wasn't at home, and she didn't look like she expected him to be there either. But I wouldn't be surprised if she does know where he is."

"Where?"

"Maybe dead, maybe out of town. If you ask me, he probably ran away from home."

"What makes you say that?"

"Because she's crazy. And she wasn't looking for him. For someone who was supposedly desperate to find her husband, and had just been told where he might be headed, she sure didn't seem very interested in searching for him. The only thing she seemed interested in was thanking me for helping her."

"And of course you fought her off?"

"Of course I fought her off. Would I look like this if I hadn't fought her off?"

"As a matter of fact you would," Jennifer said. "Wouldn't he Lorraine?"

"I'm in enough trouble, Jennifer," George sighed. "Mrs. Winslow and my wife can bury me without your help."

"I believe you, George," Lorraine assured him. She leaned her head against his chest, then reached up to kiss him. "And you know I trust you."

"You two make me sick the way you carry on," Jennifer scoffed. "I'm going over to talk to normal people. I'm going over to see Lieutenant Dickey and Mrs. Winslow."

They looked toward the science building where Lieutenant Dickey was standing with Mrs. Winslow.

She was touching the bandage on the side of his face and moving closer to him. He was not moving away.

"Pervert," Jennifer muttered.

"Slut," Lorraine muttered after her.

Jennifer headed in their direction. George and Lorraine followed. Mrs. Winslow was still caressing Dickey's bandage when they got there.

"Discover anything new?" Jennifer asked as she approached the two officers and the professor's wife.

"Mrs. Winslow has had a very stressful night," Dickey said. "Her husband is missing, and now her best friend has been murdered. I'm going to take her home."

The lieutenant guided Mrs. Winslow away from the building and toward a parking lot where his blue Chevrolet was parked. "Look after things here and make sure the forensic team gets everything," he called back to Chambers. "I'll get your report when I see you in the morning."

"Best friend?" Lorraine exclaimed to Chambers. "Did he just say that Mrs. Winslow was Professor Reid's best friend?"

"That's what she told us," Chambers informed them. "She said that she and Professor Reid had been best friends for twenty years."

Lorraine threw up her hands. "Didn't she just tell us she hardly knew Professor Reid?"

Jennifer shrugged. "I've heard so many versions, I'm really not sure what she told us anymore."

They watched as Dickey opened the passenger's door for Mrs. Winslow and then walked around to the driver's side and slid in behind the steering wheel. As the car pulled away from the parking lot, they could see the professor's wife caressing the lieutenant's bandage once again while she slid across the seat and settled close to him.

"I thought she was supposed to be afraid of him," Lorraine commented.

"Funny way to show fear," Jennifer replied.

SIX

Jennifer and Lorraine accepted Mrs. Winslow as a client. At least, Jennifer accepted her as a client. The professor's wife's request to hire her was confirmed the following morning when Mrs. Winslow arrived at Brookbaine Investigations with a check in the amount of five thousand dollars.

Jennifer was impressed. Most of the people who hired her had questions about retainers and other fees. Mrs. Winslow was not interested in discussing costs, saying it was just a down payment and more money was available if needed.

Otherwise, Mrs. Winslow was evasive. She did not want to discuss the death of her so-called best friend, Professor Reid. Instead, she went back to her story of hardly knowing the woman. She also did her best to avoid any discussion about her marriage to Professor

Winslow, and emphasized that she was hiring Jennifer solely to investigate his disappearance.

When asked about her relationship with Lieutenant Dickey, Mrs. Winslow was also evasive. She claimed she had not noticed him at the police station, and denied having ever met him until he gave her a ride home from the university the previous evening.

She also said they had not talked about the case during the drive, and made a point of mentioning that the lieutenant was a perfect gentleman who treated her like a lady and had just dropped her off at the front door.

Thoughts of Dickey being a gentleman who would stop at just dropping a woman who looked like Mrs. Winslow at the front door, and Mrs. Winslow being a lady who would allow herself just to be dropped at the front door, were a little more than Jennifer could accept.

She surveyed her client's attire, searching for evidence of a tussle on a pillow with the lieutenant, friendly or otherwise. Although different, it was as provocative as the clothing she had worn the night before, which for Mrs. Winslow, appeared normal.

A picture of the couple sharing a sexual encounter while the lieutenant carried out his interrogation entered Jennifer's thoughts, causing her to shiver. She wasn't certain how Dickey could manage to be a detective along with whatever else he was doing with Mrs. Winslow, but suspected he had somehow managed to do both. Her suspicions were confirmed when Mrs. Winslow emphasized once again the urgency of finding her husband as soon as possible because she believed the police had already decided he was guilty of murder and would not treat him fairly.

After her new client had left her office, Jennifer stared at the check and thought about Mrs. Winslow's quickly acquired reputation for distorting the truth.

"I should believe her," she said to herself, "because there has to be trust between an investigator and a client, even liars like Mrs. Winslow. Right?"

"I don't think so," she declared to the empty room.

She picked up the telephone and called the manager of the bank where the check had been drawn. She knew him quite well, having carried out previous investigations for him.

"You know I can't do that," he stated when she asked him to verify the balance in Mrs. Winslow's account.

"I know," she replied, "but there's a possibility my client and her husband might be involved in a crime that could indirectly involve your bank since the check was written there." Then she was silent.

There was also silence at the other end of the line as she waited patiently for him to speak first. She knew he would be thinking it over and didn't want to give him any reasons to say no.

"What's your client's first name?" he eventually asked.

Jennifer whistled to herself when she was given the

information on Mrs. Winslow's account. She was still whistling when she arrived at the Brensleys' residence a short time later to pick up Lorraine. She wasn't sure yet how she would get her friend involved in the investigation, because of her distrust and dislike of Mrs. Winslow, but she was sure she would find a way. She always did.

But not at first. "I think you'd better bite that to make sure it's real," Lorraine suggested when she was shown the five thousand dollar check Jennifer had been given as a retainer.

"Of course it's real," Jennifer insisted. "Tell me what person in her right mind would give us a check for five thousand dollars if it wasn't real?" She lapsed into silence the way she had with the manager when she telephoned the bank, and waited for Lorraine to make the first move.

Lorraine didn't speak. Instead, she examined the check, searching for improprieties.

This time, Jennifer was forced to break the silence. "All right, so Mrs. Winslow isn't in her right mind. But she still gave us a check and we're going to cash it."

"In the first place," Lorraine proclaimed, "Mrs. Winslow can't be in her right mind because she doesn't have a right mind. And in the second place, what is this, we, business?"

"You and me," Jennifer replied. "Aren't you just a little bit curious about Mrs. Winslow and her missing husband, and Professor Reid's death, and Lieutenant Dickey's interest in Mrs. Winslow, not to mention his interest in you?"

George Brensley interrupted the conversation. "I'm curious about one thing."

"And what's that?" Lorraine asked. "I know. You want to go back and have another look for Mrs. Winslow's mind."

"Can you believe your wife's jealousy," Jennifer exclaimed. "Just because another woman found you attractive, practically climbed into your lap while you were driving, and tried to seduce you when you were supposed to be looking for her husband . . . I'm sure if she had a mind, she would have already given it to you."

"That's not what I'm curious about," George answered.

"Then just what are you curious about?" Lorraine demanded.

George pointed to Jennifer. "I'm curious about how long it will take her to get you involved in Mrs. Winslow's case."

"She is not going to get me involved," Lorraine insisted. "And I'm not worried. As soon as that check from Mrs. Winslow bounces, she's going to lose all interest anyway."

"I'll make a deal with you," Jennifer offered. "If this check bounces, I'll forget the whole thing. But if it doesn't bounce, you'll help me carry out this investigation, at least for a couple of days." She held her hand for Lorraine to shake. "Agreed?"

Lorraine did not extend her own hand. Although she did not want to have anything to do with Mrs. Winslow, she did want to find out what was going on with the murder, if that's what it was, and Mrs. Winslow's and Professor Winslow's involvement, and where Lieutenant Dickey fit into it all. And it always was interesting working with Jennifer, even if she did find herself in the role of a pigeon every once in a while. She looked at her husband.

"The check will probably bounce," he said. "Mrs. Winslow has lied about everything else, so she's probably lying about that too. What have you got to lose? The worst that can happen is, you get to lock her up."

"The woman is definitely a liar," Jennifer reminded her. "For all you know, her bank account could be as empty as her head."

Suspicion showed in Lorraine face. She hesitated for a moment more, then reluctantly yielded. "You did say . . . a couple of days."

"Good," Jennifer replied. "Now, when can we get started?"

"Started on what?"

"On Mrs. Winslow's case."

"Hold on just one cotton pickin' minute," Lorraine demanded. "You said there would be no case until we found out if the check bounced."

"I know," Jennifer answered, "but it's not going to bounce."

"What makes you so sure?"

"Because Mrs. Winslow isn't lying this time. She has five hundred and eighty thousand dollars in her bank account, give or take a few cents."

"How much?"

"Five hundred and eighty thousand."

"How do you know that?"

"I can't tell you because you might have me arrested. Actually, I asked somebody to take a peek at her account."

"That's dishonest."

"No it isn't. If it were dishonest, I would have had to pay him."

"Yes it is," Lorraine complained. "And it's sneaky. You said her bank account was probably as empty as her head."

"I did not. I said as far as you knew, it could be as empty as her head. It just so happens it isn't."

"That's a lot of money for Professor Winslow and Mrs. Winslow to have in one bank account," George interrupted, ignoring his wife's protests.

"Not the professor," Jennifer answered. "Just Mrs. Winslow. The bank account is in her name only. My friend couldn't find any record of Professor Winslow having an account. Of course it could be in another bank."

Lorraine's curiosity in the case was beginning to

show. "She could have emptied his account and put the money into hers, and then arranged for something to happen to him."

Jennifer shrugged. "Judging from Mrs. Winslow's ability to avoid the truth, and if she were the only one who said he does exist, I'd say you could be right. But, since the security guard at the university says he saw him, I think we can be reasonably sure he must be around here some place. Besides, George knows he exists. He was in his class in college."

"He existed when I attended Westland," George agreed. "But I don't know about today."

"I still think she could have transferred all his money into her bank account and then killed him," Lorraine said. "Then she filed a missing person's report with the police to throw them off the trail. You'll probably have to turn in your own client for the murder of her husband, and her best friend, or whatever Professor Reid was." Her face suddenly brightened. "And then I could toss her into jail for fifty years."

"Don't become too happy," Jennifer cautioned. "She couldn't have killed him. The security guard saw him just an hour before we got to the university, and Mrs. Winslow wasn't out of our sight during that time. Besides, we don't have even one ounce of proof that anything has happened to him."

"She could have killed him later. Don't forget, when she and George went to search for him, she appeared to already know where he was. I wouldn't be surprised if his body shows up."

"It must have been quite a bit later. She left the College of Science with Lieutenant Dickey, remember. And from the way she was playing with him, I'll bet they kept each other busy for quite a while, in spite of what she told me this morning about nothing happening between them."

"What about Professor Reid then? Maybe Mrs. Winslow killed her and found some way to come up with a fool proof alibi, like being at the police station. I don't know about this business of an open marriage. Any time you get one married person fooling around with another married person, there's going to be trouble. She sure had a good enough motive to kill her."

"I suppose, but why would she pay us five thousand dollars to investigate the disappearance of her husband if she's involved in murder?"

George and Lorraine looked at each other, and then sang in unison.

"Because she's crazy."

"She doesn't need us," Lorraine declared. "She needs someone with a large net. And we're the ones who are crazy. You're crazy if you get involved with her, and I'm crazy if I let you get me involved, aren't I George?"

"George!"

"I can't remember it ever stopping you before,"

George replied. He nodded toward Jennifer. "You and I both know that she'll get you involved sooner or later. It's just a matter of time. Where are you planning to start?"

"I think we should talk to Sergeant Chambers and ask if he's received any information from the medical examiner's office," Jennifer suggested. "He should have a preliminary report by now on how Professor Reid died."

"What about Lieutenant Dickey?" George asked. "Are you going to be seeing him again? It seems to me that you're not going to get a lot of cooperation from him, not after what you did to him."

"I don't understand why not," Lorraine chuckled with a sudden burst of enthusiasm. "After all, we did tell him we were sorry."

"I wish I shared your wife's warmth and affection for our dear Lieutenant Dickey," Jennifer answered. "Fortunately, Sergeant Chambers should help us. I phoned him at police headquarters before I came over. He wasn't there, but they said we would find him at the College of Science."

As they drove to the university, Jennifer went over with her new, if somewhat reluctant partner, everything that had transpired.

"So far, we have one extremely well off, oversexed college professor's wife who lies a lot," she said, "one science professor who appears to have been murdered, and one science professor, Mrs. Winslow's husband, who might be the murderer, might be missing, and might be dead."

"The evidence so far points to Professor Winslow being somehow involved in Professor Reid's death," Lorraine said, "and although there is still a possibility her death was an accident, she has almost certainly met with foul play. And what's Mrs. Winslow's role in all this. Is lying just part of her personality, or is she so frightened about her husband's safety, and so desperate to find him, that she's willing to try almost anything to get help?"

"Don't forget one slightly perverted and obnoxious police lieutenant who has been hanging around the College of Science where the crime took place, likes to make passes at beautiful women he doesn't know, and appears to know our client."

Lorraine grimaced. "Ah, Lieutenant Dickey. I'm curious as to why he would insist he had never heard of Mrs. Winslow, even though he was standing right beside her at the police station. I also wonder why she seemed so apprehensive when she first saw him, and then so friendly when they left the College of Science together. And why would she leave with him if she was so afraid of him? It was obvious that they knew each other the way they were snuggling in his police car."

"I'm sure we will be seeing the lieutenant again," Jennifer answered, "since he will probably be working on the case if it's determined that Professor Reid was murdered, and if by some miracle he's talking to us, we'll ask him."

"This is a strange case," Lorraine agreed. "Usually when investigators are hired to solve a crime, they know what the crime is. But in this instance, you've been told to ignore the crime, and instead try to find a man who is missing when we're not even sure why, or even if he is missing, at least not in the sense his wife says he is. Maybe George was right. Maybe he did run away from home."

Jennifer nodded. "I don't think she's told the truth even once since we laid eyes on her. She lied to the desk sergeant at police headquarters, she lied to us, and she lied to Dickey and Chambers. She knows she's lying and everybody else knows she's lying, but she does it anyway. The question is, why?"

"I don't know," Lorraine replied. "But I figure there has to be some truth in there somewhere. Maybe Lieutenant Dickey found it last night when he took her home."

"If that's all he was looking for."

SEVEN

Sergeant Chambers had not arrived when they entered the College of Science building, but they did spot Lieutenant Dickey in the hallway. He did not look any better. His left eye was a deeper shade of purple and almost swollen shut. He still had the bandage on the side of his head.

"Lieutenant," Jennifer called out in the sweetest, most agreeable voice she could muster. "Can we talk to you? Sergeant Chambers told us you would have some information about the professor who was found dead in the science lab."

"Chambers didn't say that," Lorraine whispered.

"I know that," Jennifer whispered back, "but he doesn't."

"You believe in putting your head smack dab in the lion's mouth, don't you," Lorraine muttered.

Dickey glared at them with his one good eye. "I don't have anything for you. What's your business in all this anyway, and what are you doing here?"

"We've been hired by Mrs. Winslow to find her husband," Jennifer informed him.

Dickey guffawed. "When you do find him, give him to me. I have a nice jail cell waiting for him."

"Why?"

"Because he murdered Professor Reid, that's why."

"What makes you say that?"

"Because his fingerprints are all over the place. They're on the lab benches, they're on the science equipment, they're on her purse, they're on the hypodermic needle he used to inject her with the truth serum . . . ."

"Truth serum?" Lorraine exclaimed. "You mean that . . . ?"

"That's right, truth serum. Winslow gave her an overdose, she was probably allergic to it, and it killed her."

"But why would he give her truth serum?"

"How the hell should I know. Maybe they were playing games. Maybe they got high on it."

"Why did she take off her clothes?"

"Maybe he was having trouble finding a place to give her the needle. What do you think? They took off their clothes because they were having an affair."

"How do you know the men's clothes were Professor Winslow's?"

"Who else would they belong to?" Dickey swung his hand in an arc as if to dismiss them. "Now get out of my way so I can find this Winslow person and arrest him for the murder of Professor Reid."

"Did you happen to learn anything from Mrs. Winslow when you took her home last night?" Lorraine asked.

Dickey didn't answer the question. "Get out of my way," he repeated again as he turned and walked away.

"Could I ask just one more question, Lieutenant?" Jennifer called after him. "What were you doing outside the College of Science building yesterday and again last evening?"

Dickey didn't answer that question either.

"See, I told you there had to be some truth in there somewhere," Jennifer said after Dickey had gone, "although I don't think the lieutenant shared it all. I'd still like to know what he was doing hanging around the College of Science."

"Truth serum?" Lorraine exclaimed. "What were they doing with truth serum?"

"I'll bet Professor Reid knew something and somebody was trying to get it from her."

"I wonder if we could get hold of some of that truth serum and give it to Mrs. Winslow," Lorraine wondered aloud.

Jennifer nodded. "That might be a good idea, unless she already has some."

"You mean she might have given the injection to Professor Reid?"

"Anything is possible at this stage."

"But Lieutenant Dickey didn't mention finding her fingerprints, just Professor Winslow's."

"True, but his prints are going to be all over the lab anyway. He works there, remember?"

"What about on her purse?"

"If they were having an affair, that wouldn't be unusual."

"What about on the hypodermic needle that was used to give her the truth serum?"

"Now, that could be unusual."

"Let's consider where they worked," Lorraine said. "In a science lab, and they conducted experiments all the time. Maybe Professor Reid discovered something and wouldn't share it."

"But why would they take off their clothes? Unless Winslow was trying the other method first. We should have asked Dickey if the crime lab report showed she had intercourse before she died."

"And why was the lieutenant so sure those were Professor Winslow's clothes? He didn't say there was identification in them, and we didn't see any. Besides, whoever was there would have taken his clothes off if he and Professor Reid were going to have sex, but how many times have you heard of a murderer taking off his clothes to kill someone?"

"Maybe Sergeant Chambers can help us," Jennifer

said as the sergeant appeared around a corner. She repeated Lorraine's question to him.

"According to Dickey, at least one person," Chambers informed them. "Professor Winslow. Although I'm still not convinced the clothes were his. There was no identification in them. Dickey just assumed they were the professor's since he had been there and was seen leaving."

"Did Professor Reid have intercourse before she was killed?" Lorraine asked.

"She had intercourse with somebody," Chambers answered. "We don't know who yet. And it looks like she consented. Other than the needle mark, there were no signs of physical abuse on her body."

"So they might have been putting their clothes back on when she was murdered."

"It's a possibility."

"Maybe we were right," Lorraine said. "Maybe whoever killed her was trying the other method first."

"Do you have any idea why Lieutenant Dickey would be hanging around the science laboratory the past few days?" Jennifer asked. "I saw him watching the building yesterday, and then we saw him here again last night, before we had our altercation with him. Was he investigating something else he won't tell us about?"

"Not that I know of," Chambers replied. "But I'll ask him. In the meantime, I would suggest you two try to stay out of his way, if that's possible."

"We'll try," Jennifer assured him. "Do you mind if we continue to call you once in a while to see what he's been up to?"

"Be my guest," the sergeant responded as he turned and walked toward the science lab where Dickey was working.

"I think that Dickey and Mrs. Winslow would make a wonderful couple," Jennifer said as they watched Chambers disappear into the laboratory. "They both have enough hangups to fill a psycho ward."

Lorraine nodded in agreement. "Let's see if we can talk to that security guard again. Maybe he'll know what Dickey was doing hanging around here. We'll also ask him what Professor Winslow was wearing when he left the building. I don't think he could help but notice a naked man with one green sock, no matter what Lieutenant Dickey says."

The guard who had been on duty the night before hadn't come in yet, but other laboratories were filling with students and several professors were in their offices. They talked to as many as possible. Most of them could not offer any information, but one of the students had been walking through the campus the evening before and had seen Professor Winslow leave.

"What was he wearing?" Jennifer asked.

"Same as always," the student answered.

"Pants and shoes?"

The student looked at her inquisitively. "Yes."

"And a jacket?"

"Yes."

"Are you sure?"

"About what?"

"Was he wearing pants and shoes and a jacket?"

"Yeah, I'm sure."

"Did you happen to see Professor Winslow and Professor Reid together in the lab?" she asked the student.

"Just Professor Reid. She taught a class until about nine-thirty."

"Did you see her and Professor Winslow together again after nine-thirty, before Professor Winslow left?"

"No, at least I didn't," the student answered. "I left right after class, but Professor Reid and Professor Winslow often worked late. He might have come in later."

"Did you happen to see anyone else leave the lab?"

"No. Sorry."

"I think our love triangle just turned into a rectangle," Lorraine said when they were alone. "Who on earth owns the men's clothes they found in the lab? And why didn't the police find identification in them? And one other thing. Where's the guy who owns the clothes, or is he walking around without them?"

Jennifer shrugged. "Perhaps Dickey's at least half right about who the murderer is. Maybe Professor Winslow discovered that Professor Reid, who he was having an affair with, was having an affair with someone else. He caught them together in the science lab and killed them."

"All right, then where's the other body?"

"Maybe he got rid of it."

"Why? And why didn't he also get rid of Professor Reid's body?"

"No time maybe? I don't know. We don't even know for sure that there is another body. Why don't we have another look around. As long as we stay out of the lieutenant's way we should be all right."

They began to check some other rooms that were not in use. They found nothing unusual until they came to an office that had a piece of green cloth wedged between the door and the frame, preventing it from closing all the way.

"I think we might have discovered our other sock," Lorraine said as she pushed the door open and examined the green material.

Without entering, they looked around. The room had been ransacked. "It appears that more than just Professor Winslow and Professor Reid had a secret that someone wanted," Jennifer commented.

"And I think we might have found our other murder victim," Lorraine replied as she stared at a partially nude body slumped over a desk.

"Would you like to tell Lieutenant Dickey, or will I tell him?" Jennifer asked.

"Tell me what?"

They turned at the sound of the demanding voice behind them. Dickey had the usual scowl on his face. Chambers was a short distance behind. The sergeant looked a little more cheerful.

"Good morning again, Lieutenant Dickey," Jennifer half sang as he approached.

"Rrrr," Dickey growled as he looked at the sock in the doorway and then at them. Without asking what they were doing there, he stepped past and into the room where the body lay.

"Has Lieutenant Dickey not had his coffee yet?" Jennifer said as she greeted Chambers.

"He says he has a headache," Chambers responded. "I think he was just reminded who gave it to him."

When Dickey emerged from the room a few minutes later, he glowered at the two women. "Well, what do you know about this one?"

"About as much as you do," Lorraine answered. "I hope your eye is feeling better?" she sympathized when she noticed Dickey nursing the side of his face.

Jennifer added her own sympathies. "And your head where I hit you with my purse?"

"Why do you two always show up where there's been a murder?" Dickey barked.

"I suppose you could say we're lucky," Jennifer said, "but the truth is, we were looking for anything that could help us find Professor Winslow for his wife, and we stumbled across this guy. Any idea who he is?"

Dickey ignored the question. "Where's the forensic team?" he asked Chambers.

"I'll get them," Chambers replied. He repeated Jennifer's question. "Any idea who the body in the office is?"

"Not yet. A male, probably one hundred and seventy or one hundred and eighty pounds, and approximately thirty or thirty-five years old. He's about as naked as the lady we found in the lab. More naked, he wasn't wearing glasses."

The others smiled at his humor. Dickey either didn't get his own joke or chose not to acknowledge it. "From the fresh puncture mark on one of his arms, I would say he probably met the same fate that she did," he continued.

"Truth serum?" Chambers asked.

"Probably. Except he had a little additional help, a bullet hole in the back of the head."

Jennifer put on her sweet voice again. "Will you let us know when you find out who he is?"

"Rrrr," Dickey grumbled, returning to his old cantankerous self. Without any indication that he was planning to leave, he turned away and walked back into the office.

"I'm beginning to think Lieutenant Dickey likes the murder victim more than he likes us," Lorraine commented.

Chambers grinned. "That's not entirely true. If you two were dead, I'm sure he'd like you better."

"Do you or the lieutenant have any ideas as to why two college professors would be given truth serum and then murdered, and another one would disappear?" Jennifer asked.

"Only that someone appears to have been trying to extract information," Chambers answered. "From what I've seen, college professors just aren't the type of people who become involved in murder. They read books, they play in their labs, they hang around together, they don't usually get themselves into this sort of thing . . . except . . . ."

"Except . . . ?"

"Except two, and maybe three of them did get involved. Two of them are dead, and one is on the run."

"If he isn't also dead."

Chambers nodded. "Yeah. Well, we'll find him, one way or another. I just hope we find him alive, and then maybe we can piece this whole thing together."

"I'm not ready to hang Professor Winslow quite yet," Jennifer declared, "although I must admit, this doesn't look good for him."

"Professor Winslow had to have been involved," Lorraine said, "and probably Mrs. Winslow too. Except it looks like the murders took place while she was at the police station filing her missing person's report."

"It gave her a convenient alibi."

"Maybe too convenient. I think we were right about

open marriages. Anytime you get that many people
fooling around together, there's going to be trouble. For
all we know, Professor Reid and the guy in the office
were caught in the act by Professor Winslow or Mrs.
Winslow."

"Right now your client and her husband are the
only suspects we have," Chambers reminded them.
"And if these murders were committed over sex, they
must have had quite a club going."

Jennifer shook her head. "No. That's not why they
were killed. Maybe they took their clothes off to have
sex, but they were killed for some other reason."

"Somebody was looking for something," Lorraine
agreed, "and when they couldn't find it, they used the
truth serum."

"But what?"

"That's where the professor comes in. Hopefully
when we find him, we'll find the answer. We can also
ask your client, if we ever discover when she's telling
the truth and when she's lying."

Dickey finished his examination of the room and
waved to the forensic team to take over. "Let's go," he
said to Chambers as he walked past them. "Let's find
this Winslow and hang another murder on him for
killing Professor Bentley."

"Is that the name of the victim?" Chambers asked
as he fell in behind.

"That's who his identification says he is. He's listed
as one of the professors who worked in the science

department with Winslow and Reid. And Winslow killed him."

Jennifer and Lorraine followed. "Do you have even one piece of evidence that shows Professor Winslow was involved in his death?" Jennifer demanded.

"I have two victims who were killed with truth serum, a bullet hole in one of them, and a professor on the run," Dickey snapped back. "His fingerprints were all over the murder scene in the lab, and they're going to be all over this one too."

"So much for innocent until proven guilty," Jennifer murmured.

"You just make sure you call me if you hear from him," Dickey ordered.

"We will," Lorraine assured him.

"No we won't," Jennifer said after Dickey was out of hearing range. "Not until we find out what our client's husband's role is in all this."

"We will too," Lorraine insisted. "If it weren't for Dickey and Chambers, we wouldn't even know what's going on. Besides, your client's husband might just be the murderer, not to mention what your client might be."

"Have you noticed something peculiar here?" Jennifer said as they neared the main office of the College of Science.

"What?"

"When I talk about Mrs. Winslow, she's our client. When you talk about her, she's my client."

"That's because I want you to receive all the credit for whatever we get ourselves into," Lorraine replied.

"Don't be silly," Jennifer said. "I want you to receive at least half the credit."

"I was afraid of that," Lorraine sighed. "Could you just promise me one thing. If we do find Professor Winslow, promise me you'll take him to police headquarters and give him to Lieutenant Dickey."

"And what about our client? Don't we owe her anything? She did give us five thousand dollars to find her husband."

"Oh, all right. If we find Professor Winslow, we'll turn him over to Mrs. Winslow."

"Good."

"And then we'll turn them both over to Lieutenant Dickey."

EIGHT

The dean of the College of Science wasn't in when Jennifer and Lorraine arrived at his office, but his secretary said she would try to help them.

"Professor Reid was an awfully nice lady," she said. "Brilliant too. She was always discovering something new. The students loved her. I can't imagine anyone wanting to kill her."

"Do you know if she might have discovered or developed anything new lately?" Jennifer asked. "Something important, or secretive, that someone would kill her for?"

"No," the secretary answered, "but then I never paid that much attention to what she worked on. I just know she invented things. She and Professor Winslow worked together quite often. Perhaps you could ask him."

"We'd like to, but we can't find him," Lorraine said. "Did you know that he was missing?"

"Oh dear," she answered. "I hope he's all right."

"Do you know Professor Winslow?"

"Yes. He's a nice man and very well liked by everybody at the university, much like Professor Reid."

"Do you know if they were in any kind of trouble, maybe strange people hanging around them? Were they worried about anything?"

"I really didn't know that much about what they were doing or who they might have known," the secretary said. "Perhaps Dean MacRae could help you, but as far as I know they weren't in any trouble."

"Do you know when the dean will return?" Lorraine asked.

"The day after tomorrow," she replied. "I can make an appointment for you, if you like. He should be able to see you then."

They waited while the secretary entered their names in her appointment book. When she finished, Jennifer asked if she knew Professor Bentley.

She hesitated a few seconds, and then as if choosing each word carefully, spoke slowly. "I know him. But not very well."

"What kind of person was he?" Jennifer asked.

The secretary was silent.

"You might help us catch his murderer."

"Murderer? You mean he was murdered too?"

"I'm afraid so. He was found dead in his office a little while ago."

The secretary chose her words carefully again. "I don't know exactly how to say this," she stammered. "I don't want to speak badly about the dead, but Professor Bentley was not a very nice person. He was arrogant and rude, and people were afraid of him. Ever since he came here from England . . . ."

"He's from England?"

"Yes. He's been here about six months. He arrived approximately the same time that Professor Winslow returned."

"This could be a coincidence," Jennifer said, "but Professor Winslow's wife is from England, and she's been married to him for approximately six months. Do you know her?"

"Not very well," the secretary replied. "But I know about her. Have you seen the way she dresses? Professor Winslow taught in England for a year, and when he came back, he brought her with him. They were married."

"Did Professor Bentley work with Professor Reid and Professor Winslow?"

"Professor Reid spent some time with him."

"Did the Winslows know him?"

"I don't know about Professor Winslow, but Mrs. Winslow did. I saw her talking to him a couple times. I heard him call her Mrs. Smythe once, and I wondered about it, so I inquired. I had to get some information for Professor Winslow from the university where he taught in England, and I asked the secretary who worked for him there. She said that before Mrs. Winslow married Professor Winslow, she had been married to a Professor Smythe who taught in the same science department. They had only been married for six months when he was killed in some kind of laboratory accident."

"Did you say six months?"

"Yes. And she married Professor Winslow shortly after."

"Did the professor's secretary in England say what kind of accident?"

"An overdose of something. If they had taken the time to ask me, I could have told them what the overdose was."

"What?"

"Mrs. Winslow."

"You mean his wife gave him an overdose?"

"I mean his wife was the overdose. They said they found him in his lab one day, shortly after Mrs. Winslow had left. He was almost nude with a big smile on his face."

"He was smiling?"

"Well I don't know about that part, but I was told he was, and I believe it. She's put a smile on quite a few faces around here too."

"Do you know if there was an official cause of death?"

"They said he died from an overdose of truth serum. But I don't believe it. Nobody dies from truth serum, do they? I think he was giving her the other kind of serum and just ran out of it, if you know what I mean."

"I think I know what you mean," Jennifer said with a smile. "Did Mrs. Smythe . . . Mrs. Winslow always live in England?"

"No. Professor Winslow's secretary said she came from Austria."

"But she's English, isn't she?"

"I don't think so. I was told she's Austrian, or German."

"But her accent?"

"Her accent probably sounds English to people from other countries. It depends on where she learned the language. I was told she immigrated to England with Professor Smythe from Austria. She lived there with her former husband."

"Professor Smythe."

"No. Professor Helmitten."

"She had another husband?"

"Yes. When Helmitten died, she married Professor Smythe."

Jennifer was silent for a moment. "Do you by any chance know how long she had been married to Professor Helmitten before he died?"

"No, but I don't think it was a long time."

"Do you know how he died?"

"No. I was just told they found him in his laboratory one day."

"Naked, with a smile on his face?"

The secretary smiled. "I don't know. Probably. I wouldn't be surprised. They didn't give him very long to live after he married her. He was fairly old, you know."

"Do you know if she has any more husbands lying around?" Jennifer asked.

"That's all I know about."

Jennifer thanked her for the information. "Would you also give what you told us to the police," she said. "It could help them in their investigation."

"I will," the secretary answered. "A Lieutenant Dickey called and left a message that he would be coming in this morning."

Jennifer thanked her again. "I have a feeling our client has been experimenting more than her husband has," she said to Lorraine as they left the office and walked toward the parking lot.

"And it could be that we finally have a connection of some kind," Lorraine replied.

Jennifer nodded. "Do you think Bentley and the Winslows might have been up to something in Europe before they came here, and brought it with them?"

"That's what I was thinking. Now all we have to do is figure out what."

"We also have to find out what happened to Mrs. Winslow's first husband, Professor Helmitten. It will be interesting if we discover he died from an overdose of truth serum."

"If he did, it puts our client right smack dab in the middle of three murders."

"Thank you for calling her our client," Jennifer replied. "I'm not sure I want full responsibility for her right now. It looks like she could be into something up to her neck."

"Et tu Brutus? And after all the money she's given you to find her husband."

"You're absolutely right. As far as we're concerned, Mrs. Winslow is innocent, at least until Lieutenant Dickey finds her and her professor husband guilty and throws them both into jail, or until our five thousand dollars runs out. Let's take another drive over to the Winslows' residence and see if she's home. She knows a lot more than what she's told us so far, and I'd like to hear about it."

"Why don't we take a lie detector with us," Lorraine suggested. "Then maybe we can make some logical sense out of what she's telling us."

"You're so cynical," Jennifer accused. "Just because she's lied once or twice, doesn't mean she'll lie all the time."

Lorraine shook her head. "She hasn't lied just once or twice. She hasn't told the truth once or twice. She's lied to everyone who has ever talked to her."

"Precisely. And that will make it easier for us, because we'll be expecting her to lie."

"I'll know when she's lying," Lorraine said with a twisted smirk.

"How?"

"Anytime she's talking to us. We should send Lieutenant Dickey over to interrogate her. I'll bet he has more effective ways to get information than we have, especially after the way she crawled all over him when he was driving her home last night."

"I'm sure Dickey has already interrogated her," Jennifer said. "That and a few other things."

No one was home when they arrived at the Winslow residence. Jennifer knocked on the front door for several minutes. When there was still no answer, she tried the door knob. It turned in her hand. She slowly pushed open the door.

"Is anybody here?" she called out, pushing the door open all the way. She called out one more time, then stepped into the foyer and motioned for Lorraine to join her.

"We can't go in there unless we have the police present and obtained a search warrant," Lorraine protested.

"Who do we know that's going to provide a search warrant so we can investigate our own client?" Jennifer replied. "Besides, she could be in trouble."

Lorraine gave a half-hearted nod of agreement. "Well let's at least be careful."

They called out for Mrs. Winslow as they proceeded from room to room, until they reached the master bedroom. As Jennifer pushed the door open, they could see the empty drawers in a dresser and the women's clothes that were piled on the bed and packed in an open suitcase.

Jennifer opened a drawer in another dresser and stared at the clothes that were still there. "Do you notice anything unusual here?" she asked as she opened the remaining drawers.

"What?"

"Professor Winslow is the one who's supposed to be gone, right?"

"Yes."

"And Mrs. Winslow is still supposed to be here, right?"

"Yes."

"Then how come his clothes are still in the drawers and hers are in the suitcase?"

Lorraine looked at the men's clothing in the dresser drawers again. "If we're seeing what we think we're seeing, the professor either left town without his clothes or he's still here."

"And Mrs. Winslow is getting ready to leave. How do you feel about sitting on a stakeout for a few hours, and then following her?"

"Do you think she'll return?"

"Probably," Jennifer replied. "It doesn't look like she's gone yet. It just looks like she, or whoever the suitcase belongs to, hasn't finished packing."

They left the bedroom and the rest of the house the

way they had found it and parked down the street where there was a clear view of the house. As they waited for Mrs. Winslow to make her next move, the afternoon dragged on and shadows of evening began to stretch across the road.

"How can you do this for a living?" Lorraine asked after they had been waiting for three hours.

"What?"

"Sit for hours and watch a house."

"It's usually a little easier than this," Jennifer said, grinning at her discomfort. "I usually have some idea of when the person is coming or going, but sometimes I just have to wait."

"I have to go to the bathroom."

"You should have gone before you left home."

"I did go before I left home, but that was eight hours ago."

Jennifer laughed. "Oh, all right. There's a motel down at the end of the street with a restaurant attached to it. Go down there and use their restroom. And get us some coffee. If I'm not here when you get back, it means that Mrs. Winslow came home and left again, and I'm following her."

"And what do I do?"

"You can have my coffee. I'll be here, but if I'm not, you'll have to call George to come and get you, or take a taxi."

Lorraine walked the half block to the restaurant where she used their facilities and then ordered coffee and sandwiches. As she was leaving, she noticed a man and woman coming out of one of the motel rooms that was adjacent to the building.

She recognized the woman immediately as Mrs. Winslow. But it was the man Mrs. Winslow was with who attracted her attention. He was the same person she and Jennifer had seen in the photograph at the College of Science.

"Professor Winslow?" she exclaimed.

NINE

Professor Winslow and Mrs. Winslow stood for a few seconds outside the door to their motel room. They looked around the area in front of the building, then walked quickly into the parking lot. Mrs. Winslow unlocked an older green colored Pontiac, waited for the professor to get in the passenger's side, then slid in behind the steering wheel.

She appeared to be ready to start the engine when they were distracted by an automobile that had entered the parking lot and stopped in front of the motel office. They sat motionless as they waited for the driver to emerge.

"Lieutenant Dickey," Lorraine exclaimed to herself as she recognized the lieutenant and the blue Chevrolet he had been driving the night before. "How did he get here?"

Dickey got out of the car and entered the office. A minute later he reappeared and walked along the sidewalk in front of the motel. He examined each number as he advanced until he came to the door of the room the Winslows had left a few minutes earlier.

Lorraine peered into the semidarkness of the parking lot where Mrs. Winslow and the professor were hidden. They had sunk down into the car seat, obviously afraid they might be discovered.

"Probably with good reason," she decided. Mrs. Winslow had told them she didn't trust the police to treat her husband fairly, and Lieutenant Dickey had already decided the professor was guilty of two murders.

The lieutenant knocked on the door, then leaned against the building and scanned the surrounding area while he waited for someone to answer. When there was no response, he fumbled with the lock, and the door swung inward.

He quickly inspected the interior of the room from the doorway, then disappeared inside. A few minutes later he came out and closed the door behind him. He looked around the area once more, then walked off in the direction of his car.

Lorraine considered calling out to him, but quickly changed her mind. She didn't trust him. She was also sure he somehow knew the Winslows, or at least Mrs. Winslow, in spite of her denial that she had ever met him before the previous evening. What if he was searching for the professor for reasons other than to arrest him. If she did call out, she could be putting the Winslows, and maybe even herself, in danger.

The Winslows also waited for the lieutenant to leave. When he was out of sight, Mrs. Winslow started the engine and backed the Pontiac out of the parking space. Lorraine expected her to leave in the opposite direction so that they could make their escape, but instead, she turned in the same direction that Dickey's Chevrolet had gone, and pursued him down the street.

"Why the hell would they be following Dickey?" Lorraine murmured in surprise. She made sure of the direction the two cars were heading, and then ran the half block to where Jennifer was patiently waiting for Mrs. Winslow to come home.

"I saw them, I saw them," she gasped as she pulled open the door of the car and slid in. "Mrs. Winslow and Professor Winslow."

"Where?" Jennifer exclaimed.

"At the restaurant. They came out of a motel room, got into a car and headed north. I got their license plate number. I also saw Lieutenant Dickey. He was searching for them, or was following them, and now they're following him."

Jennifer started the car, pulled it into gear, and swung it into a driveway. The ten year old Porsche screeched back out onto the street and they sped off in the direction that Lorraine had last seen the Winslows and Dickey.

"Are you sure it was Professor Winslow and Mrs. Winslow that you saw at the motel?" Jennifer asked. "And Lieutenant Dickey?"

"I'm sure," Lorraine replied. "Dickey was driving his blue Chev, and the Winslows are in an older green Pontiac sedan."

"And the Winslows were following Dickey?"

"That's what it looked like. When Dickey pulled out of the parking lot, they took off down the street after him. I just hope we can catch them before they catch him, or he catches them, or whatever they're doing."

"Don't worry, we'll catch them," Jennifer said as she stared into the busy traffic ahead. "By the way, the next time I tell you to go to the bathroom before you leave home . . . ."

"Yes?"

"Don't listen to me. If it wasn't for you, we'd still be watching an empty house."

"No thanks needed," Lorraine answered. "I was happy to do it. Boy, was I happy to do it. Sorry about your coffee. I left it on a curb in the parking lot."

She suddenly stiffened against the back of the seat. "There they are. Right in front of us. And there's Dickey's car, just ahead of them."

Dickey didn't appear to be in much of a hurry and didn't show any indication that he was worried about being followed. Neither did the Winslows, and Jennifer had no trouble keeping both cars in sight for the next several blocks. When the lieutenant pulled onto a side street, and then into the parking lot of an apartment complex, Mrs. Winslow didn't try to follow, but instead parked on the street. She and the professor climbed out and walked quickly into the complex.

Jennifer parked on the street a few yards behind the Pontiac. "Do you suppose Dickey lives here?" she said. "The Winslows appear to know where he's going."

"I don't know," Lorraine answered, "but I'm going to find out. You stay here while I follow them, and if Dickey or the Winslows come back unexpectedly, sound the horn."

Jennifer smiled. "Don't worry. If Mrs. Winslow and Professor Winslow come out, I'll just hand him over to her and thank her for the five thousand dollars. And then we'll hand both of them over to Lieutenant Dickey, or the Westland Police Department, or whoever wants them."

Lorraine quietly closed the car door and hurried in the direction of the apartment complex. She stopped when she reached the corner of a building, then gradually moved forward until the Winslows came into view. A few feet ahead, the couple was cautiously moving along a sidewalk.

The sound of footsteps from the direction of the apartment parking lot caused both Lorraine and the Winslows to stop and listen. Lorraine quickly stepped into the shadow of the building. The Winslows had also taken cover as they waited for the other person to pass by. When he appeared, the glow from a street light temporarily lit up the taped bandage on the side of Lieutenant Dickey's head.

When he had passed by, Professor Winslow stepped out of the shadows. A glint of bluish silver appeared in his hand as he raised a pistol and aimed it squarely at the lieutenant's back.

Lorraine was about to scream out a warning, when the sound of a group of people approaching caused Winslow to lower his weapon and step back into the shadows.

Lorraine also remained hidden as she watched the lieutenant make his way around the pool area and approach an apartment on the other side. He stood at the door for a moment and looked around, much like he had at the motel, then entered.

After the door had closed, the Winslows left their hiding place and started back toward the street. Lorraine let them pass and then followed. When she arrived at Jennifer's car, the Pontiac was already half way down the block, and Jennifer was lightly tapping the horn.

"I thought you said that if they came out, you were going to grab them, thank Mrs. Winslow for the five thousand dollars, and then hand them over to the police," Lorraine exclaimed as she slid into the Porsche.

"I know," Jennifer said, "but my curiosity got the best of me. I thought we could follow them and see

what else they might be up to. How about Dickey?
Did you see him?"

"I saw him," Lorraine answered. "And so did the
Winslows. Apparently he lives here, and they knew it.
And get this. It looked like the professor was getting
ready to shoot him. At least he had a gun in his hand
and it was aimed squarely at Dickey's back. Why
would they want to shoot Dickey?"

"Hmm." Jennifer nodded her head and smiled
crookedly as she considered the question. "Now why
would anybody want to shoot Lieutenant Dickey? Or
better yet, why wouldn't anybody want to shoot
Lieutenant Dickey?"

"Surely nobody could hate him that much," Lorraine
said. "Other than perhaps us. The Winslows had to be
following him for some reason. There's more going on
here than just one overzealous police officer trying to
catch one innocent, or maybe not so innocent, university
professor. When they saw him at the motel, I had the
impression they were terrified of him, and not just
because he was a cop."

"Maybe we'll find out what they're up to when we
find out where they're going," Jennifer said as the
Pontiac came into sight again. She handed Lorraine
her cell phone. "I think you'd better let your husband
know you're going to be a little late getting home this
evening."

"Couldn't I just go home and let him know in
person," Lorraine said. It was more of a rhetorical

question than a statement. She knew when Jennifer started on the trail of someone, she usually didn't stop until they stopped.

George wasn't home, so Lorraine left a message. It went something like, "I'm with Jennifer. She's on the trail of two suspects. One of them is the person you met recently who tried to seduce you, and the other is the husband of the person who tried to seduce you. And yes, they're together. See you when I get home. Love you."

"I have a question," she said as she disconnected the phone. "I hate to keep bringing up Mrs. Winslow's mind, but what person in her right mind would pay us five thousand dollars to look for a man she's already with?"

"A crazy woman?" Jennifer answered. "Or maybe a very smart woman. Maybe she wasn't with her husband all this time. Maybe she didn't know where he was, and she just found him herself a little while before you did. Or maybe they're in cahoots and she did that to throw everyone off the trail."

"One of them, or both of them, had to be involved in the murders at the College of Science. And even if they weren't directly implicated, they must have known something about what had gone on."

"But if they're working together, then why was she preparing to leave town without him?"

"I don't know," Lorraine responded, "but I have another question."

"What?"

"Where are we going?"

The Winslow's car had left the heavier congestion of the city streets and pulled onto the interstate. Half an hour and thirty miles later when they pulled off again, the lights of Westland were a distant glow on the horizon behind them.

The road they were now on climbed and fell as it twisted through the mountainous terrain, and for moments they lost sight of the car they were pursuing, but then as the road straightened out, they picked it up again. Occasionally, Jennifer would slow down or accelerate her own car to avoid losing them.

The brake lights on the Winslow's car lit up as it slowed at an intersection and turned onto another side road. Jennifer accelerated so they could keep them in sight, but when she swung around the corner in the direction the Pontiac had taken, the car had disappeared.

"Where the hell did they go?" she exclaimed.

"It's hilly here and they're going to disappear every once in a while," Lorraine said. "We'll catch them."

"You're damn right we'll catch them," Jennifer cursed. "We're not going to chase them all the way out here just to lose them."

Although the road they were on wasn't as wide as the main road, it was paved and they were able to travel at a relatively fast speed. Jennifer's Porsche lunged over the hills and into the dips as they raced to catch up to the Pontiac, but it was still nowhere in sight. The Winslows had completely disappeared.

"We should have seen them by now," Lorraine said as she searched the darkness at the side of the road for places the other car might have gone. "Unless they discovered we were after them, and turned off somewhere."

Jennifer glanced in the rear view mirror. "I don't think we have to worry about us finding them," she replied. "I think they just found us. Either they have, or someone else has. Look behind us."

Lorraine turned to look at the headlights that were just a few feet away from the rear window. "It can't be the Winslows," she said. "The lights are too high for a car. It's a pickup truck or something bigger. They're probably just passing through."

Jennifer slowed down and moved to the right to let the pickup truck go by. It continued to follow closely behind with its lights piercing the rear window of the Porsche.

"What do you suggest we do now?" Lorraine asked.

"I suppose we could make a run for it," Jennifer offered. "Except for one little obstacle."

"What's that?"

"The truck in front of us."

Lorraine took her eyes off the vehicle that was following to look at the pickup truck that filled the road ahead. It had slowed down and was straddling the middle of the narrow pavement, preventing them from passing. Suddenly it veered and swung sideways to a stop, completely blocking any chance of escape.

Jennifer brought her own car to a halt. The beams of light from the Porsche lay motionless along the black strip of pavement, stirring only occasionally when the polluted blue and grey air that was stirred up when the truck ahead came to a stop drifted through them. The glow lit up the unshaven faces of the men who had jumped from the cab and were now crouched behind the fenders. The rest of the light filtered off into the dust and the darkness beyond.

At the same time, the truck behind came to a stop in the middle of the pavement, cutting off any chance of escape in that direction. Men had jumped from the cab and taken positions behind the opened doors. In the faint glow beyond the headlights that shone through the rear window of the Porsche, Jennifer and Lorraine could see the rifles they were carrying.

TEN

Lorraine breathed deeply as she tried to settle her pounding heart. She looked across at Jennifer, hoping her friend would have some kind of answer to explain the situation they were in, and at the same time, knowing she wouldn't have an answer.

"What the hell is going on?" she swore nervously as she looked in one direction and then in the other. She picked up the cell phone, only to be met with an out of range message.

"They must think we're someone else," Jennifer answered. Although she was determined not to show any fear, her own heart was beating faster. "I didn't see any signs that said private property or no trespassing. Maybe we stumbled into a game preserve or a restricted forestry area."

"Those people don't look like forest rangers to me,"

Lorraine said, "and if we're on a game preserve, I think we could be the game."

Jennifer reached into her handbag, pulled out her thirty-eight revolver, and laid it on the seat beside her. She opened the glove compartment and retrieved a smaller revolver which she handed to Lorraine.

Lorraine let the gun dangle by its barrel between her fingers. "You expect me to shoot my way out of here with this," she scoffed. "Do you see what's in front of us and behind us? There must be five or six of them, and they all have rifles."

"I guess that eliminates that idea," Jennifer replied. She had picked up the thirty-eight, but then placed it on the seat beside her again. "Do you have any other suggestions?"

"Well, I know we're not going to shoot our way out." Lorraine looked at the small handgun that Jennifer had given her. "I'm not even sure my bullets would go that far. Maybe we can negotiate with them."

"With what?"

"You're right. I don't think we're in a very good position to negotiate."

"We could always make a break for it," Jennifer suggested, looking into the darkness of the desert.

Lorraine broke into a nervous laughter. "Would you look at the way I'm dressed. I'm wearing high heels and a skirt."

"I told you not to wear high heels."

"Ten hours ago you also told me we were only going for a short drive to the university to see Lieutenant Dickey and Sergeant Chambers."

Jennifer looked at Lorraine's clothing. "What you need are cowboy boots and blue jeans."

"A good horse wouldn't hurt either," Lorraine sniped. "You know what we're trying to do here, don't you."

"What?"

"We're trying to talk ourselves out of being scared."

"Is it working?"

"No."

"I didn't think so. Did you happen to notice if those men were wearing uniforms? Maybe they're cops or security people."

"Cops don't drive pickup trucks. They drive police cars. They're probably gangsters of some kind."

"Gangsters don't drive pickup trucks either. They drive Cadillacs."

"You there in the car," a voice from behind them boomed. "Climb out of there slowly with your hands in the air."

The two women looked at each other for a moment before Lorraine broke the silence. "I don't know about you, but I'm going to climb out of here slowly with my hands in the air." She opened the car door and stepped onto the edge of the road with her arms held high over her head.

Jennifer did the same on the driver's side. They peered into the glow beyond the headlights in an effort to see the man who had given the order.

"If they are security people or policemen, maybe we could tell them we know Lieutenant Dickey," Lorraine suggested. "If they know the Winslows, maybe they also know him. We could say he's your husband or something."

"I would rather be shot," Jennifer muttered. "Why don't you tell them he's your husband?"

"I can't."

"Why not?"

"I'm already married."

Jennifer smirked at Lorraine across the car. She turned her attention to the man who had given the orders. "Who are you?" she yelled.

Her question wasn't answered. "Who the hell are you?" the man yelled back. "And what are you doing here?"

"We're very close associates of Lieutenant Dickey of the Westland Police Department," Lorraine replied. She curled a finger and pointed it at Jennifer. "In fact, this is Mrs. Dickey."

There was no response until one of the men behind them cocked a rifle.

"I'm Lorraine Brensley," Lorraine quickly added. "I'm a prosecuting attorney for the City of Westland. And this is Jennifer Brookbaine. She's a private investigator. Who are you?"

The man ignored her question. "What are you doing here?" he demanded again.

"We were just out for a drive," Jennifer replied defiantly. "That isn't against the law, is it?"

"Out here? At this time of night?"

Jennifer and Lorraine looked around. Even if it had been daylight, they would not have known where they were.

"Where are we anyway?" Lorraine asked.

"Lieutenant Dickey knows exactly where we are," Jennifer reminded her and the man with the gun, deciding that being married to a police officer couldn't hurt their situation.

The man stared at Jennifer with a puzzled look. "You call your husband . . . Lieutenant . . . Dickey?"

"They don't get along all that well," Lorraine explained.

"Lieutenant Dickey is a dirty, rotten, low down, miserable slime bag," Jennifer proclaimed. "We don't like him and he doesn't like us. If you were to shoot us right now, he'd probably say, thank you."

Lorraine glared at her across the car. "Will you be quiet, or at least try to say something nice about him."

"I'd rather be dead," Jennifer blurted.

The man smiled as though he might give Jennifer her wish.

"Don't listen to her," Lorraine pleaded. "She just had a fight with him. You're not going to shoot us, are you?"

"I haven't decided yet," he said. "You still haven't told me what you're doing here."

"We were following a client and she turned down this road and then disappeared," Lorraine replied. "Did you happen to see a green Ponti . . . ?"

"You're on private property," he snapped, cutting her off.

"We're very sorry," Lorraine apologized. "We didn't know . . . ."

"Do you know J.D. Hursh?" the man asked.

"I've heard of him," Lorraine answered. "He owns one of the largest ranches in the state."

"Well, you're on it," he snapped again. "This is his property and you're trespassing."

"So what are you going to do about it?" Jennifer bellowed back. "Shoot us?"

Lorraine grimaced. "Will you quit saying that." She turned to the man who was asking the questions. "We really are sorry," she apologized again.

The man who was doing the talking was obviously in charge. He was tall and fairly good looking, and with his cowboy hat and western attire, would have been at home in a western movie.

The other men appeared to be ranch workers. They wore blue jeans and boots, and looked like they had not shaved for several days. As Jennifer and Lorraine glanced around them at the desolate area, they began to appreciate that he was there. As rough as his voice was, he appeared to be a stabilizing factor. They would not have wanted to meet the other men without him.

The clean shaven man bent one leg and rested the butt of his rifle on his knee. The other end pointed into the air. "Now, one more time," he said. "What are you doing here?"

"We've already told you what we're doing here," Jennifer answered. "We were following a client and she came up this road. Do you know Professor Winslow and Mrs. Winslow?"

"Who?"

"Mrs. Winslow and her husband, Professor Winslow. They just came up this road. You must know them."

"I don't know any Mrs. Winslow, or Professor Winslow," he replied. "You must have seen someone else who works on the ranch."

"Perhaps you're right," Lorraine agreed as she moved closer to the car. "Well, we'd better be getting home."

The man took the rifle butt off his knee and held the gun in both hands. "I don't think so," he said, "not until you've answered a few more questions." He used the barrel of the rifle to brush Jennifer aside, then grabbed the door of the car and swung it open as far as it would go. He reached in and retrieved their handbags. His gaze fell on the two guns that were resting on the seats.

"This certainly isn't ladylike," he remarked, holding Jennifer's thirty-eight revolver in the palm of his hand and moving it up and down as if to weigh it. He lifted the smaller revolver and showed it to Lorraine. "Now, this is much more ladylike. This one belongs to you, doesn't it?"

He dumped the contents of their purses onto the driver's seat and shuffled them around with the barrel of Jennifer's revolver. "Family portrait?" he asked, looking at the photo of the Winslows.

"That's our client and her husband," Jennifer informed him.

He examined the photograph for a few seconds and then pushed it aside. If he recognized the Winslows, he didn't give any indication. He picked up their wallets from the pile and flipped each open.

"You're a private investigator?"

"That's right," Jennifer replied.

"And you said you're a prosecuting attorney?"

"Yes," Lorraine answered.

He rubbed his chin as if pondering what his next move should be. "Mighty strange combination," he finally commented.

"Do you think we could go now?" Lorraine asked. "You know why we're here. Obviously we made a mistake coming onto your property and we're very sorry."

"I don't think so," he responded, as if still undecided what he should do with them. "I think you'd better come with us."

"Now wait just one damned minute," Jennifer

declared. "We've already told you why we're here. We were following a client."

"Didn't you just say a few minutes ago that you were out for a drive?"

"That's true," Jennifer stammered, "but . . . ."

"Why would you be following your own client?"

"It does seem a little unusual," Jennifer explained, "but if you knew our client . . . ."

"And why do you keep referring to the person you were following as being her client too," he said, jerking his thumb in Lorraine's direction. "Since when do prosecuting attorneys have clients?"

Jennifer looked at Lorraine, hoping she would help give an explanation.

"Don't look at me," Lorraine declared. "It was your idea to make her, our client."

"Let me get this straight," the man continued. "You were following a college professor and his wife who happen to be your clients."

"No," Jennifer corrected him. "Just Mrs. Winslow is our client."

"And why did Mrs. Winslow hire you?"

"To find her husband, Professor Winslow."

"The same Professor Winslow who you claim was in the car with your client, Mrs. Winslow?"

"That's right."

He rubbed his chin, then turned to Lorraine and waved a finger in the air as if preparing to make a point. His finger dropped to his chin again before he raised it once more. "And this Mrs. Winslow is also your client?"

"That's what she says," Lorraine replied.

"And you two were hired by Mrs. Winslow to find Professor Winslow who just happened to be in the same car with Mrs. Winslow?"

"That's right."

"She actually paid you to do this?"

"Yes."

"A lot?"

"Quite a bit."

"Just out of curiosity, why would she pay you to find her husband if she already knew where he was?"

"We don't know."

"But we were attempting to find out when you and your band of . . . ." Jennifer hesitated. "Your band of thugs, ambushed us."

"Haven't you forgotten something?" the man said, his eyes narrowing. He spoke softly as if prodding a child for an answer to a question in a kindergarten class.

Jennifer could sense him weakening and her own voice rose as her confidence increased. "What?"

His voice remained soft. "Haven't you forgotten who's trespassing and who's holding the guns?"

"Oh."

"We haven't forgotten," Lorraine broke in. "And we really do appreciate your help in letting us know, Mr . . . Mr . . . Ah . . . ?"

"Jack."

"Mr. Jack."

"Just Jack," he said with a smile.

"Thank you Jack," Lorraine said, trying to keep her voice as soft as his had become. "We didn't know we were trespassing, and we really are very sorry, but could I possibly ask why you and your band of, one, two, three . . . ." She turned to count the men behind her. "Four, five gentlemen, were patrolling a deserted road with guns?"

"Cattle rustlers."

Jack swaggered and his rifle returned to his knee as he leaned toward them. His head nodded a couple times as if satisfying himself with the answer he had given.

"Cattle rustlers?" Lorraine repeated.

"Cattle rustlers."

"Jack. Do we look like cattle rustlers?"

Jack peered at them as if trying to decide if they looked like rustlers.

"Where the hell were we going to put the cattle?" Jennifer trumpeted. "In the back seat?"

"I don't know," he said. "The other night, we had a very nice family visit us, a father, a mother, and their three kids. They had a heifer strapped to the front fender of their car like you would a deer." He leaned sideways and looked past them at the front fender of their car as if expecting a heifer to be strapped to it. His gaze returned to them for a second and then he stretched his neck to look into the back seat.

"Jack?"

"Yes," he said, responding to Jennifer.

"Do you see the way we're dressed?"

"Very nicely," he commented as he nodded in approval. "To tell you the truth, when you got out of the car, I was torn between shooting you and asking you out for dinner."

"Look Jack," Lorraine said. "Can we cut the bullshit here?"

Jack's face changed to amused surprise at the new tone Lorraine's voice had taken.

"You know we're not cattle rustlers, don't you?"

"I know," he answered.

"And you know we didn't just indiscriminately drive up this road, don't you?"

"I know."

"And you believed us when we told you that we were just following our client?"

"No."

"Why not?"

"Number one, your client didn't come down this road because we would have seen her. Number two, nobody follows their own client."

Before she could answer, he spoke again. "Number three, prosecuting attorneys don't have clients. Number four, if I were a private investigator, and I saw my client with the man, her husband, that she had hired me to follow, I would have just stopped them and said, here he is."

Lorraine began to speak, but before she could say anything, he continued.

"And number five, we're going to take you in for a little more questioning, no matter what your excuse is for being here."

Jennifer threw up her hands in disgust. "Just who the hell do you think you are?"

Jack smiled crookedly. "Just a hired thug."

"Now just hold on right there, Mr . . . Mr . . . Uh, Jack, or whoever you are," Jennifer said, her voice rising again. "You and your band of . . . your band can't detain us like this." She shook her finger at him and then pointed it at Lorraine. "My friend here happens to be a pretty good lawyer, and if you don't let us go we're going to sue your ass off, you and your boss J.D. Hursh, or whatever his name is."

"Whew," Jack sighed. He shrugged and lifted his eyes to the sky in defeat. "Do you realize how much trouble I'll be in with J.D. if I get him involved in a lawsuit?"

"You'll be in plenty trouble," Jennifer emphasized, pressing her advantage.

"I guess we won't insist you come with us for questioning after all," he said.

Jennifer and Lorraine watched in puzzlement as he cradled his rifle in the crook of his arms.

"Shoot them."

Jack gave the order, then turned and walked away. "And don't leave their bodies lying around where J.D.

will find them," he yelled back over his shoulder after he had gone a few feet.

"Wait, wait, wait, wait, wait," Lorraine pleaded. She turned in circles and her hands were held out toward the men as though she could use them to stop the bullets. "We'll come with you."

Lorraine screamed the last words so Jack would be sure to hear them.

Jack stopped and then slowly turned. He moved one hand slightly to form a cup around his ear the way a person would when he wanted someone to repeat something.

"We would like to come with you," she said. "We just didn't know it meant so much to you."

"And you won't sue?"

"Of course we won't sue," Lorraine answered. She gestured toward Jennifer. "That was her idea."

"Go ahead and shoot, you coward," Jennifer snarled. "I dare you."

"Perhaps we could shoot just her," Jack suggested to Lorraine.

"Right now, that would be all right with me," Lorraine replied.

"Naw," he said. "You'd probably tell everybody."

"No I wouldn't," Lorraine assured him. "In fact, I'm beginning to wonder if she needs to be shot."

"But what if J.D. found her?"

"You could tell him you mistook her for a cow or something."

"Hmm," Jack pondered. "I can definitely see a resemblance."

Jennifer glowered at them. "Look," she snarled. "Either shoot me or take me in for questioning, but quit insulting me."

"I think we'll take her in for questioning," Jack said. "It wouldn't be fair to leave her out here with the coyotes."

"Thank you," Jennifer muttered.

"I like coyotes," he added with a twisted grin.

Jack's grin disappeared as he grabbed the stock of his rifle and waved the barrel at Jennifer's Porsche. His voice took on the authoritative boom they had been met with when he first stopped them and demanded to know who they were.

"Now, I want you two ladies to get into your little ol' car there," he ordered, "and follow that pickup. And keep close to it. I don't want you getting lost."

One of the unshaven men had picked up their belongings and stuffed them back into their purses. Jennifer's thirty-eight was stuck under his belt. He pointed Lorraine's smaller gun into the night and then turned it sideways and examined it as if trying to determine if it was real.

"Can we please have our belongings back now?" Jennifer asked. She took a step toward the man and reached for their handbags. She stopped when Jack waved his rifle and motioned again for them to get into the car.

"I'll take those," he said. He took the purses and guns from the man, waited for Lorraine and Jennifer to close the doors of the car, and then walked to the truck that was stopped behind. The other men went with him or climbed into the truck ahead.

As the small procession of two pickup trucks and the Porsche slowly moved away, the bouncing headlights of the rear pickup shone through the window of the car. The men could see Jennifer looking over her shoulder. One finger, her middle one, was pointed firmly in the air in their direction.

"The one on the left would kill us if she could," Jack said to the other passengers. "The one on the right is telling her to keep her mouth shut."

ELEVEN

"Maybe we can use your finger to stop the bullets after Jack and his men begin shooting at us," Lorraine suggested.

"Shoot this Jack," Jennifer snarled. Her face contorted into a sneer and her rigid middle finger extended once more in the direction of the truck that was following.

"Will you cut that out," Lorraine chided. "And don't give him any ideas. He just might decide to do it."

"Me, yeah," Jennifer scoffed as she shook her head up and down. "He'd shoot me like a cow, and then he'd leave me out in the desert to be eaten by his coyotes. But not you. Oh no, not you. You and Jack would be standing over my dead body, and you would be saying, shoot her again Jack."

Lorraine couldn't help but laugh at her friend. "But he didn't shoot you. And I don't think he has any intentions of shooting you, or me. And hopefully we're headed toward civilization."

Jennifer was a little more cynical. "Or maybe farther out into the desert. Do you see any civilization around here? They're probably still finding bodies out here that disappeared a hundred and fifty years ago."

"Well at least we know Jack didn't do it," Lorraine shot back. "He can't be more than thirty or forty, so I don't think he was around a hundred years ago. Besides, Jack isn't going to shoot us, or he would have done it already."

"Give him time," Jennifer said. "Maybe he just hasn't found the right spot yet."

"If he intended to shoot us, why would he trust us to drive our own car?"

"Because he has five thugs with guns aimed at us. Six if you include Jack. Does that look like he trusts us?"

When Lorraine spoke again, she was a little more resigned. "No, but thinking that Jack trusts us and might possibly let us go makes me feel better than contemplating being shot like a cow. I'm still hoping he likes us, at least a little bit."

"Well, he likes at least one of us a little bit," Jennifer commented wryly. "You and Jack seemed to hit it off pretty good back there."

"That's because I didn't try to antagonize Jack," Lorraine mimicked, "like someone else I know. You don't call a bunch of cowboys, or whatever those men were, a band of thugs, and then encourage them to go ahead and shoot you, if you want to make them your friends."

Jennifer smiled sheepishly. "It was kind of dumb, wasn't it?"

"Yes, it was, but then it's the kind of thing I've come to expect from you."

"That makes me feel better. But at least we're still alive, so something we did must have worked. I'm still wondering why Jack needed so many men with loaded rifles with him to stop two women on a deserted road . . . unless he thought we might be someone else."

"Maybe the Winslows, or whoever the Winslows are involved with? Do you think that Jack was looking for them when he found us? Do you think he knows them?"

"Yes I do," Jennifer answered. "I didn't believe him for one minute when he said he doesn't know them. I didn't believe him when he said he hasn't seen them either. I also didn't believe that cockamamie story he told us about looking for rustlers or that he's taking us some place for questioning. In fact, I didn't believe anything he told us, other than his threat to shoot us. And do you know what?"

"What?"

"Neither did you."

"Hmm," Lorraine pondered. "Maybe not, but I'll tell you what I do believe."

"What?"

"I believe you're up to something."

Jennifer had let her foot up on the accelerator and was allowing more distance between the Porsche and the pickup in front of them.

"Do you have something in mind," Lorraine asked, "or did you forget Jack's instructions to stay close to the truck ahead?"

"I didn't forget. But just because Jack hasn't shot us yet, doesn't mean he won't have us shot. If we can find a main road that looks like it goes somewhere, I'm taking off. Or would you rather wait and see what else he has in store for us?"

"I think I'd rather escape, if you think we can get away with it."

The only roads they had seen, other than the one they were on, were little more than dirt paths that led off into the desert. Then in the lights from the pickup truck ahead, they could make out what appeared to be a main intersection where a car had approached from a side road and stopped. They looked in the direction it had come from. In the distance they could see lights.

"It could be a town," Lorraine said excitedly.

Jennifer didn't answer. Instead, she slammed on the brakes and the Porsche slid into the intersection. She twisted the steering wheel and pushed her foot down hard on the accelerator as the car skidded sideways around the corner and shot forward along the side road.

For a moment, the occupants in the rear truck didn't react, then the driver skidded the truck around the corner after them. At the same time, the truck ahead swung into the dirt by the side of the road, peeled back onto the pavement in a cloud of dust, and headed back to the intersection.

The side road was filled with sharp twists and turns, and Jennifer had to alternately step on the accelerator and then the brakes as they raced toward the lights in the distance. The pickup trucks had fallen behind and were nowhere in sight when she swung the car around the final curve that stood between them and their destination.

A large industrial complex lay half a mile away. There was one main building and several other smaller buildings that stretched out from it like tentacles. In the lights from the well lit yard they had seen from the highway, they could make out what appeared to be long corridors that connected the structures.

"It's not a town," Lorraine said. "It looks like a warehouse, or a factory of some kind."

"I don't care what it is," Jennifer replied. "I see cars and lights, and that means people."

A high fence topped with barbed wire surrounded the entire complex, and a guard house stood at the only entrance. If there was a security guard on duty, he didn't have time to react before Jennifer raced by and braked to a stop beside the main doorway to the largest building.

They jumped out of the Porsche and ran up the sidewalk to the building. The door wasn't locked, and it thudded open against a wall as they ran inside. They found themselves in the main office area, where except for lights in the foyer and a few adjoining offices, the place was in semidarkness. They quickly checked the rooms where the lights were burning and found them empty.

At one end of the office was another doorway. Through the glass in the door they could see a long dimly lit corridor that led farther into the building. They entered and searched for signs of employees that could be working late. There were none, until they reached the end of the corridor and stopped at a set of double doors. Through the glazed windows they could see lights. The shadow of a person passed in front of the glass.

Lorraine grabbed the handle and pushed. The doors were locked. They banged frantically and yelled to whoever was on the other side. If the people in the room could hear them, they did not respond. They continued to yell until the sound of the front door opening and footsteps in the office area caused them to turn around.

"Jack and his merry band of thugs," Jennifer

muttered. She looked around the area they were in. Small narrow corridors led off to the left and right. They were dark and appeared to be unoccupied.

"Which way?" she whispered to Lorraine.

"Neither," Lorraine said as she picked up a chair. With one motion, she smashed it through the window of the door. The glass shattered into the room and bright light flooded across them and into the corridor.

Several people were working in what appeared to be a laboratory. All wore protective clothing that covered them from head to foot. Oxygen tanks were strapped to their backs. They stopped what they were doing and stared through the heavy masks they were wearing.

"Help us," Lorraine shouted at a hooded figure closest to them. "Unlock the door, please."

The people inside didn't move.

Lorraine reached through the opening left by the broken window and searched with her fingers for a lock on the other side.

"Stop!" the one nearest the door shouted, his words muffled by his mask.

"You'd better do as he says," a voice from the hallway echoed.

They turned to look at Jack who had been joined by the men from the two pickup trucks. They all had their rifles held at the ready.

"These people know we're here," Lorraine yelled. "Don't you, people," she screamed as she returned her attention to the room.

"Don't you, people," she screamed again when there was no reaction from the workers inside the laboratory.

The figures on the other side of the door still did not move as they stared back at her.

"They are people, aren't they?" Jennifer said as she looked through the broken glass. "You are people, aren't you?" she yelled over Lorraine's shoulder.

"We're people," the one nearest the door yelled back. "What are you doing here?"

"We need your help," Lorraine shouted. "We're being kidnapped by these men. We need you to call the police."

The figure leaned against the door and looked past them at the men who were holding the guns. "Hello Jack," he called out, his words still muffled by his mask.

"Hello Ralph," Jack replied. "I'm sorry about the mess."

"That's O.K.," the man known as Ralph replied. "Where did you get the beauties?"

"We found them back on the road."

"He kidnapped us back on the road," Jennifer shouted. "You've got to help us."

They couldn't see the expression on Ralph's face because of the mask, but they were not encouraged when he began to turn away from the door.

"See you again Jack," he said with a wave. "Don't do anything to them that I wouldn't do." With that,

Ralph motioned for another worker to clean up the glass, and walked off.

"Help us, damn you," Jennifer yelled after him.

Either Ralph could not hear her, or had chosen not to listen. He had gone to the other end of the room.

Lorraine reached through the door once more and felt with her fingers for a latch.

"I don't think you should do that," Jack advised.

"Why not?"

"Didn't you see what they're wearing in there?"

"Yes."

"Tell me."

"Oxygen masks and protective lab clothing of some kind."

"Do you know why?"

"No."

"Well neither do I, but you can bet it ain't for no small reason. They work with some funny stuff in there, hormones and the like. I heard that one man took his mask off and three weeks later he was growing breasts."

Lorraine continued to search for a way into the room. "In case you haven't noticed, Jack, the thought of growing breasts doesn't exactly scare me, and in Jennifer's case it might even be appreciated."

"Thank you," Jennifer muttered.

"The breasts he grew had hair on 'em," Jack added.

"Mmm," Lorraine murmured as she pulled her arm back through the door.

"Well I don't care," Jennifer snarled. "I'd rather have a hairy chest than be taken out to the desert and shot like a cow by you and your merry band of low life thugs." She reached for the door and shook the handle.

"Of course that isn't necessarily what will happen to you," Jack warned. "They could be experimenting with something else in there. Worse than hormones."

Jennifer continued to twist the handle.

"It could kill you."

She looked into the room, then at Jack. She went back to shaking the door.

"Painfully," Jack added.

Jennifer stopped. She turned her head to the side and stared down the empty corridor. She kept one hand on the door while the other hand lightly rubbed her cheek as she thought it over. "You're going to shoot us now anyway, aren't you," she said, expecting a yes answer.

"Don't be ridiculous," Jack replied. "If I were going to shoot you, I would have done it the first time I laid eyes on you. Or if not then, I surely would have shot you after our first conversation."

"See," Lorraine said optimistically. "He isn't going to shoot us."

Jack smiled. "I'm going to leave you out in the desert and let the coyotes have you."

"See," Jennifer said. "I was right."

"Now just one minute, Mr . . . Mr . . . Mr . . . Jack," Lorraine stammered. "You can't shoot us, or leave us out in the desert for your coyotes, or anything else. Now we have witnesses. These people have seen us. They know we're here, and if we disappear, how are you going to explain that?"

"Ralph. Hey Ralph," Jack called out. "Do you know who these women are?"

The man in the oxygen mask had left the laboratory through another doorway and was approaching from the direction of a side corridor.

"Reporters?" he guessed as he removed his mask. "Trespassers, spies, enemy agents? You're enemy agents, aren't you?" he accused Jennifer and Lorraine. "Damn you people, why can't you ever invent anything on your own?"

"We're not enemy agents," Lorraine protested. "I'm a prosecuting attorney and she's a . . . ."

Ralph cut her off. "Yeah, and the last person who sneaked in here said he was a school teacher or something. What are you going to do with them Jack?"

"Shoot them I suppose," Jack replied.

"Shooting's too good for them," Ralph said with a sneer. "I'd take them out in the desert and let the coyotes have them."

"Jack," Lorraine broke in. "Remember when you were just going to take us some place for further questioning?"

"Yeah?"

"Do you think we could do that now?"

"That depends," Jack answered hesitantly.

"On what?" Jennifer snapped.

"Will you try to escape again?"

Jennifer didn't answer.

"Of course we won't try to escape," Lorraine assured him. "Do you think we could please go and be questioned now?"

Jack hesitated again as he looked at Lorraine. "I don't know, I trust you . . . ." His eyes moved to Jennifer.

"I'll make sure she doesn't try anything," Lorraine promised. "She'll do everything you say. When you say drive, she'll drive. In fact she doesn't have to drive. I'll drive."

Jack shook his head. "You won't have to drive."

"You can drive our car then. You're going to drive it anyway, aren't you?"

"No," Jack said. "We'll let her drive." He swung his rifle and motioned for them to move back down the hallway, then gave Jennifer a tap on the rear with the barrel of his rifle. The other men kept their rifles at the ready.

They continued to watch carefully as the two women walked out of the building and climbed into the Porsche. A short time later, the procession of two trucks and the car drove away from the complex with Jennifer at the wheel.

"Jack has something up his sleeve," she said suspiciously as they drove past the guard house at the main gate where a guard was now standing watch. "I know it."

"He trusts you," Lorraine assured her. "I think he likes you too. Did you see the way he looked at you, and then gave you a tap with his rifle barrel?"

"What?"

"Men do things like that," Lorraine continued. "Remember in the old cowboy movies, the way the hero used to look at his horse?"

"Are you saying that Jack thinks I look like a cowboy's horse?"

"Of course not."

"Good."

"Remember in the movies, when the hero had a sidekick, and the sidekick used to ride an animal that looked like it was part horse and part mule, and it was ornery and stubborn, but the sidekick loved it anyway?"

"Yes . . . ."

"Well that's the way Jack looks at you."

"How long have you been working for Jack?" Jennifer demanded.

"What do you mean?"

"I mean it's obvious that you think more of Jack and his murdering band of cutthroats than you do of the person who used to be your best friend."

"That's not true," Lorraine declared. "I still like you, and so does Jack. Why else would he trust you to drive your own car when he could have thrown us into the back of his truck and driven it himself?"

Jennifer didn't answer. She looked at Lorraine and shrugged. Her eyes returned to the road as her car began to fall a little farther away from the truck ahead. They were jolted back into their seats as the truck behind nudged the rear of the Porsche and pushed them closer.

"So much for trusting us," she muttered.

TWELVE

Behind them, in the rearview mirror, Jennifer could see mostly headlights from the pickup truck as the driver nudged her car one more time, forcing it closer to the truck ahead.

Beyond the glaring lights, standing up in the bed of the truck with his rifle resting on the cab, was a member of Jack's security force. In the gleam from her own headlights, she could see another man in the truck ahead with his rifle resting on the tailgate.

As the small procession prepared to turn the corner at the intersection where she and Lorraine had taken off earlier and made their race for freedom, she looked longingly in the direction they had traveled when they first drove in on the main road, and then in the opposite direction that took them farther away from Westland.

"I know what you're thinking," Lorraine informed her. "And don't do it." Not taking any chances, she grabbed the steering wheel and helped Jennifer guide the car the rest of the way around the corner.

"At least we're heading back toward civilization," she said hopefully as she looked off into the distance. "I see more lights ahead."

Jennifer surveyed the area around them. They had left the barrenness of the desert and were now on a narrower long winding driveway. In the glow from the headlights, she could see neatly trimmed shrubbery and grass that lined either side, and columns of tall trees. Beyond the trees, white fences surrounded fields of green pastures. Lights flickered through the windows of buildings in the distance.

"I'm not impressed," she replied. "I still remember the last time we thought we'd reached civilization."

They drove for another quarter mile until the lane twisted sharply and the trees spread open to form a wide circle around a manicured lawn. Porch lights at the front entrance of a rambling one story ranch house illuminated the driveway.

As the procession of vehicles came to a stop in front of the house, a tall slim man with silvery gray hair appeared in the doorway. Like Jack and the other men who had stopped them on the highway, he was dressed in western attire. He wore neatly pressed blue jeans with a large silver buckled belt and a blue checkered shirt.

Jennifer and Lorraine studied the man's face, searching for signs in the way he carried himself that might provide some indication of the type of person he was, or of what their fate might be. There were no clues. His face was pleasant enough, but it showed no emotion. It did not change as he watched the two women in the Porsche, and the armed men in the pickup trucks that accompanied them, come to a stop.

"We have some visitors for you, Mr. Hursh," Jack called out as he climbed down from his truck and walked to the Porsche. He grabbed the handle on the driver's door and swung it open.

"After you," he said to Jennifer, motioning gallantly with his rifle.

Jennifer glared at him as she swung her legs slowly out of the car, but offered no resistance.

"You too," he ordered Lorraine.

Lorraine opened her door and climbed out. She walked around to where Jennifer was standing with Jack.

The silver haired man's somber expression suddenly changed and he burst into laughter. "Do you mean to tell me that this is what all the commotion has been about?"

Jack grinned. "This is it. But be careful. They're more dangerous than they look, especially this one." He nudged Jennifer with the barrel of his rifle and pushed her in the direction of the house.

"The one we have to worry about the most was packing this," he continued as he displayed the thirty-eight revolver he had taken from Jennifer.

He held Lorraine's smaller pistol in the air so that it dangled between two fingers. "I believe this belongs to the other one. I think it's a gun, but I'm not sure."

"It's big enough to put a hole in your empty head," Jennifer growled. Her remark earned her another tap on the backside with Jack's rifle barrel.

"Give Ms. Brookbaine and Ms. Brensley back their belongings," Hursh instructed, "and their weapons."

Jennifer and Lorraine stared at him, wondering how he knew their names.

Jack also stared at him in disbelief. "Are you sure?"

"Of course I'm sure," Hursh replied. "They're not going to shoot anyone." His attention shifted to the two women. His words were aimed mostly at Jennifer. "Are you?"

"I wouldn't bet against the one with the thirty-eight," Jack said before either of the women could answer. "I wouldn't be surprised if she shot me, and you, and everybody else on the ranch."

"What about the other one?"

"I think she'd probably be on our side," Jack snorted with some satisfaction in his voice.

The older man hesitated for a moment as he rubbed his chin with a hand and gazed at the two women. "Well, if they shoot us, they shoot us. Give them back their guns."

Jack shook his head from side to side in weak disapproval as he walked the short distance to his pickup truck and retrieved the handbags he had taken from them earlier. He emptied the bullets from Jennifer's revolver and dumped them in her handbag, then did the same with Lorraine's. He placed the weapons inside the bags, closed the clasps as if to provide some kind of barrier, and reluctantly handed them over.

"Thank you," Lorraine said in a flat tone as she took her purse.

Jennifer ignored Jack. Instead, she addressed his boss as she swung the strap of her handbag over her shoulder. "May we please go now?"

"It's a pleasure to finally meet you," he said, brushing aside her request. "Jack has told me quite a bit about you."

Jennifer and Lorraine didn't say anything, but continued to look at him with puzzlement.

"Jack has a phone in his truck," he said, answering the question they had both wanted to ask regarding how he knew their identities. "We had to install our own communications system so we can get telephone reception out here."

"May we please go now?" Jennifer repeated. Her request was a little stronger than it had been the first time.

"Not quite yet," Hursh responded, still keeping a pleasant tone in his voice. He lowered his head and raised his eyebrows the way a parent would talk to a daughter who had come in late. "There are still a few questions to be answered about what you're doing out here at this time of night."

"We were following a client," Jennifer shouted in disgust. "Didn't this . . . this Jack tell you that on his telephone?"

"Yes. He told me that. He also told me he didn't believe you."

"Well, it's the truth."

"What do you say Jack?" Hursh asked, turning to his security man.

"I say they were snooping."

"Snooping at what?" Jennifer screeched. "Your cows, your coyotes, your hormone factory."

Hursh looked at them inquisitively. "Hormones?"

"They broke into one of the experimental labs," Jack explained.

"And there's something going on in that building we were in, isn't there?" Lorraine accused them both. "Something illegal, or at least something you don't want people to know about."

Neither man answered.

"Why are you experimenting with hormones or whatever that stuff is that grows breasts and hair and kills people?" she demanded. "Just what is going on there anyway?"

"We use some of the information to help us breed a better strain of cattle," Jack answered.

Jennifer screwed up her face. "Bullshit, if you'll pardon the expression. But there's probably some of that up there too. I know there's a hell of a lot of it down here. Since when do you need to grow hair on cattle?"

Jack looked at Hursh as if seeking approval before answering the accusation. "It's not that we need to grow hair on cattle. It's just an experimental lab that . . . ."

Jennifer finished his sentence. "That grows hair, and breasts, and kills people."

"Painfully," Lorraine added. "Look, Mr. Hursh, we don't really care what you do up there, or down here. You can grow breasts on cattle, or hair on people, or whatever you like. We didn't know we were trespassing on your property and we're sorry. We're also sorry if we caused you any trouble. We just want to leave."

Jack looked at Hursh again. "Do you want me to call the authorities?"

"Oh, please, please do," Lorraine responded. "Please call the authorities. They know who our client is, and they can also tell you who we are."

"O.K.," Jack said. "Who do we call?"

"Lieutenant Dickey . . . ."

"No, no, no, no, no," Jennifer interrupted before Lorraine could go any further.

Jack looked at her in surprise. "No? You don't want me to call your husband?"

"No. I don't mean no," Jennifer stammered. "It's just that we don't know him all that well."

"You're married to a man you don't know?"

Jennifer gestured to Lorraine. "It was her idea that I marry him."

Jack looked at Lorraine. She met his stare with a shrug and a blank expression.

"Why don't you call Sergeant Chambers of the Westland Police Department?" Jennifer proposed. "I have his telephone number."

Rifles moved to the ready as Jennifer reached into her handbag. She smiled with amusement at the men perched on the pickup trucks, then pulled a business card from a compartment. She wrote the telephone number for the precinct where Chambers worked, and handed it to Jack.

"What do you propose we do until we get our answers?" Hursh asked.

"Lock them in the tool shed?" Jack suggested, a little too cheerfully.

"Perhaps the ladies would like to join me for a refreshment?"

"We would," Lorraine replied, "but we really must be going."

"Nonsense," Hursh insisted. "You have time for one drink, perhaps a coffee, or something else . . . or you could stay with Jack."

"Coffee would be fine," Jennifer quickly interjected. The thought of spending more time with Jack and the other security men made Hursh's proposition seem more appealing.

"And then we really must be going," Lorraine emphasized.

Jack stepped aside and held out his arm in the same gallant way he had when he told them to get out of the car. "I'll keep some room for them in the tool shed," he said as they passed. "Just in case."

The older man held the door open and they stepped onto a tiled foyer inside the entrance. It overlooked a huge room which appeared to be a den or study. One wall was covered with oak bookcases filled with shooting trophies. Western oil paintings hung on the other walls. At the far end of the room, several rifles rested on a gun rack.

"Please make yourselves at home," he said as he guided them down the steps. He went to a bar that stretched along one wall. "You said you would like coffee, didn't you?"

Lorraine ignored his offer. Instead, she looked at him coldly. "Mr. Hursh. Would you mind telling us why you're keeping us here against our will?"

Hursh poured coffee into three cups. "I don't like to think I'm keeping you here against your will," he replied. "But you were trespassing. And according to Jack, you illegally entered a top secret experimental facility and broke down a door. Jack also said you were prepared to throw yourself into a potentially dangerous laboratory, rather than accompany him to see me."

"Top secret?" Lorraine responded.

"I would throw myself into a room full of anything rather than go anywhere with Jack and his band of thugs," Jennifer said with as much indignation as she could muster.

"I'm sure Jack will be interested in hearing that," Hursh replied.

"No he won't," Lorraine broke in. "Please don't listen to her, Mr. Hursh. I think, deep down, Jack and Jennifer really like each other."

"Like I want to grow hair on my chest," Jennifer snorted. "Like I . . . ."

"Shut up, shut up, shut up!"

Lorraine enunciated each word slowly. "I would somehow like to think that there might somehow be a slim possibility that we might somehow be allowed to go home sometime this evening. And you are not helping."

Hursh smiled at Lorraine. "Is she your friend?"

"Sometimes."

"Jack said something about, if there was a fight, you might be on our side."

"Probably."

"Good. I have a feeling we could use all the help we can get."

"Now just one . . . ."

"Shut up," Lorraine ordered again, cutting Jennifer off in mid sentence. "Be quiet, right now."

Jennifer pouted. "Could I at least have my coffee?"

"Of course." Hursh handed them each a cup of coffee and then gestured toward a large sofa. "Please make yourselves comfortable."

They sipped on their drinks for a few seconds before Lorraine broke the silence. "Jack said the experiments at that building we were in had something to do with raising cattle. Is that right?"

Hursh was silent.

"What would chemicals or hormones that are used to raise cattle have to do with growing hair on our chests?"

Hursh smiled. "Is that what he told you?"

"Yes. And what about the chemicals they're using that might kill people?"

"Some more coffee?" Hursh offered.

"We would prefer an honest answer, if you don't mind," Lorraine said. "We're still a little curious about what's going on over there, that has us in so much trouble with you and Jack."

"We're also more than just a little suspicious," Jennifer added.

"I'm not altogether sure," Hursh said, "and I'm not so sure I should be talking about it."

Jennifer and Lorraine looked at him distrustfully.

Hursh hesitantly continued. "What I mean is, I've never paid that much attention to what goes on out there. The buildings have been there for years. They were used primarily during the Second World War to manufacture weapons and other materials. They had been closed, but then the science department at Westland University asked if they could put them back into operation for some experiments. I told them they could. I'm not sure whether the experiments are a secret or not, and that's why I'm not so sure I should be talking about them."

"The College of Science is using the buildings?" Lorraine exclaimed.

"Yes."

"Do you know Professor Winslow?"

"Oh, yes, Professor Winslow, and his wife. They're the ones you say you were following."

"That's right. You do know them then, don't you."

"I'm afraid not," he answered. "But then I don't know most of the people who work out there. Why were you following these Winslows anyway?"

"Like we told Jack, Mrs. Winslow is Jennifer's client. We think her husband, Professor Winslow, is somehow involved with the murders of two other professors at the university. Mrs. Winslow asked us to find him, and tonight we found them both, together. I suppose we should have stopped them, but we were curious about what they were up to. That's when we followed them. And they led us to your ranch."

It was Hursh's turn to look suspicious. "That's a strange story."

"It's the truth though," Lorraine assured him. "Even if it is strange. Maybe if we told you about Mrs. Winslow, it would help you to understand."

For the next few minutes, they related how they first met Mrs. Winslow at the police station, became involved with the murders, and then began working for her.

"She's a good liar," Hursh remarked when they had finished telling him about her.

"That's because she gets a lot of practice," Lorraine responded. "I don't think Mrs. Winslow even knows what the truth is."

"And what about you?" Jennifer asked pointedly.

"What about me?" Hursh replied.

"Are you good at lying?"

"Lying is not one of my weaknesses," he said. "I have enough other vices to get me into trouble, like good brandy and beautiful women." He raised his glass and smiled at them as he made the comment.

They looked at him suspiciously.

"Don't worry," he laughed, guessing what they were thinking. "You're safe. Do you know how old I am? I'm sixty-four years old. My days of chasing young fillies like you are long gone. Now, I'm not saying I didn't enjoy it when I was young, but that was quite a few years ago."

"I think we might have just been insulted," Jennifer remarked.

"You don't look sixty-four," Lorraine said.

"Thank you," he answered, "I guess working on the ranch has kept me young."

Lorraine studied his face, still searching for clues that would tell her what type of person they were dealing with. Her gaze moved past him to the walls and shelves that were covered with guns and trophies.

"Do you hunt?"

"Only for food or stray animals that bother the cattle," he informed them. "Although I used to shoot quite a bit. I still enjoy riding out into the desert and shooting a tin can off a tree stump. Perhaps you would like to join me sometime."

"Perhaps," Jennifer answered noncommittally.

"We would like to join you," Lorraine said. "But before we can come back and go shooting with you, we have to leave." She waited for his reaction.

"Of course you can leave," he said. "I'm usually a pretty good judge of character, and I knew you were telling the truth. But that was still a strange story you told about the Winslows."

"If you knew we were telling the truth, why did you keep us here?"

"Jack. He was so sure you were up to something, I couldn't disappoint him. Once he talks to your friend at the Westland Police Department and confirms everything for himself, he'll be satisfied. Jack is a good man you know."

Their conversation was interrupted by a door opening. Jack appeared in the foyer.

"I spoke to your Sergeant Chambers," he informed them. "He confirmed your story about working for the woman you said you were following."

"Well, that's that," Jennifer said, rising from the sofa.

"I also asked him about your husband, Lieutenant Dickey."

"Oh, oh." Jennifer sat down again. She put her hands to her cheeks, expecting the worst.

"And?" Lorraine asked.

"It took me a little while to get an answer," Jack said. He smiled and pointed at Jennifer. "When I told him that Lieutenant Dickey was married to her, he couldn't stop laughing. He said he didn't know about any marriage. But I had already figured that out. However, he did say you knew the lieutenant intimately."

"And?" Lorraine asked again.

"That's about it," Jack replied. "Chambers said you two spent an intimate evening with the lieutenant that he will never forget."

"I forgot about that," Jennifer exclaimed, taking her hands away from her cheeks.

"I asked for a telephone number so I could speak to him," Jack continued.

"Oh?"

"I wasn't able to get through to him. But I'll talk to him sooner or later."

"He won't be able to tell you anything," Lorraine

said. "He and Jennifer once shared a very fast and painful romance, but it didn't last long. Jennifer broke it off and Lieutenant Dickey was deeply hurt. Isn't that right, Jennifer?"

"He certainly was hurt," Jennifer agreed.

"And now he doesn't want to see her ever again. Isn't that right Jennifer?"

"I don't think he wants to see either one of us ever again."

Jack looked at them with puzzlement but didn't pursue it. "If they're ready to leave, I'll take them to the main road," he offered, "if that's all right with you, Mr. Hursh?"

"That's fine Jack," Hursh replied. He returned his attention to the women. "I'm sorry I couldn't help you with your professor and your client, but if there's ever anything we can do to assist you, we'll be happy to. But could I suggest you call first, just to let Jack know you're coming?"

He guided them to the door and said goodnight. They followed Jack down the sidewalk to where they had left their car and the pickup trucks that were still parked at either end, blocking it in. The men who had escorted them to the ranch house were leaning against the vehicles, talking.

"I think you know the procedure, just follow that pickup truck," he ordered as they approached the Porsche. He turned before getting into his own truck. "And stay close."

"Well, what did you think of him?" Jennifer asked as they followed the lead truck away from the ranch house.

"Jack?"

"J.D. Hursh. Is he just a hard working rancher, or a mad scientist."

"He didn't have us killed."

"That's a plus. Do you think he knows Mrs. Winslow and the professor?"

"He says he doesn't."

"Do you believe him?"

"I don't know."

"I don't see how he could help but know them if they make a regular habit of coming out here. Unless Jack has something going on with them that he doesn't know about. That wouldn't surprise me either. I wouldn't trust him as far as I could throw one of his hairy cattle."

"It does seem kind of peculiar that Jack spotted us coming up the road to the ranch, but claims he didn't see the Winslows. Of course, they could have turned off somewhere. We only saw a couple of side roads on the drive in, but there are probably plenty of other roads."

"It all fits. Professor Winslow does experiments at the College of Science. The College of Science is carrying out experiments here at the ranch. And we saw Professor Winslow and Mrs. Winslow come out here. We even saw somebody doing the experiments.

For all we know, the professor was behind one of those masks at the building we broke into."

They had passed the road that led off to the experimental building they had been in earlier, and were approaching the area where the Winslows had disappeared, when two sets of headlights appeared from behind. In the beams of light from the rear pickup, they could make out the two figures inside the first car as it went by.

"Did you see what I just saw?" Jennifer exclaimed as the automobile passed.

"I saw it," Lorraine answered. "But I'm not sure I believe it. Mrs. Winslow and Professor Winslow!"

"It was them all right," Jennifer said. "And do you see what else I see?"

Even before the other car had caught up to them, they could tell it was a blue Chevrolet. As it raced by, the driver came into view.

"Lieutenant Dickey," Lorraine exclaimed. "How did he get out here?"

THIRTEEN

"I don't know where they came from," Jennifer said as Lieutenant Dickey's Chevrolet and the Winslow's Pontiac sped away, "but we're going to find out. And this time we're not going to lose them, Jack or no Jack."

Lorraine had already guessed what Jennifer had in mind. "I suppose Jack can only shoot us or leave us out in the desert with his coyotes and cows," she said philosophically.

Jennifer pushed the accelerator to the floor and pulled out to go around the lead pickup truck. She didn't get far. She was almost past when the driver swerved sideways in front of them, forcing her to brake to a stop. The truck behind also came to a halt in much the same way it had when they first met Jack and his men.

"Does this scene look familiar to you?" Lorraine asked.

"Not for long," Jennifer muttered. She swung her door open, climbed out, and marched toward the rear pickup truck where Jack was patiently waiting and watching.

"Didn't you see them?" she called out.

Jack didn't speak as he climbed out of the pickup and walked to meet her. His rifle was cradled in his arms.

"The two people in the Pontiac," Jennifer yelled. "The Winslows. Didn't you see them?"

Jack still didn't say anything.

"And the other car. Lieutenant Dickey. Didn't you see him?"

Jack finally spoke. "Your husband?"

"Look you asshole," Jennifer said, her voice rising, "those two people in the first car were our client and her husband. And the man in the second car was Lieutenant Dickey. You know it and I know it. So get your damn pickup trucks out of our way and let us go after them."

Jack's eyes narrowed and he gripped the stock of the rifle a little tighter. "All I saw were some people in some cars, and two very foolish women who were trying to take off again."

"Bullshit," Jennifer screamed. "Just what the hell were we supposed to be escaping from? J.D. Hursh already said we could leave."

"J.D. said you could leave," Jack corrected her. "I didn't."

Jennifer was suddenly silent as she realized the position they were in. Once again they found themselves wedged between pickup trucks and armed men in a desolate area of the desert.

"Jack . . . ."

Jack looked past Jennifer to Lorraine.

"Jack. Don't you think we're being just a little foolish here?"

Jack chose not to speak as he waited for Lorraine to continue.

"You know that we wouldn't have tried to take off the way we did unless there was a good reason, don't you?"

"I know," Jack acknowledged.

"And you know that we weren't really trying to escape, don't you?"

"I know."

"And you must have had a pretty good idea that the people in the car were our clients."

"I figured they must be somebody you knew."

Lorraine attempted to keep her voice as quiet and free of annoyance as she could. "Then why would you not let us go after them?"

Jack answered in a steady voice that was as quiet and annoyance free as Lorraine's had been. "Because I don't give a damn about you two, or your damn clients."

"Oh."

"Now, what I would suggest is that you two ladies get back into your little ol' car there, and follow that pickup truck there, and if you're lucky, you might just make it back to the main road without being shot or run over."

Jennifer and Lorraine looked at each other, then deciding that further conversation with Jack would be pointless, walked back to the Porsche.

"I don't think we're going to catch Dickey, or the Winslows, tonight," Jennifer said as the procession of vehicles started slowly down the road. "If Jack has anything to do with it."

"I don't think so either," Lorraine agreed. "They're probably halfway to Westland by now, thanks to our slow driver ahead. I think Jack is deliberately holding us up."

"I know he's holding us up," Jennifer growled. "I wouldn't be surprised if he's giving his friends, the Winslows, time to get away. Dickey too. But maybe we can still find them anyway. We know where Dickey lives. I'm sure he won't mind if we drop by and ask him what he's been up to tonight."

Lorraine nodded. "What's the worst he can do? Shoot us? Lock us up?"

"I'm not worried about him," Jennifer replied. "I don't know about the Winslows though. If it wasn't going to bother them to shoot Dickey, maybe it won't bother them to shoot us."

"I don't think they'll go back to the motel, because they know Dickey found them there," Lorraine said. "I suppose they might go home, since their clothes are still there, but I wouldn't count on that either. They're probably on their way out of town."

"We can check anyway, unless Dickey already has them in custody . . . ."

"Or is having a cup of coffee with them . . . ."

"From the way Dickey and Mrs. Winslow were looking at each other when they left the university, I wouldn't be surprised if it was coffee, and maybe a cigarette. No. We thought it was sexual, but there's something else going on here. They know each other from somewhere else, something that happened before the murders at the College of Science took place."

Lorraine shrugged. "I wouldn't even try to guess what they see in each other, but I agree there has to be something going on between them."

"And tell me this, how did Dickey end up out here at the Hursh ranch? As far as we know, he didn't follow us, and he couldn't have been ahead of us."

"He wasn't. He was still at his apartment when we left to follow the Winslows. They're doing something out here, and he had to have known where to go to find them."

When they finally reached the entrance at the edge of the ranch, and freedom, the lead truck pulled onto the shoulder to let them pass. Jack flipped a half wave from the other truck as they pulled onto the main road, then swung his own truck around and drove away. In his rear view mirror he could see Jennifer's middle finger waving goodbye above her car. Although he couldn't hear what she was saying, he was sure she was making use of the descriptive words and phrases she had been saving for him and his merry band of cut throats.

The drive back to Westland was uneventful. They did not encounter the Winslows or Dickey, and did not expect to. They decided to stop at the lieutenant's apartment first since it was on the way back and would save them a trip later. They left the Porsche on the street beside the apartment complex and walked between the buildings until they could see the door of the apartment the lieutenant had gone into earlier. A light could be seen through a curtained window as they approached.

"I'm not optimistic about him being here," Lorraine said. "He's probably still out chasing our client and her husband, if he isn't already with them. But we might as well find out." She walked the last few steps and knocked confidently on the door. They heard a noise on the other side and then the door opened. It was not Lieutenant Dickey who answered.

"Sergeant Chambers," Lorraine exclaimed. "What are you doing here?"

"I live here," Chambers responded with an amused smile. "Unless you know something I don't know. A better question might be, what are you two doing here?" He held the door open and waved them into the living room. "Come in, and sit down."

"We can't stay long," Lorraine replied. "We were looking for Lieutenant Dickey. We saw him enter your apartment earlier this evening and thought he lived here."

"Dickey dropped off some information a while ago." Anticipating their next question, the sergeant picked up a folder from a table and handed it to Jennifer.

"It's the results of the forensic tests they ran on the murdered professors. They show that Professor Reid and Professor Bentley had intercourse just before they were killed. Professor Bentley had also been given truth serum. It probably was enough to kill him, but if it didn't, the bullet in his head would have finished the job."

"So it appears they were putting their clothes back on, rather than taking them off when they were murdered."

"It looks that way. Dickey thinks that Professor Winslow must have caught them in the act, got jealous, and murdered them both."

"But why was Bentley found in his office? If Winslow discovered them in the lab, wouldn't he have killed him and left him there? And why was Bentley's office ransacked?"

"Search me. All I know is what Dickey told me. He said they found the professor's fingerprints all over the place." Chamber's face took on an inquisitive appearance. "Why were you following Lieutenant Dickey anyway?"

"We weren't," Jennifer replied. "We were following the Winslows, and they were following Dickey, or he was following them. We're not sure which. Anyway, we were trying to find out where the Winslows were going, and Dickey kept popping up. We wanted to find out why."

"I'm afraid you'll have to ask Lieutenant Dickey or the Winslows that one," Chambers said. "Did you say the Winslows, like in Mrs. Winslow and Professor Winslow?"

"That's what she said," Lorraine answered. "We found Mrs. Winslow with the professor, and we followed them here because they were following Dickey. We thought they were going to shoot him, until he entered your apartment. Then we followed the Winslows again, but we lost them. Then we found them again, but this time, instead of them following Dickey, he was following them. Does any of this make sense to you?"

Chambers shook his head. "Nope. But perhaps you can help me with a question I was asked tonight that didn't make much sense either. Some man from the Hursh ranch telephoned and asked about you two and the lieutenant. He was under the impression that Dickey was married to one of you."

"That would have been Jack, J.D. Hursh's security

man. He somehow got the idea that Jennifer was Mrs. Dickey."

Chambers stared at them with bewilderment. "I would have liked to have seen that wedding."

He was about to ask another question regarding Jennifer's marriage to the lieutenant, then changed his mind. "I'll phone Dickey and ask him what he's been up to," he offered. "I'll also ask him if he's aware that he has a wife."

The Sergeant dialed Dickey's home number. After getting no answer, he dialed the police station. "He's not home," he said, "and the precinct doesn't know where he is. He wasn't scheduled to work tonight, although he sometimes carries out investigations on his own time, so if he was following the Winslows, maybe he's still doing it, or maybe he's already picked them up. You might have to wait until the morning to get an answer from him about where he was and what he's been up to."

"Or maybe we can ask the Winslows," Jennifer replied, "if the lieutenant doesn't have them, that is. We don't expect them to be there, but we're on our way to their place now to see if they might have gone home. Would you know of any other reason, other than trying to solve a murder, that Lieutenant Dickey would be interested in them?"

"Nope. I just know he's convinced that Professor Winslow killed the other professors. If I had one concern, it would be what he might do to the professor when he catches him. Dickey's not known for his tact, you know."

"We're familiar with Lieutenant Dickey's tact, or rather the lack of it. Maybe we'll get lucky and they'll be there."

Chambers reached for his coat. "I'm going with you. I'll get my car and meet you there in a few minutes. I still haven't made up my mind yet as to whether Professor Winslow is just missing, or whether he's the prime suspect in a murder investigation, but whatever is going on, it could be a dangerous situation."

Jennifer nodded her head in agreement. "It would be reassuring to have you along, although I kind of doubt that they're even going to be home, especially if they discovered that Lieutenant Dickey was following them. They're probably out of town by now, or in another motel. Or maybe Dickey already has them. But we're going to have a look anyway."

"Whatever you do, don't approach them until I get there," Chambers cautioned. "If there's any trouble, I don't want you trying to handle it by yourselves."

"We won't," Jennifer assured him, "unless they try to leave."

They left Chambers and headed for the Winslows' residence. The drive took considerably less time than it had when the traffic was heavier and they were going in the opposite direction. They soon passed the university and the motel where Lorraine had first seen Mrs. Winslow and the professor together. There was no sign of the Pontiac in the parking lot. Jennifer turned down the street that led to the Winslows' neighborhood.

As they neared the professor's house, they strained to get a better look at a car that was parked in the driveway. Even in the darkness, they could make out the lines of the automobile they had been following earlier. The gleam of the headlights from the Porsche confirmed their suspicions.

"The green Pontiac," Jennifer exclaimed. "It looks like they did decide to come home."

"Maybe our luck is about to change," Lorraine said. "I kind of wish we hadn't told Chambers we'd wait for him. I'd like to grab Mrs. Winslow by the throat, and Professor Winslow too, and choke the truth out of them."

"Actually, we did tell him we would wait, but we also said we'd prevent the Winslows from leaving if they attempted to escape," Jennifer replied. "How do we know they're not planning to escape?" Before Lorraine could say anything, she had opened the car door and started to climb out. "And I'm going to do it. Don't try to stop me."

"I'm not going to try to stop you," Lorraine assured her. "I'm going to help you. And I don't even care if we get the truth. I just want to choke her."

They walked up the path to the house and knocked on the front door. There was no sound for several seconds, then Mrs. Winslow opened the door. She was dressed in a black negligee that was only partially covered by a kimono.

She greeted Jennifer with a cheerful smile. "Miss Brookbaine, how nice to see you. Won't you please come in. Do you have some information for me about my husband? Come into the kitchen and you can tell me all about it. I was just about to make myself a cup of coffee."

Jennifer and Lorraine glanced at each other as Mrs. Winslow closed the door behind them and led the way to the kitchen area. She finally looked at Lorraine. "And how are you, Miss . . . ?"

"Mrs.," Lorraine replied. "Mrs. Lorraine Brensley." Her voice grew colder. "I'm sure you remember my husband."

"Oh yes, the nice man at the police station who offered to help me search for my husband. Have you brought me some news about the professor? Have you found him?"

Jennifer and Lorraine looked at each other. "Mrs. Winslow," Lorraine exclaimed in astonishment. "We have not found your husband. But we have a feeling that you have."

"What do you mean?"

"You know very well what we mean. You picked up Professor Winslow at the motel across from the university earlier this evening, and we followed you while you followed Lieutenant Dickey, then you led us on a merry chase out to the Hursh ranch."

Lorraine looked past Mrs. Winslow in an attempt to see the rest of the house. "Now where is he?"

Mrs. Winslow ignored her, and instead looked at Jennifer as if to ask what was going on.

"We saw you with your husband tonight," Jennifer informed her. "We followed you to the Hursh ranch, and then we saw Lieutenant Dickey following you back to the city."

Mrs. Winslow looked baffled. "You couldn't have seen me. I've been here most of the evening, so you certainly didn't see me at this Hursh ranch. And if you saw my husband, why didn't you bring him home?"

Jennifer held up a finger as if to answer, then without speaking, dropped it again. "Why didn't we bring him home?" she asked Lorraine.

"Because this woman was with him," Lorraine replied in exasperation. Her eyes were round and her face was turning red. Her finger shook in Mrs. Winslow's direction. "We saw them. We saw them together. We saw them in that Pontiac that's sitting outside in the driveway."

"What Pontiac?" Mrs. Winslow asked innocently.

"What Pontiac? Come with me and I'll show you what Pontiac." Lorraine's voice was rising in volume as she motioned for Mrs. Winslow to follow her to the front of the house.

"That Ponti . . . ."

Mrs. Winslow and Jennifer followed Lorraine's

outstretched finger as they stared in the direction of the empty driveway.

"What Pontiac?" Mrs. Winslow repeated.

"What Pontiac?" Lieutenant Dickey repeated after her as he walked up the driveway.

FOURTEEN

"What Pontiac?" Lieutenant Dickey demanded once again.

"What Pontiac!!!" The tone in Lorraine's voice had become brusque and more serious, much like the one she would use when cross-examining a witness in a courtroom trial. "I'll tell you what Pontiac."

"Mrs. Winslow," she said.

"Yes?"

"Are you Jennifer Brookbaine's client?"

"Yes."

"And did you hire Jennifer Brookbaine to find your husband?"

"Yes."

"Would you please answer a question truthfully for me?"

"Of course."

"Where's the Pontiac that you and your husband were driving earlier this evening, that was parked in your driveway when we arrived here?"

Mrs. Winslow shrugged. "We don't own a Pontiac. We own a Ford. It's in the garage."

Lorraine's voice had lost its courtroom manner. "Then who the hell owns the Pontiac?" She screamed in exasperation.

With a look of puzzlement, Mrs. Winslow opened her hands in a gesture of confused ignorance as she stared past Lorraine to Lieutenant Dickey.

"What Pontiac?"

"Why didn't we park in front of the driveway and block the damn thing in," Lorraine muttered. "Then we could have shown her what Pontiac."

"What Pontiac?" Lieutenant Dickey demanded one more time.

"There was a green Pontiac car in their driveway," Lorraine exclaimed. "Not five minutes ago. It was the same car that we saw Mrs. Winslow and Professor Winslow in earlier tonight."

"What the hell are you talking about?" Dickey demanded.

"I'm talking about the green Pontiac I saw Mrs. Winslow and her husband driving," Lorraine said. "I'm talking about the green Pontiac they were in when they followed you from the motel down the street to Sergeant Chambers apartment. I'm talking about the green Pontiac we followed to the J.D. Hursh ranch where they fool around with hormones or whatever it is the professor does out there. I'm talking about the green Pontiac with Mrs. Winslow and her husband still in it, that you followed from the Hursh ranch back to the city. That is, unless she dropped him off somewhere."

Lorraine turned to Mrs. Winslow. "Now where is it?"

"Do you know what they're talking about?" Dickey asked the professor's wife.

"No. And they did not see me and my husband together tonight," Mrs. Winslow emphasized again. "I've been with a friend most of the day and all of this evening."

"Can you prove it?" Lorraine growled.

Mrs. Winslow looked at Lieutenant Dickey. "Do I have to?"

Lorraine didn't wait for Dickey to answer. "It's either that or explain a green Pontiac that was parked in your driveway until five minutes ago."

Mrs. Winslow was quiet for a moment as though thinking it over, then she turned toward the rear of the house.

"Professor Hampson," she called out.

There was no sound.

"Professor Hampson," she called again. "Would you come here please."

A few seconds passed, then they heard a rustling at the other end of the house. A man opened the door of the bedroom that Jennifer and Lorraine had been in that afternoon. His clothing was askew and he tucked in his shirt tail as he shuffled hesitantly down the hallway. His hair was mussed and his face was flushed with embarrassment and telltale signs of smeared lipstick. He looked like a man who would rather have been anywhere else than where he was at that moment.

"Tell these two ladies and Lieutenant Dickey where I was all evening," Mrs. Winslow ordered him.

He didn't speak.

"Well??!!" Lorraine exclaimed.

"With me," he stammered. It was difficult to tell if his answer was a statement or a question.

"Here?"

"For the past little while."

"And before that we were at a movie," Mrs. Winslow added.

"Oh yeah, what was playing?" Lorraine demanded of Hampson.

Mrs. Winslow didn't wait for Professor Hampson to answer. "It was a drive-in. How would we know what was playing?"

"Was Professor Winslow with you?" Lorraine asked Hampson.

Again Mrs. Winslow answered for him. "Professor Winslow has been missing for more than two days."

Lorraine addressed Hampson again. "What are you doing here?"

Dickey interrupted before Hampson could answer. "Never mind what he's doing here. What are you doing here?"

"We were searching for our client's husband," Jennifer answered. "Would you mind telling us where you were tonight, and why you're here? Did Sergeant Chambers get in touch with you?"

"The dispatcher down at the station said Chambers was going to meet you here," Dickey replied. "What is this business about someone being married to me?"

Jennifer didn't answer his question. "Where were you tonight?" she asked again.

Dickey didn't answer Jennifer's question either. "Haven't you forgotten who the police officer is, and who is bothering this lady and this gentleman. And possibly obstructing justice," he added as though he could use additional charges if he wanted.

"Perhaps we did forget for just one moment," Lorraine apologized sarcastically. "Are you telling us that you don't know anything about what went on here, and at the motel down at the end of the street, and out at the Hursh ranch tonight?"

Lieutenant Dickey's head cocked sideways as his unswollen eye glared at one of them and then at the other. "I'm telling you that you two . . . ladies," he spat out the word, ladies, "are acting more than just a little strange. And I don't like it. Why were you following me around tonight anyway, and why were you at the Hursh Ranch?"

"We followed you and the Winslows to Sergeant Chamber's apartment," Lorraine said. "Or at least we followed the Winslows to his apartment. They were following you. And before that, I saw you at Professor Winslow's motel room. And after that, we saw you chasing the Winslows away from the Hursh ranch. What were you doing there?"

Before Dickey could answer with a question of his own, another voice called out from the street. "I thought I told you to wait until I got here."

Sergeant Chambers was coming up the driveway. He did not appear to be very happy. "I thought I told you to wait for me," he repeated angrily.

Jennifer and Lorraine were silent for a moment. Finally, Lorraine answered. "We were going to wait. But then we saw the Pontiac they were driving, and we were afraid that Professor Winslow might get away again."

"So where is he?"

"Who?"

"Who do you think? Professor Winslow."

Jennifer came to Lorraine's defense. "I would say, and I'm just guessing of course, that Professor Winslow is in a green Pontiac, somewhere in this city, making a clean getaway, while we're standing here asking each other what we've been doing."

"That's unacceptable," Chambers snapped. "You've interfered with police business and possibly assisted in the escape of a suspect in a murder investigation."

Jennifer became more subdued. "We're sorry. We should have waited."

Dickey pointed a finger at Lorraine, then at Jennifer, and then at the street. "I want you, and you, to get the hell out of here while Sergeant Chambers and I see if we can straighten this mess out." His finger moved toward Mrs. Winslow. "And you owe this lady an apology for upsetting her."

"Well, I guess we'd better be going then," Jennifer announced sheepishly. "I'm sorry we had to bother you at this late hour," she said to Mrs. Winslow. She took one more suspicious look at Professor Hampson. "We'll let you know if we find out anything more about your husband."

"I guess we sure wrung the truth out of her," Lorraine offered as they walked down the sidewalk to Jennifer's car.

Jennifer couldn't help but laugh. "Either she's still lying her head off, along with everybody else, or you and I are blind and stupid."

"We're not blind," Lorraine said. "We saw her and her husband together tonight. But I don't know about us not being stupid, because somebody thinks we are. We know we saw the Winslows chasing Dickey, and Dickey chasing the Winslows, and a ranch where people work in a laboratory with dangerous hormones, and who knows what, and a green Pontiac that was parked right there in that driveway, and a blue Chev that Dickey was driving at the police station, and the university, and out at the ranch. And yet we seem to be the only two people who don't know what's going on."

"I know one thing," Jennifer said, "and that is, why Mrs. Winslow invited us into the kitchen. She wasn't making coffee. She just wanted us at that side of the house so we wouldn't hear the Pontiac starting and backing out of the driveway. I'll bet Professor Winslow was the driver. She's obviously trying to protect her husband."

"And all while she's having sex with Professor Hampson, or whoever he is, in the back bedroom. We know that Mrs. Winslow lies, but would somebody please tell me why Hampson would lie about being with her all night, unless he's part of what's going on. And why is Dickey lying? I think we were right about what we said earlier. He knows Mrs. Winslow and probably Professor Winslow a whole lot better than it appears on the surface."

"I feel bad about Sergeant Chambers. He sure was upset. It looks like we did ruin an opportunity to find the professor."

"He had every right to lose his temper. We went back on our word to wait for him, and our enthusiasm to find Professor Winslow was probably the reason he got away."

They looked back in the direction of the house once more before they climbed into the Porsche. Sergeant Chambers and Lieutenant Dickey were still talking to

Mrs. Winslow and Professor Hampson at the front doorway. Every once in a while a finger was pointed in their direction.

"Do you remember exactly how we got ourselves into this mess?" Lorraine commented as they drove away. "Oh yes, now I recall. You said, of course we'll be happy to help you, Mrs. Winslow."

"It's not fair for you to give me all the credit," Jennifer replied. "After all, it was your husband who introduced us."

"I still haven't forgiven him for that," Lorraine grumbled.

"I have," Jennifer answered. "I don't care if Mrs. Winslow is crazy, and a liar. George made us five thousand dollars when he introduced us to her. And all we had to do was nearly get ourselves killed."

Lorraine grimaced. "I think I feel something funny growing on my chest."

FIFTEEN

"It's nice of you to come home," George Brensley said with a cheerful smile as Jennifer and Lorraine walked into the Brensleys' residence. "I was beginning to worry about you. I wondered if perhaps your policeman friend, Lieutenant Dickey, had thrown you into jail again." He looked at his watch and then at the two women, as if expecting some kind of explanation for the late hour.

"We did see the lieutenant," Jennifer volunteered. "In fact we just left him, along with Sergeant Chambers and our client, a few minutes ago. And you're right. Our policeman friend did threaten to lock us up again. Personally, I think he just wanted to spend more time with your wife."

Lorraine made a face at Jennifer, then put her arms around her husband and hugged him tightly. "You don't know how nice it is to be home," she said with a sigh of relief.

"Anything exciting happen today?" George inquired. "Other than meeting Lieutenant Dickey?"

Jennifer smiled innocently and shrugged as though she couldn't think of anything of any importance that had taken place. She knew she didn't have to. Lorraine always shared whatever she was involved in with her husband.

Lorraine gazed back at George for a moment while she took in a deep breath. Then she exhaled with a noisy sigh as she spread her hands in an air of exaggerated insignificance.

"Oh, not too much happened," she began, speaking slowly and forming each word carefully. "We went to the university this morning and discovered that Professor Reid had been killed by truth serum. After that, we found the body of another science professor who was also killed by truth serum, except he had some help from a bullet in the head. They were having sex just before they were murdered, and Lieutenant Dickey thinks our client's husband, the person we're supposed to be searching for, did it, the murder, not the sex, although he might have been doing some of that too."

George didn't say anything as he waited for his wife to continue. When she did, her words came out a little faster. "Then we went to the science department office to see the dean. He wasn't in, but his secretary told us that our client, Mrs. Winslow, had been married twice before, to a college professor in England and before that to another professor in Austria. One apparently died from an overdose of truth serum just before she married Professor Winslow, and the other died not long before that under mysterious circumstances, although we suspect it was also from truth serum. Then we went to Mrs. Winslow's home to ask her about her previous marriages, except she wasn't there."

"But," Lorraine continued, "although Mrs. Winslow wasn't home, we did find her, because I had to go to the bathroom. She was coming out of a motel room with guess who? That's right, her present husband, the very same Professor Winslow that she hired us to locate for her. And then guess who else showed up? Our good friend, Lieutenant Dickey."

Lorraine's finger moved rapidly back and forth as she drew imaginary maps in the air to indicate where they had been and to describe what they had been doing. Her speech quickened and her voice raised in excitement as she went on with her story.

"Unfortunately we lost our client, along with her husband and the lieutenant, not to mention our sandwiches and coffee, because I had to run back to the Winslows' house where Jennifer was waiting so she could follow Mrs. Winslow if she came home, which she never did because she was at the motel with her husband. We eventually found them again and they led us to Dickey's apartment, except it wasn't his apartment, it was Sergeant Chamber's apartment. I thought the Winslows were going to shoot Dickey there, but I guess they changed their minds, because they left and we followed them to a hormone factory out in the middle of the desert where we lost them again. That's where we were kidnapped by a bunch of murderous thugs."

"Kidnapped?" George exclaimed. "Murderous thugs?"

"That's right. They took us to meet a rancher by the name of J.D. Hursh, who might just be a mad scientist."

Lorraine was about to continue when George interrupted. "He's an interesting man, isn't he."

"Who?"

"Hursh?"

"You know J.D. Hursh?"

"Not real well, but I know about him, and I've met him a few times."

"What do you know?"

"I know he's very rich."

"What else?"

"He owns a large ranch north of here."

"That's the one we were on," Jennifer said. "What else do you know about him?"

"And also a man named Jack," Lorraine added. "He appears to be the head security guard on the ranch. He's also the one who kidnapped us."

"Jack O'Dell," George informed them. "He's been working for Hursh as long as I can remember."

"So you know Jack . . . ?"

"I can't say I know him personally, but I do know him. I saw him every once in a while when I met with Hursh."

"Would you trust him?" Lorraine inquired.

"I don't know if I would, but then I've never given it any thought. But Hursh does."

"Just what does Jack do, other than being Hursh's security guard and leader of his band of thugs?" Jennifer asked.

"As far as I know, he pretty much runs the ranch. And he has to be good at it. You can imagine what must be involved in operating a place that size."

"Quite a bit, I suppose."

"Well, Hursh wouldn't leave the management of that much property to Jack if he wasn't certain he could do the job."

"What's Jack like?"

"I suppose he's not a bad guy, although he does sometimes have a temper. I saw him throw a reporter who was bothering Hursh against a wall one day. I also saw him shoot at some trespassers on the ranch. He didn't aim to hit them, but he shot at them just the same."

"Does he do anything else, other than beating up reporters and shooting at trespassers, and kidnapping innocent people, and being a security guard?"

"I would say that's enough," George replied, "except he's more than just a security guard. He's Hursh's personal body guard and manager."

"Anything else?"

"No. Not that I can think of."

"Darn," Jennifer exclaimed. "I was kind of hoping we'd discover he was a mass murderer or something."

"I'm glad he wasn't a mass murderer," Lorraine declared. "Especially tonight. But that doesn't mean he can't still be involved in something illegal. We may not be finished with Mr. Jack O'Dell yet. There are still a few more questions that I'd like answered about Jack and J.D. Hursh, and their association with that laboratory we were in."

"And also about their relationship with Professor Winslow and Mrs. Winslow," Jennifer added. "Why would a professor from the university, who could be involved in two murders, go to the Hursh ranch and then disappear? And why does Hursh have that factory on his property?"

"The so called hormone factory?" George inquired.

"Yes."

"I don't know about the professor," George replied, "but maybe I can help you with the factory. In the past, Hursh has worked very closely with the government on a lot of top secret projects, fuels and propellants, and stuff like that. Are you sure about the hormones?"

"They said hormones. But I supposed they could be making just about anything. But why on the ranch?"

"I don't know, although I've heard that Hursh is very patriotic. So was his father. During the Second World War, his father let the government build several experimental laboratories on the ranch, and some of them are still there. Hursh has about fifty thousand acres, so most people don't even know the labs exist. He also owns quite a few manufacturing companies throughout the world."

"Are the government projects the only ones he allows on the ranch?"

"No, I don't think so. I've been told he has several other laboratories and workshops on his property besides the ones the government uses. I wouldn't be surprised if your Professor Winslow has worked, or maybe still works in one of them."

"And they must have discovered something new," Jennifer said, "something valuable, and somebody was trying to get it away from them."

"The question is, did they?" Lorraine asked.

Jennifer shook her head. "I don't believe they did, otherwise Winslow would probably also be dead."

"Unless he's the murderer."

"I'm not convinced yet that he is. But I am certain that he and Professor Reid developed something, and somebody was willing to kill to get it. They murdered Professor Reid and Bentley, and probably tried to murder Winslow, but he somehow escaped."

"Do you think that was why Mrs. Winslow went to the police?"

"Maybe. Maybe she was desperate. Her husband had just disappeared and she was hoping they could find him before the murderers did."

"Don't forget that when I went with Mrs. Winslow to her house to look for the professor, she acted like she already knew where he was," George reminded them.

"She probably did at that stage," Jennifer said. "She probably saw him at the motel, or maybe she saw his car parked there. Or maybe she knew all along. When the security guard told us he had seen the professor, maybe she knew right where he'd be."

"But why did she hire you to find him if she already knew where he was?" Lorraine asked.

"I'm still trying to figure that one out," Jennifer answered. "Five thousand dollars, and the offer of even more, is a lot of money for someone to pay to find a person when they already know where he is."

"Unless she didn't hire you to find her husband," Lorraine said. "Maybe she hired you to find someone else."

"That doesn't make sense."

"Yes it does, if you think about who your client is. Have you heard her tell the truth, even once?"

Jennifer thought for a moment. "No."

"Then why would she tell the truth about that? She could have us searching for somebody, and we don't even know who."

"The murderers?"

"Could be. Maybe she wants us to find them before they find her husband."

"So now we're looking for somebody other than her husband?"

"Oh no. We could be looking for someone else, but we're still looking for the professor too. He still has some questions to answer. We'd better let Lieutenant Dickey and Sergeant Chambers know what we know, or at least what we think we know."

"I don't think we should talk to Dickey and Chambers just yet," Jennifer said. "They're not very happy with us right now, and we don't even know if we're right. Besides, the lieutenant has already decided the professor is guilty of murder. We'd better get something a little more substantial before we go to them."

"You could be right," Lorraine agreed. "We can't trust Dickey. I know I saw him at the motel where the Winslows were staying. And we both saw the Winslows following him, and then him following the Winslows. They seemed to be following each other around all night, and yet they both deny it. Why?"

"How did Dickey discover they were at the motel and then at the ranch?" George asked.

"Who knows," Lorraine answered. "Maybe the blow Jennifer gave him on the head with her handbag made him clairvoyant. Or maybe Mrs. Winslow gave him something that made him want to keep coming back."

"I wouldn't be surprised if he's been following Mrs. Winslow all along because he thinks she'll lead him to her husband," Jennifer remarked.

"If he was, he's smarter than we are. Maybe we should start following Dickey. He can lead us to her, she can lead us to her husband, and we can give them both to Dickey."

Jennifer shook her head. "And we can go riding off into the sunset. Oh no. We're not going to get off that easy. There's something else going on here that we don't know about yet, and it's more complicated than just one missing college professor who might have murdered some other professors. Dickey is somehow involved with the Winslows, or at the very least, isn't telling what he knows about them."

"The more we talk to people, the more I think that our client, Mrs. Winslow, or Smythe, or Helmitten, or whoever she is, is the connection. She seems to be the one who's involved in all this, and not her husband. It sounds to me like Professor Winslow could be just another victim."

"You could be right. We should find out a little more about her relationships with the professors when we talk to Dean MacRae."

"Dean MacRae?" George asked.

"The dean of the College of Science," Jennifer said. "We have an appointment with him. We're hoping he can give us some information on Professor Winslow, as well as the murdered professors, here and in England

and Austria, and maybe beyond. For all we know, Mrs. Winslow could have had even more husbands we haven't heard about yet."

"Our appointment with the dean isn't until the day after tomorrow," Lorraine reminded her, "so that should give us enough time to stop off at the prosecutor's office to see if we have anything in our files on the Winslows, and everybody else involved in these murders, especially Jack O'Dell and the hormone factory out at the Hursh ranch."

As she spoke, Lorraine pulled out the front of her blouse and looked down.

"What's she doing?" George inquired.

"I believe she could be looking for hair," Jennifer answered as she pulled out the front of her own blouse.

George's forehead creased as he prepared to ask a question, and then relaxed in understanding. "I think I know why you two are best friends."

SIXTEEN

The prosecuting attorney's office where Lorraine worked was quiet, except for a few personnel who were doing paperwork.

"I hope you checked your purse at the security desk," Geri Burdet said with a grin as Lorraine and Jennifer entered the records room.

Lorraine looked at the records administrator inquisitively.

"I heard about your exploits with Lieutenant Dickey," Burdet explained.

"Very funny Geri," Lorraine retorted. "It wasn't even my purse. And how did you hear about all this anyway?"

"You should know that news travels fast around here," Burdet replied.

"Just how much did you hear?"

"Only that Dickey had you arrested for prostitution after you beat him up."

Lorraine grimaced as she looked at Jennifer. "You did this to me."

"I did not," Jennifer replied in self defense. "We did it together."

"Who is this?" Burdet asked.

"This is my accomplice. She helped me beat up Lieutenant Dickey. For what it's worth, she's also my madam."

"Congratulations Madame," Burdet said, holding out her hand for Jennifer to shake. "They should have put your picture in the office newsletter, alongside Lorraine's."

Lorraine's eyes opened wider and she looked at her suspiciously. "Picture . . . ? Newsletter . . . ?"

"Sure. Nobody becomes as famous as you without getting their picture in the newsletter. Lieutenant Dickey's is there too, except his is a before and after shot. By the way, how're tricks?"

"Not bad," Lorraine answered. "Say, how would you like us to give you a before and after shot?"

"After what you did to Dickey. No thanks. I've heard that public defenders are requesting their clients be sent straight to jail rather than face you in a courtroom. Now, which story is true? I've heard so many, and they're all good. Who hit him with the brick?"

"We did not hit him with a brick. I hit him with my fist. The madam here hit him with her purse."

"Then who shot him?"

"Nobody shot him. But it's not such a bad idea. Who's been telling you these stories anyway?"

"Everyone. Some people, the ones whose reputations aren't going to be affected by your criminal activities, have made you into sort of a hero. But I wouldn't worry about it. They'll all forget about it, in say, a year or so."

"Thanks," Lorraine said. "Now I feel much better. Why does everybody hate Lieutenant Dickey so much?"

"Because he's a mean egotistical bastard who has no ethics, but then you know that. He uses people, and he doesn't care who he hurts in the process. Just hope you don't meet him again for a while. He's being laughed at, so he's probably more dangerous than ever right now."

"We'll try to be careful," Lorraine said, "but unfortunately, we seem to be meeting him every time we turn around. He and Jennifer are working on the same case, the disappearance of a Professor Sheridan Winslow. He teaches science at Westland University. Ever hear of him?"

"No, can't say that I have. Is that why you're here on your vacation, looking for information on this Winslow?"

"We came down to get some information on him, and also on a man by the name of Jack O'Dell, and his boss, J.D. Hursh."

"I've heard of J.D. Hursh. He's a rich man. And very powerful."

"How about O'Dell?"

"Hursh's manager? Yep. I've got quite a file going on him. I make a habit of collecting information on people who've visited our courts more than once."

"More than once?"

"It seems that Jack is very protective about the Hursh ranch. He doesn't take kindly to strangers."

"We've experienced Jack's kindness to strangers," Jennifer said. "How about Hursh?"

"He has a pretty thick historical file, but other than that, not too much. Never been in trouble, at least that we know of."

"What about Lieutenant Dickey?"

Burdet laughed. "Everybody's searched his file, looking for something. It's full of complaints because of his methods, but he manages to wriggle out of most of them. Fortunately he has a partner that bails him out."

"Sergeant Chambers?"

"That's him. Nice guy. Dickey nails them to the wall, and Chambers pries them loose, or at least the ones that are innocent. He's been on the police force longer than Dickey. But he's only been in homicide a short time. Before that he worked undercover, and he was pretty good at it. Apparently he was responsible for breaking up several crime rings."

"How come he quit undercover work?"

"Too old. He's in his forties. They say it's a young person's job. If you ask me, it's not a job for anybody who values their hide."

"What about Dickey?"

"He's been on the force for fourteen years, and in homicide for ten. I'll get his file for you. Anybody else you want?"

Lorraine gave Burdet a list of names that included Hursh, Jack O'Dell, the Winslows, and Professor Reid and Bentley. The clerk disappeared into a row of file cabinets. When she returned, she had several folders and a computer print out.

"George was right about Hursh's wealth," Lorraine said as she examined his file. "He owns several ranches and quite a few companies in the United States, as well as interests around the world. He inherited most of the businesses when his father passed away. A couple of them were the object of an attempted corporate takeover a few years ago, but apparently Hursh won."

"Jack O'Dell's file is almost as big as his," Jennifer commented as she thumbed through O'Dell's folder. "His assault on the reporter is listed. So are a couple of other assaults that were thrown out."

"Here's something of interest. It's a photocopy of a story in the business section of the newspaper regarding one of Hursh's manufacturing companies in Europe. It doesn't mention anything about him being over there, but someone else has."

"Let me guess. Jack O'Dell?'

"You got it. It says he represented Hursh at an international conference in England."

"Was he there six months ago?"

"As a matter of fact, he was. That's when this story was printed."

"That could tie him in with at least one of the murders over there."

"What do we have on the professors?"

Jennifer looked again at the printout. "They're mentioned, at least Winslow and Reid and Bentley are."

"There's nothing on Mrs. Winslow," Burdet said, "and I ran her name through the computer under her present, as well as her previous husband's names. If she were there, I would have found her. Could she have another name?"

"Who knows," Jennifer answered. "I got her full name off the check she gave me. But with her marriage record, I suppose she could have just about any name."

"I could only find information on Sheridan Winslow," Burdet said. "There was no mention of him having a wife."

"That's strange, if you consider that she came into the country at the same time the professor did, and she came as his wife."

"Do you think that Mrs. Winslow could be here illegally?"

"I wouldn't be surprised. That's another question we'll have to ask when we see her again."

"Oh, one other thing," Lorraine added, handing Burdet a slip of paper. "We have two license plate numbers, and we want to find out who the cars are registered to. Could you check them out for us?"

"Certainly." The clerk read the information and then entered the license plate numbers into her computer. She looked at the screen in puzzlement. "According to this, they both belong to the Westland Police Department."

"Both of them?"

"Actually, they're both supposed to be out of service. One is a four year old Pontiac. The other is a three year old Chevrolet. This says they were sent to a storage compound and put up for auction. The Pontiac was sold. The Chev's still there."

"Is the Pontiac green and the Chevrolet blue?"

Burdet examined her screen. "As a matter of fact they are."

"Any record on who bought the Pontiac?"

"A Mr. William Aroyo bought it."

"Any address?"

Burdet handed Lorraine the information she had written. "I think you will find it interesting."

"The Hursh Ranch," Lorraine exclaimed. "Aroyo's address is listed as the Hursh Ranch. He must live and work there. Do you have any other information on him?"

Burdet disappeared into her files again. When she returned, she handed Lorraine a folder with a picture of Aroyo in it.

"This guy was with Jack when we were stopped at the ranch," Lorraine exclaimed, "and he has a record as long as my arm. I wonder how he got his job?"

"Jack?"

"Maybe. He would probably do the hiring."

"You might also be interested in this," Burdet said. "The Chev hasn't been auctioned off yet, but it's not in storage either. Apparently it's out on a case. Would you like to know who has it?"

"Lieutenant Dickey?"

"Right. How did you know?"

"We've seen him in it. What we're trying to figure out now is what he's doing with it, and why he won't admit that he has it."

"Well, good luck," Burdet told them. "And if you need anything else, let me know."

Lorraine thanked her for the assistance. They took the printouts and folders to a nearby table and sat down to examine the sheets of information laid out before them.

"There doesn't seem to be anything spectacular on any of the professors," Lorraine commented, "except they've all had security clearances at one time or another by the government."

"What branch?" Jennifer asked.

"FBI."

"You know why the FBI investigated them, don't you?"

"Security. All of these professors appear to have had access to government projects."

"There's also another reason," Jennifer said. "The FBI investigates people before they come into the country. Do you see where Reid and Bentley came from? They taught in England and Austria at the same universities as Winslow and Smythe. And they all applied for work permits and visas at about the same time."

"Do you think they might have been into something together in Europe?"

"Maybe. Maybe that's the connection. Except their backgrounds are different. The only thing they have in common is Mrs. Winslow, and there's nothing on her."

"What about Dickey?"

"Nothing there either. Just a list of complaints. It seems he's done something to just about everybody."

"What about this?" Lorraine said. "He was issued a passport seven months ago."

"Do you think the lieutenant might have taken a little trip to Europe?" Jennifer asked.

"I know he took a trip to Europe. And it was six months ago. He went to England on some kind of crime prevention seminar. It was approximately the same time Jack was there and Professor Smythe was murdered."

"Surely you're not suggesting that Lieutenant Dickey is involved in a murder."

"All right then, tell me why he's been following us and the Winslows around in an automobile which he denies driving. And tell me why he was hanging around the College of Science and then insisted on going to the university to investigate Professor Winslow's disappearance and Professor Reid's murder, when we both know he should have been home with an ice pack on his head."

"Because he's a sex pervert. He got one look at Mrs. Winslow's legs and plunging neckline when she went to the police station to file her missing person's report, and when the call came in, he grabbed it. You saw the way they were crawling all over each other when they left the university."

"What if Mrs. Winslow didn't go to the station to file a missing person's report? What if she really went there to see Dickey, and when she saw the condition he was in, she panicked and made up the story about her husband being missing?"

"You're really reaching you know. The man only arrested us for prostitution. That's not enough reason to hang four murders on him."

"He's practically ruined my career," Lorraine reminded her. "He should be in jail for murder."

Jennifer studied the files again. "Let's see, in all, we have four college professors who have traveled to other countries, been involved in secret experiments, and who have been murdered, supposedly by truth serum."

"Four that we've heard of. For all we know, there could be more."

"We also have one police lieutenant and one security guard, or ranch manager, or whatever Jack O'Dell is, who were in England when one of the murders took place."

"And we have one professor who has disappeared and is probably running for his life. Except, we saw him with the very woman, namely his wife, whom we suspect is involved somehow in all the murders. For all we know, she might even be trying to kill him, if she hasn't already."

"Let's not forget who's working for this woman who is supposedly involved in all these murders."

"You . . . and me," Lorraine said with a sigh. "At least until your . . . our five thousand dollars is used up."

"Ten thousand," Jennifer corrected her.

"What?"

"Ten thousand," Jennifer repeated. "I meant to tell you. I found another check for five thousand dollars under my door this morning."

SEVENTEEN

Lorraine gazed around the room for a moment without speaking. Finally, she furrowed her brow and looked at her friend. "Did your . . . our . . . renewed client happen to mention anything about what she expected you . . . us . . . to do with the five . . . ten thousand dollars she gave you?"

"No," Jennifer answered, choosing to ignore the emphasis that Lorraine was putting on her words. "She just left a note saying we were doing a very good job and she would like us to carry on."

"Carry on with what? She doesn't even know what we've been doing, or at least according to her she doesn't know what we've been doing, even when we've been following her around. We've hardly talked to her since you took this case, and when we have talked to her, she's lied to us."

Jennifer opened her hands in an unknowing gesture. "I guess carry on with looking for Professor Winslow, and whoever else she has us looking for."

"There's only one person I'm looking for," Lorraine answered, "and that's your client's husband. When we locate him, we're going to find everybody else who's involved in this affair."

"One thing we do know, it's a lot more than just a love triangle, or sex club, or whatever else it appears to be."

"It's at least a rectangle, if we include the two in Europe, and maybe beyond. And all those professors weren't given truth serum because someone wanted to know what kind of sex they enjoyed. The farther we go, the more it looks like espionage or selling secrets, or something more sinister."

"I think that's exactly what it is. Someone is extracting scientific discoveries from college professors with truth serum, then killing them and selling the information."

"Mrs. Winslow?"

"Or someone who is using Mrs. Winslow."

"Dickey?"

"Will you leave Dickey alone. Look at his record. The man has been a policeman for fourteen years, and all he has against him are a bunch of petty complaints. If he were going to be corrupted, he would have done it before now. The worst he's done is travel to Europe when a murder was being committed."

"Maybe he hasn't met a sex crazed woman with five hundred and eighty thousand dollars before now."

"That's true."

"Look what she's got us doing," Lorraine said, "and she only gave us five, excuse me, ten thousand dollars."

Jennifer shrugged. "Who knows. Anything could be possible. How about, while Dickey is keeping an eye on us, we'll try to keep an eye on him. What's our next step going to be?"

"What about the FBI," Lorraine answered. "They should be able to tell us who came into the country legally, and who didn't come into the country legally. They might also have additional information on the murdered professors and Mrs. Winslow."

Jennifer's face lit up. "Good idea. I dated a local agent a few times. Agent Addison. Maybe he can help."

"You called your date . . . Agent . . . Addison?"

"We only dated a few times."

"What's he like?"

"Not bad, except he's an agent first and a date second. Even on a personal level, everything he said was put in the form of a question."

"What did you say?"

"I said, not until I knew him better."

Jennifer telephoned the Federal Bureau of Investigation and asked the receptionist to connect her with Agent Addison's office. When she informed him she was calling about the professors who had been murdered, and the possibility that someone might be buying and selling secret scientific experiments, he requested that they come to see him immediately. His request was put more in the form of an order.

"He wants to see us right now," Jennifer said as she helped Lorraine gather up the files and return them to Geri Burdet.

The agent was waiting for them when they arrived. He led them to his office and motioned for them to be seated. "Now, what do you know about some murders that you need to see me about?" he inquired as he sat down behind his desk.

"We're looking for information on the murders of two college professors at the university," Jennifer said. "And also their status in the country."

"Just what have you heard about them?" Addison asked.

"We would like to know what you've heard about them," Jennifer replied. "I would think the FBI would know about things like that."

Lorraine kicked her under the desk.

"What we're saying," Jennifer continued, "is that when two college professors, who could be involved in spying, espionage, selling secrets to the enemy, or whatever, are murdered, you might possibly have heard about it."

Addison stared at them. "What do you know about it?"

"Then you are aware of it?" Jennifer retorted.

"It came across my desk. What's your role in all this?"

"The same as yours. We were expecting you to help us."

"Sorry, but if you have information about the murders of Professor Reid and Professor Bentley, you'd better give it to me."

"Ah ha," Jennifer declared at the mention of the two names. "So you do know about them."

"I said it came across my desk. I didn't say I knew about them. But you obviously know something, or you wouldn't be here. Now let's have it."

"What do you mean, let's have it?" Jennifer shot back. "Let's have it from you."

Addison's eyes narrowed and he leaned across his desk. "If you don't start coughing up answers to my questions, you might just find yourself an accessory to something."

Jennifer's eyes also narrowed and she leaned back across his desk from the opposite direction. "And if you don't start answering my questions, the next time we go out together, you're not going to find yourself an accessory to anything."

Addison began to answer, then hesitated. "Hey wait a minute, I wasn't an accessory to anything the last time we went out together."

"And that's the way it's going to be the next time we go out, unless you start spitting out answers. Now what do you know about . . . ?"

"Never mind what I know," Addison interrupted. "What do you know?"

The two investigators were leaning closer to each other and rising higher off their chairs. "I'm not telling you what I know until you tell me what you know," Jennifer exclaimed.

Lorraine kicked her once again under the table. "Agent Addison," she said, "we were investigating the disappearance of a missing university professor when we came across two other professors who had been murdered. We also stumbled onto something else that appears to be extremely serious and could involve additional murders and maybe even national security. We want to help you, but we would also appreciate it if you could help us."

"Fair enough," Addison agreed. "Just what is it you want to know?"

"We would like to know if these professors were involved in selling secrets, and what you can tell us about Professor Winslow and his wife. She's hired us to find him, and as far as we know, she already knows where he is. We saw her with him."

"You won't be finding Professor Winslow."

"Why not?"

"Because the professor is dead. The Westland Police Department found him out in the desert yesterday afternoon. He was pumped full of truth serum. Whoever did it also roughed him up pretty bad before they killed him."

Jennifer looked at Lorraine and then back at Addison. "You wouldn't lie to us, would you?"

"Why would I lie to you?"

"Oh, I don't know. Everybody else has in this investigation."

"I think you'd better have them examine the body one more time," Lorraine suggested. "It can't be the professor, because we saw him last night."

"They already have," Addison answered. "Twice. And you must have seen someone else. This guy was wearing Winslow's clothes, he was carrying Winslow's identification . . . ."

Jennifer cut him off. "That doesn't prove anything. They could have been planted on the body."

"He had Winslow's fingerprints."

"Oh."

"The body they found was your Professor Winslow all right."

"Did they find him out at the Hursh ranch?"

"No, on the other side of town."

"Do you know who did it?"

Addison shook his head. "No, not yet."

"Mrs. Winslow?"

"What makes you suspect her?"

"We just don't trust her."

"No. But we're keeping her under surveillance. She was with one of our agents when Professor Winslow was killed. We're concerned that whoever murdered him might try to kill her."

"Is your agent's name by any chance, Professor Hampson?"

"His name is Hampson, but he's not a professor. Mrs. Winslow called us in a panic last night. She said someone was following her and she was afraid he was going to kill her. So we asked Agent Hampson to stay with her."

"Does Agent Hampson do most of his work with his clothes off?"

"Huh?"

"Never mind. You'd have to know our client. Why did he tell us that he'd been with her all evening?"

"Because he didn't know you, or know what your role was at that time. He didn't see any need to give you information."

"Where's Mrs. Winslow now?"

"I can't tell you that."

"At the Hursh ranch?"

"What do you know about the Hursh ranch?"

Lorraine told him about following Professor Winslow and Mrs. Winslow to the ranch, losing them, and then finding what they called the hormone factory.

Addison chose to ignore the reference to Professor Winslow. "Do you know Hursh personally?"

"No. We just met him once."

"I heard he's quite the womanizer."

"He used to be, but not anymore. He says he's settled down."

Addison was about to ask another question, then

changed his mind. "Don't talk to anybody about what you saw out there," he cautioned, "or it could cost some of our agents, and possibly you, your lives."

"Just what did we see?" Jennifer demanded. "All I can remember were people in oxygen masks."

"I'm not at liberty to tell you that right now," he said. "But I'll let you know as soon as I get some more information."

Jennifer and Lorraine rose to leave. As they neared the doorway, Addison called after them.

"Ms. Brookbaine, you forgot something."

"What?" Jennifer asked, turning around.

Addison didn't say anything. Instead, he motioned with a finger for her to return to his desk.

Jennifer walked back across the room. In a few seconds she returned.

"All right, one more time," she called back as she joined Lorraine where she was waiting by the door. "But you'll get nothing from me."

"Was he cross examining you again?" Lorraine asked as they walked down the hall.

Jennifer smiled. "No. He just wanted to know if I would go out to dinner with him on Friday night. I said I would."

"What was that business of, he'll get nothing from you?"

"It had something to do with getting another chance at becoming an accessory."

"And is he?"

"Is he what?"

"Is he going to get another chance to become an accessory?"

"Of course not. Maybe. Anyway, I'll wait and see what kind of dinner he buys me."

Lorraine was muttering as they walked out of the building.

"What's the matter?" Jennifer asked.

"Oh nothing," Lorraine replied. "It's just that we're being paid ten thousand dollars to find a dead person, and now we can't talk about something when we wouldn't even know what we were talking about if we did talk about it, because it might get us killed."

"Yep," Jennifer replied. "Whoever said, what you don't know can't hurt you, certainly hasn't met our Mrs. Winslow."

EIGHTEEN

They decided to track down Mrs. Winslow so that they could question her and extract more lies. Her residence was the first stop.

"We'll probably get FBI Agent Hampson, or Professor Hampson, or whoever he is," Jennifer said as she rang the doorbell.

When there was no answer, she rang several more times and then knocked. There was still no response. She checked to see if the door was unlocked. It was. When it swung open, they saw the reason for their client not being there. The house was full of bullet holes.

They found Agent Hampson in the master bedroom. He had been shot in the arm, but otherwise he was all right. All he had on were his undershorts.

"Caught with our pants down, were we, Professor Hampson," Jennifer remarked.

"What happened?" Lorraine exclaimed.

"Two hooded men," Agent Hampson answered. "They broke in. When I confronted them, they started shooting at me. They took Mrs. Winslow with them."

"From the looks of this place, she could be in serious trouble," Jennifer said as she looked at the damage done by the bullets.

"I wouldn't worry about her being in trouble," Hampson replied. "I got the impression she went along with them willingly. I heard them talking when they were leaving, and they seemed real friendly, as though they knew each other. They were more intent on shooting me, so I ran for cover in here."

"Did you hear anything else?"

"One of them said they had some business to take care of and then they had a meeting with someone named Jack."

"Jack O'Dell?"

"I didn't hear a last name."

"How long ago did they leave?"

"About ten minutes ago. I've already called for help. I didn't have much to report about the two men because of the hoods. The only one they'll recognize is Mrs. Winslow."

Agent Addison and several other FBI agents arrived a few minutes later. Addison already knew what had taken place at the Winslows' residence. They asked if he had any information on their client's whereabouts. He said he didn't.

"I'm afraid Mrs. Winslow and the men she went with gave us the slip," he admitted. "Unless of course, she didn't go willingly and has been kidnapped. I'll make sure you're the first to know if we locate her."

"What about her husband?" Lorraine asked.

"I told you, he's dead."

Lorraine didn't pursue the matter. She was mumbling once again as they drove away from the Winslow residence and toward Westland University for their scheduled appointment with Dean MacRae at the College of Science.

"I think I could use some of that truth serum that somebody's been giving the professors," she said.

"Who do you want to give it to?" Jennifer asked. "Dickey? Mrs. Winslow? Addison? I think Addison could use some."

"No. Me. I'm beginning to doubt myself. You and I are the only two people who ever see anybody. Everybody else we meet says they don't exist."

"That's because everybody else we meet is lying their heads off and covering up something," Jennifer said.

"How do you cover up fingerprints?"

"I don't know. How do you cover up an entire college professor?"

Lorraine shook her head. "We did see him. Didn't we?"

"We saw him all right, in spite of what Addison says. And we're going to find him if it kills us."

"I wish you would quit asking people to kill us," Lorraine sighed.

Jennifer ignored the comment. She was looking into the rear view mirror. "Maybe we can ask Lieutenant Dickey to help us."

"Why?"

"Because I think he's right behind us."

Lorraine turned so she could see the car that was trailing them. It was a blue Chevrolet like the one Dickey had been driving.

Jennifer pulled over to the curb and waited for the Chevrolet to pass. "What say we find out once and for all why the lieutenant finds us so interesting," she suggested.

"It looks like he's decided to be a little shy," Lorraine said as she watched the driver of the other car also pull over half a block behind. "I suppose we could wait for him to make up his mind about what he plans to do, or I could just take a walk back there and ask him."

She climbed out of the Porsche and marched in the direction of the Chevrolet. Before she could get there the driver swung the automobile into traffic and accelerated. He disappeared down a side street, but not before she had an opportunity to recognize the lieutenant.

"Why doesn't he just ride around with us," Jennifer replied when Lorraine told her who the driver was. "He seems to go everywhere we go."

"Do the two men in the other car also go everywhere we go?" Lorraine asked as Jennifer pulled the Porsche into traffic.

"What men?"

"There were two men in another car that was parked just behind Dickey. Dickey's gone but they're still following us."

"I wonder who they are."

"FBI?"

"Maybe."

"Agent Addison?"

"I wouldn't be surprised. Or some other agents. I don't think my friend Addison is a completely trustworthy fellow. He's probably having us followed to see what we're up to."

"Is this the same Agent Addison that you're going out to dinner with on Friday night?"

"Yep. Problem is, he's still an FBI agent first and a date second."

"Then why on earth did you agree to go out with him?"

"Because he's a nice guy. Besides, while he's trying to find out what I know, I can maybe find out what else he knows about the Winslows."

They decided not to lose the car behind them, and instead continued on to the university. When they arrived, the other car parked a few spaces away. The driver and occupant made no effort to avoid being seen.

"Either they think we're blind, or they're not very good at tailing someone," Jennifer remarked. "We'd have to have our heads up our behinds not to see them."

"Maybe that's the idea. Maybe they want us to know we're being followed."

"Could be. Let's find out." Jennifer climbed out, walked the few steps back to the car that had been following them, and knocked on the side window.

"Hi," she said to the driver.

"Hi," he replied.

"Well, it's not Agent Addison," Jennifer informed Lorraine as she peered in at the driver and his passenger.

"Addison asked us to keep an eye on you," the driver said sheepishly.

"Why?"

"Addison's worried about you. He told us we were to follow you and make sure you were all right." The agent hesitated, then continued with a confused smile. "He said he didn't want anything to happen to you before Friday evening."

Jennifer's face twisted into a smirk. "You tell Agent Addison that I have no intention of letting anything happen to me, at least until I've had dinner."

They left the two bewildered agents sitting in the car and walked to the science building. Dean MacRae's secretary gave them directions to the laboratory where the dean was working. There they found an older white haired man who was holding two beakers at arms length while he poured a solution from one to the other. His brow was furrowed in nervous apprehension and his eyes were squinted so that they were nearly closed.

The substance was popping, and each time he poured, the popping grew louder. Eventually, after one last loud crackling fizzle, the noise subsided and a bluish white mist rose from the beaker. He blew the mist from the top of the container like a drinker would blow the foam off a mug of beer, and drank it down with one swallow.

"Ah," he sighed, holding one hand to his mouth to cover a silent burp. He licked some of the foamy liquid off his mustache and blew away the rest. Then he burped again as he tapped his stomach with his rolled up hand. "I haven't seen the heartburn yet that could live through one of those."

"It's an antacid?" Lorraine exclaimed.

"That and a few other things," he replied. "It's a combination of sodium, starch, sugar, some other ingredients, and nitrodyhydrocinoxide."

"Nitrodyhydro . . . ?"

"Nitrodyhydrocinoxide. And I have trouble spelling it too. You would think I wouldn't since I invented it, but I do. It's an industrial type chemical I'm working on. The military seems to like it, except it's a little too volatile for them. I haven't quite perfected it yet, but in the meantime, it does one heck of a job on heartburn. The secret's in the popping."

"Why the popping?"

"Because if you use too much, or if you don't get all the popping out, it can be extremely dangerous. I just used a small drop."

"I can imagine," Lorraine agreed.

"I gave some to one of our lab animals before the last pop was removed," he continued. "That was before we knew it could be dangerous. Poor Herman."

"Herman?"

"Herman, our laboratory mouse. We're still finding pieces of him around the room." He held the container out toward Lorraine. "Would you like to try some?"

Lorraine put up her hands. "No thank you, I feel fine."

"Me too," Jennifer exclaimed as she held up her hands. She looked around the room for signs of Herman.

"What can I do for you then?" he inquired.

"We'd like to ask you some questions regarding the murders of Professor Reid and Professor Bentley, and the disappearance of Professor Winslow, if you don't mind," Jennifer informed him. "Are you Dean MacRae?"

"That I am, Lass." The professor emitted another silent burp and tapped his stomach again. "According to the FBI, Professor Winslow is dead. They were here a little while ago asking me what I knew about him."

"The FBI has told us the same thing," Lorraine

replied, "but his wife hired us to locate him, and we think we saw him with her. So now we don't know if he's dead or not."

"Why don't you just ask her?"

Lorraine shrugged in embarrassment. "We'd like to, but we can't find her."

"Then why are you still working for her?"

"Because she keeps sending us money. We think she wants us to continue searching for her husband, or possibly for whoever murdered her husband, if he has been murdered. We also worry that she could be in danger herself. She might have been kidnapped because she could know something about whatever it was that Professor Winslow and Professor Reid discovered."

"You mean the truth serum?"

"We mean whatever it was the murderers were using the truth serum to find out about."

"That was it. The truth serum. Didn't you know?"

Lorraine and Jennifer looked at each other and then back at Dean MacRae.

"You mean . . . ?"

"Yup. They had discovered truth serum."

"But truth serum has already been discovered."

"Not this truth serum. Actually, it's a brand new type of serum, and Professor Winslow and Professor Reid had perfected it to such a degree that they could put a drop in your coffee and you would spill your guts over lunch."

"Is that what Professor Winslow was doing out at the Hursh ranch? Developing this new type of truth serum?"

The dean hesitated a moment before he spoke again. "That, and other things. He worked with Professor Reid, here, and at the ranch. Trouble is, the formula for the new truth serum disappeared along with Professor Winslow."

"Then what are the murderers using?"

"They're also using truth serum, but it's not as advanced as the serum that Professor Winslow developed. And it kills people. They increased the potency to get as much information as they can in the shortest possible time."

"How do you know all this?"

"I just know," he replied. "Please be very careful. If they think you know something, it could cost you your lives."

"You're the second person to tell us that today. Do you really think we're in danger?"

"Yes, I do. These people are desperate to get that formula, and they'll kill anybody they think has information about it."

"Do you know these people?"

"I know about them."

"How?"

The dean did not answer Lorraine's question. "Just take my word for it," he said. "They're extremely dangerous."

"That's probably why Agent Addison told us not to talk about whatever we might have seen at the ranch," Jennifer said, "even though we're not even sure what we might have seen."

Dean MacRae opened his arms in a wide gesture. "Imagine the power the person who possesses this formula would have. There would be no more need for hypodermic needles. A few drops in your food or drink is all that would be required to find out everything you know."

"How do you know it works?" Lorraine asked. "How can you really be sure there is such a truth serum?"

"Because I've tried it," he answered. "Professor Winslow and Professor Reid had tested it on themselves, but they knew each other so well they weren't totally convinced. So I volunteered. They gave me a few drops in a glass of water, and I told them things about myself that even I had forgotten. And it seemed so natural. We just chatted like you and I are doing right now, except I was telling them my entire life story without any reservations whatsoever. If they asked a question, I answered it, simple as that, and I answered it with every grain of truth I had in my body."

"You knew you were telling them everything they wanted to know?"

"Yes, but it didn't seem important to me. I told them about my sex life like you would tell me about the weather."

"And what about afterwards?"

"There's sort of a sobering up period when they play back on a tape recorder everything you told them, and you realize your sex life wasn't as great as you thought it was. But by then it's too late. They know everything that you know and you're left somewhat embarrassed, at least I was. How would you like to tell me about every intimate sexual moment you have ever experienced, know you're doing it without putting any importance whatsoever on what you are saying, and then in a half hour or so, think back on what you've done."

Lorraine shuddered. Jennifer appeared to be considering the information the professor had just given them.

"Imagine the damage they could do. With a few drops in the punch bowl at a Pentagon cocktail party, three hundred government officials could be telling top secrets to foreign agents and not even care that they're doing it."

"Do you have a sample of this truth serum?" Lorraine asked.

"No. The only person who had a sample of it was Professor Winslow, and when he disappeared, so did the serum."

"What about Professor Reid? Did she know what the formula was?"

"Probably. What one of them knew, the other almost always knew."

"Then why didn't the murderers get the formula from her when they gave her the truth serum using the hypodermic needle?"

"Like I said before, their serum wasn't as effective, and they probably had to increase the potency and the amount to make it work. My guess is she died before she could give them the complete formula, or else they wouldn't still be looking for it."

"Did Professor Bentley know the formula?"

"I don't think so. He didn't get along very well with Professor Winslow, although he did seem to have some kind of relationship with Professor Reid. I think he was just using her to get information. The agents who killed her probably thought he knew what she knew, so they questioned him in the same way, then killed him."

"Agents?"

"Foreign agents, and people in this country who work for them. They steal secret information and then sell it to enemy governments. Using the truth serum is just one of the ways they do it."

"Do they also use sex?" Jennifer asked.

"Could you be thinking of something specific?" he replied.

"As a matter of fact, I am. Do you know Professor Winslow's wife?"

Jennifer watched for a reaction. Her question was met with a slight smile from MacRae. "She's a mighty sociable lady."

Jennifer didn't miss the expression on his face. "Could there be a sex club or something like that going on in the science department?" she asked bluntly. "And did Mrs. Winslow use sex to obtain information from college professors?"

"If she did she could have obtained a heck of a lot," he answered, "because she sure used it a lot. But as far as I was concerned, Mrs. Winslow just had an open marriage and used sex to obtain pleasure. What else she used it for, I don't know. Of course you realize I'm not under the influence of truth serum, so you might not be getting the whole story."

"I understand," Jennifer replied. "Was she by any chance looking for her next husband?"

"Why do you ask that?"

Jennifer told him what they had discovered about Mrs. Winslow's previous marriages in Europe.

"You've certainly done your homework," he declared when she had finished, neither confirming or denying that he knew anything about Mrs. Winslow's relationships. "I can only keep repeating that we're all in a certain amount of danger by just being involved with her."

"Were you involved with her?"

The dean smiled again. "I've already told you, I'm not under the influence of truth serum."

Jennifer let the subject drop. After receiving the dean's permission to look through Professor Reid's laboratory again, they left him working with his formula.

"If you ask me, Mrs. Winslow opened her marriage for just about anybody who wanted to take advantage of it," she said to Lorraine as they walked away.

"Including Dean MacRae?"

"Including Dean MacRae. Did you see the smile on his face?"

"I saw it. But asking him if he was involved in some kind of sex club, that was a little tacky."

"Yes it was, wasn't it," Jennifer replied with a grin of satisfaction. There was no sign of an apology in her voice.

"I still think there's something in here we could be overlooking," Lorraine said when they reached the laboratory where Professor Reid had been murdered. She opened a drawer and examined the contents.

Jennifer looked through the glass door of a cupboard at what she assumed were liquid chemicals. "At least now we know what we're looking for," she answered. "Truth serum."

"I have a question for you."

"What?"

"What does truth serum look like?"

They stared at the hundreds of test tubes that lined the walls and filled the cabinets. The only chemical they saw that looked familiar at all was one with the same name that Dean MacRae had used for his heartburn remedy.

Lorraine read the label. "Nitrodyhydrocinoxide."

"I think the name itself would be enough to kill you," Jennifer said wryly. "We'd better not touch anything in these cabinets in case we blow ourselves up."

"Why don't we ask Dean MacRae if he'll help," Lorraine suggested. "Maybe he can tell us what's in some of these bottles."

"Good idea," Jennifer replied. "I'll keep looking around here if you want to go get him."

Lorraine left Jennifer in the room and headed to the lab where Dean MacRae was working. "Can you help us?" she asked. "We don't know what truth serum looks like."

"It doesn't matter," he replied. "There isn't any there anyway. The police have already taken away anything that even remotely resembles the ingredients in truth serum. They even took my bottle of antacid tablets because they thought it looked suspicious."

"Could we ask you to search with us anyway?" Lorraine asked again. "We really think there might be something there that the police have overlooked, and we don't know what all the substances are. The only thing we recognized was a bottle of your nitrodyhydro . . . ."

Dean MacRae's face brightened and he broke into a broad smile. "My nitrodyhydrocinoxide. I've been looking for that. I'll be happy to go with you."

The dean gathered his wrinkled laboratory smock together and straightened his tie. "I hope you didn't touch it," he said, "because like I mentioned before, it does tend to be a little volatile."

Together, they walked back to the laboratory where Jennifer and Lorraine had been searching for the truth serum. Jennifer had not moved from the location where she had been standing when they found the nitrodyhydrocinoxide.

The only difference Lorraine could see was the way Jennifer was standing. The contents of her handbag were strewn about a laboratory table and her hands were raised high in the air.

NINETEEN

Before Lorraine or Dean MacRae could react, the laboratory door closed behind them. They turned to see a man in a black hood. At the other side of the room was another man, also wearing a hood. They both had guns.

"Get over there," the man at the door ordered, motioning toward the table where Jennifer had placed her belongings.

"And empty your pockets," he added. "And your purse."

"Now just one minute," Lorraine declared. "You can't do this . . . ."

"Get over there," he ordered again, waving the gun in her direction.

"But . . . ."

"Get over there," the man ordered a third time. He

pointed the gun directly at her and his finger pressed on the trigger.

"All right, I'm going," Lorraine sputtered, partly in anger and partly in fear.

She turned her handbag upside down and emptied its contents. The small pistol that Jennifer had given her at the Hursh ranch made a loud thunk as it hit the table.

"Who are you?" she demanded. "And what do you want?"

The man ignored her protests. He sorted through her belongings with the barrel of his gun, but saw nothing that interested him.

"Move over there," he growled, motioning for her to join Jennifer where she was standing beside one of the glass cabinets.

"What's going on?" Lorraine mouthed silently as she neared her.

Jennifer shook her head slightly and shrugged. "I don't know," she whispered back.

"You," the man snapped at Dean MacRae. "Get over here."

MacRae did as he was told. The gunman pulled the dean's pockets inside out and quickly went through his wallet. Not finding what he was looking for, he threw the contents on a table

"What do you know about Professor Winslow and his formula for truth serum?" he demanded, pushing the barrel of his gun against the dean's chest.

"Professor Winslow is dead," MacRae answered. "The FBI found him out in the desert, pumped full of your truth serum."

The man pushed the gun a little harder. "This will be the last time. What do you know about Professor Winslow's truth serum?"

"He's telling you the truth," Lorraine called out. "The professor is dead. The FBI told us the same thing."

"We'll find out." The gunman pointed MacRae toward a chair. "Sit down."

When the dean was seated, the man pushed his gun into a holster under his arm and reached beneath his coat on the other side. He pulled a flat black container from an inside pocket, flipped open the top, removed a hypodermic needle, and pressed the plunger to force out any air that had been trapped inside.

Dean MacRae's eyes opened wide and he made an effort to get up. The other man pinned his arms from behind and pulled him back into the chair.

The first man rolled up the sleeve of the dean's lab coat, then inserted the needle into his arm and pushed the plunger. The dean continued to move for a few seconds, then he relaxed.

"Now," the gunman demanded. "What do you know about Professor Winslow and his truth serum?"

"I was told that he's dead."

"When was the last time you saw him?"

"A few days ago."

"Where?"

"At the lab."

"This lab?"

"No."

"Where then? What lab did you see Professor Winslow at?"

"The lab at the ranch."

"The Hursh ranch?"

"Yes."

"What was he doing?"

"Developing his truth serum."

"Did you help him?"

"Yes."

"How?"

"I gave him one of the ingredients."

"For the truth serum?"

"Yes."

"Does Professor Winslow know what this ingredient is?"

"Yes."

"Does he know what's in it?"

"No."

"Who does know?"

"Just me."

"What is it called?"

"Nitrodyhydrocinoxide."

"Where is it?"

"I don't know."

"Who does know?"

The dean hesitated for a moment, then nodded toward Lorraine. "She does."

The gunman looked at Lorraine, then returned his attention to Dean MacRae. "Exactly what is in this nitrodyhydro . . . this formula of yours?"

The dean did not answer. He had begun to sway back and forth in the chair.

"What are the ingredients?"

The dean mumbled something that was incoherent. Then his eyes slowly closed and his head fell to his chest.

The man shook him and slapped his face. "What are the ingredients, damn you?"

The dean did not respond, even though the gunman continued to slap him and shake him. Finally, the other gunman released him and he slumped to the floor.

The man who had been doing the questioning bent over the dean and felt for a pulse. "He's dead," he said to the other man, "but you don't need him anymore."

The second man still did not speak. Instead, he motioned with the barrel of his gun toward Jennifer and Lorraine.

The first gunman nodded. "Now that we know what the other ingredient in the truth serum is, we'll find out exactly where it is."

He retrieved the black container from the lab bench where he had placed it when he was interrogating

Dean MacRae and removed another full hypodermic needle. Then he pulled his gun from his holster and advanced toward the two women.

"Get over here," he ordered, motioning to Lorraine.

"I don't think so," Lorraine replied.

"Get over here," he ordered again.

Before he could steady his arm and point the gun directly at her, the two women glanced at each other and ducked behind a bench. A bullet from his gun penetrated the wood above their heads as they took cover.

"Where's your gun?" Lorraine whispered.

"Over on the table with the rest of my things," Jennifer whispered back. "Where's yours?"

"Same place."

Lorraine glanced around the end of the bench but quickly pulled back when the gunman fired another shot.

"Now what?"

Behind them was a cabinet. The glass doors were locked, but inside they could see the vial that had nitrodyhydrocinoxide marked clearly on the label. Without hesitating, Lorraine smashed the leg of a stool through the glass, grabbed the vial, and threw it in the direction of the gunmen.

She had hoped it would explode. It didn't. They could hear a clunk as the container landed without breaking and rolled across the floor.

There was no sound for several seconds as Lorraine

frantically searched for something else she could throw. Then they heard another sound. The vial containing the nitrodyhydrocinoxide was popping.

At first the noise was hardly noticeable. Then the pops began to increase in number and grow louder in much the same way they had seen the substance react in Dean MacRae's laboratory. Finally, the solution gave one long last crackling fizzle and exploded.

When the explosions had subsided, they slowly lifted their heads over the top of the bench. The gunmen were not in sight. Instead, they saw a large cloud of fizzing bluish white mist rising from the floor and hanging over the room.

"My gosh," Lorraine gasped.

"My God," Jennifer exclaimed. "Where are they?"

They quickly retrieved their guns and moved cautiously to where they thought the gunmen had been standing when Lorraine threw the container.

The gunman who had been doing the talking was lying on the floor. A piece of glass from the vial protruded from his neck. Blood flowed from the wound and covered the area around his head. His eyes stared at the ceiling in death through the slits in the black hood.

The other gunman was gone.

"Don't move!"

They slowly turned, expecting to see the other hooded gunman again. Instead, they found themselves staring at Agent Addison.

Addison stared back at them, and then around the room. "What the hell happened here?" he asked in astonishment.

Lorraine pointed to the body of the gunman on the floor. "That man killed Dean MacRae, and then he tried to kill us. There's another one too. He left the laboratory just before you got here."

"I know," Addison said. "Our men are after him now. We saw him run out of the building."

Another agent who had entered the room with Addison went over and looked at Dean MacRae. "This one's dead all right," he informed them. He came back and looked at the piece of glass that protruded from the masked gunman's throat. "So is this one."

Just then, another man entered the room. He was one of the two agents that had followed them from FBI headquarters to the university.

"We lost him," he told Addison. "He disappeared into one of the buildings, and when we got to the other side he was gone."

Jennifer and Lorraine joined Addison where he was going through the dead man's pockets. He had removed the hood and was studying his features.

"Recognize him?" he asked.

Jennifer examined the man's face. "He's one of the thugs that was with Jack the night they stopped us at the Hursh ranch."

"And the other one?"

"That's Dean MacRae, the head of the science department here at the university."

"How does he fit into all this?"

"We're not quite sure. We came to ask him some questions about Professor Winslow's disappearance, and the other murders that occurred here. And I think he gave us the answer. Professor Winslow had discovered a new type of truth serum, one that is very effective, and the two men that broke in wanted it. They thought Dean MacRae knew what it was, or at least knew some of the ingredients."

"Tell me everything that took place," Addison directed, "from the time you met the dean, until what happened here, in detail."

Lorraine told him about their meeting with the dean and their search for Professor Winslow's truth serum. "That man, and the other man, the one that got away, killed Dean MacRae," she explained. "They didn't use the new truth serum. They used some other kind of serum that gets the truth but kills whoever they give it to. But they didn't seem to care. After they killed him, they tried to kill us."

Addison looked at the damaged laboratory and then pointed to the piece of glass in the gunman's neck. "What happened to the room, and where did this come from?"

"We threw a bottle of some stuff we found in the cabinet at them, and it exploded."

"What stuff?"

"Nitrodyhydro . . . something or other. It's some kind of chemical that Dean MacRae invented."

"Do you know what this man is?" the FBI agent asked, pointing to the gunman.

"Yes. We already told you," Jennifer answered. "He works for Jack O'Dell."

"You know who he is, but do you know what he really is?" Addison pressed.

Jennifer looked at Lorraine and then back at Addison. She shook her head.

"He's an international terrorist. You two are very lucky to be alive."

"No kidding," Jennifer replied. She looked one way and then the other at the damage in the room. "If you knew he was a terrorist, why did you wait so long to come and rescue us? We would have been happy to see you."

"Because we just got here."

Lorraine pointed to the other agent. "But he followed us here."

"Sorry," the agent replied. "But we got a report that Mrs. Winslow was somewhere at the university. We thought she might come back here to the science department, and she did. Anyway, my partner spotted her. He trailed her and saw her meet this man and another man. Then he lost them. He told me he had seen the other man snooping around here before and thought he looked suspicious. He didn't get a really good look at him."

"He didn't happen to have a black eye and a bandage on the side of his head, did he?" Lorraine asked.

"My partner didn't mention it," the agent said, "but I'll ask him."

"He did have a bandage on the side of his head," another agent said as he entered the room. "I couldn't make out if he had a black eye, but he did look a lot like the same guy we saw running away from this laboratory."

Addison gazed at the women inquisitively. "Did you have someone in mind?"

"Do you happen to know Lieutenant Dickey of the Westland Police Department?" Lorraine asked.

"No."

"Well, I won't be surprised if you meet him in a few minutes," she predicted. "And then you'll see what I mean."

"What makes you say that?"

"Oh, just a feeling. Every time there's a dead body, Lieutenant Dickey seems to show up."

"That doesn't prove anything," Jennifer exclaimed. "Every time there's a dead body, we seem to show up."

"But we don't have a black eye and a bandage on the side of our head."

Addison looked at Lorraine. "Are you saying this Lieutenant Dickey looks like the man that our agent saw running away."

"I'm just saying that I won't be surprised if you get to meet Lieutenant Dickey for yourself in about five minutes," Lorraine repeated with an air of confidence.

Addison dismissed Lorraine's prediction and was about to go over once again the events that had taken place in the laboratory, when they were interrupted by footsteps in the hallway.

The door opened and Lieutenant Dickey entered.

TWENTY

"Has it been five minutes already?" Jennifer commented.

They watched as Dickey slowly moved around the room, ignoring the FBI agents. He looked at the bodies of the terrorist and Dean MacRae with his good eye and the black and purple eye that had begun to lose some of its swelling. Then he stared at the people who were standing there.

"What's going on here?" he demanded.

Agent Addison examined Dickey's black eye and the bandage on his head. "Maybe you can tell us?" he shot back without answering the lieutenant's question.

"That's the man we saw with Mrs. Winslow and with this dead guy on the floor," the agent who had attempted to catch the terrorist said. He pulled his gun and pointed it at Dickey.

Dickey looked at him coldly. "I happen to be Lieutenant Dickey of the Westland Police Department. Now what's going on here?"

"This is official FBI business," Addison informed him. "You'll find out what happened here in due course, if you don't know already."

"And exactly what is that supposed to mean?" Dickey demanded.

"What do you think it means?"

Dickey glared at Addison and the man who held the gun. "It means you think I know something about what happened here. And if you think that, you've got shit for brains."

"Where were you twenty minutes ago?" Addison asked.

"I was out in the parking lot watching your comedy patrol lose a suspect."

"What were you doing there?"

Dickey spit out his answer. "I was waiting for these two . . . ladies."

Jennifer was getting used to Dickey spitting out answers. "Then it *was you* following us."

"I said I was waiting for you."

"Were you tailing them?" Addison asked when Dickey refused to tell Jennifer if he was the person following them in the Chevrolet. Then he repeated his own questions. "What were you doing in the parking lot? And how did you know these two . . . ladies . . . would be here at the College of Science?"

"That's none of your damn business," Dickey growled. His angry expression relaxed a little. "I saw their names in an appointment book in the science department office."

"Why all the interest in them?" Addison asked suspiciously.

"Because I thought they'd lead me to a suspect in a couple homicides I'm investigating. Instead, they've handed me another murder scene."

Addison stiffened. "This is not your murder scene. This investigation falls under the jurisdiction of the Federal Bureau of Investigation, and me. This is my murder scene."

Lieutenant Dickey also stiffened. "This is not your murder scene. This investigation falls under the jurisdiction of the Westland Police Department, and me. This is my murder scene."

Dickey's voice rose in an authoritative growl as he gestured toward the dean and the terrorist. "That is my body, and that is my body, and so is every other body these two ... ladies ... supply me with. And I'll thank you to keep your hands off them. Now, what happened here?"

Addison pointed to Dean MacRae and then to the gunman. "This man was killed by that man, and that man was killed by these two ... ladies. And that is all you need to know."

"To hell that's all I need to know," Dickey shouted. "In the first place, this happens to be an official crime scene of the Westland Police Department, and I'm conducting the investigation of . . . MY . . . murder."

"In the first place, second place, and third place," Addison shouted back, "this is not . . . YOUR . . . crime scene, this is . . . MY . . . crime scene, I'm conducting the investigation of . . . MY . . . murder, and you're my prime suspect."

Dickey continued to glare at him. "And just what the hell makes you think I'm a suspect?"

"Your black eye and your bandaged head."

"WHAT!"

"And these two ladies," Addison added.

Lieutenant Dickey's face had turned a scarlet red. He glared at Jennifer and Lorraine with something they perceived to be slightly beyond hatred.

"These two . . . ladies . . . as you so loosely refer to them, have already been picked up once for prostitution and assaulting a police officer, and if they don't start cooperating, they are about to be picked up again as accomplices to murder." He leaned toward them as he spoke the last words. "Now, what do you two know about what's going on here?"

"Don't answer that question," Addison ordered. "What happened here involves top-secret government security."

"Bullshit," Dickey yelled. "What happened here involves this corpse and that corpse, and this woman and that woman, and me and the Westland Police Department, and nobody else."

Addison leaned forward until his face was almost touching the lieutenant's. "What happened here does not involve you at all, except as a suspect." He turned to Jennifer and Lorraine. "You two are free to go."

"But we don't want to go," Jennifer replied. "We want to stay and . . . ."

"I said you are free to go," Addison said again, jerking his thumb in the direction of the door. This time it was more of an order than a suggestion. "And don't talk to anybody about what happened here."

Addison glanced at Dickey and the other agents, then leaned toward Jennifer and whispered, "I'll see you on Friday."

Even after they had been ushered out of the laboratory and into the hallway, and the door was closed behind them, Jennifer and Lorraine could hear Dickey and Addison debating who owned the crime scene.

"These are . . . MY . . . murders," Dickey shouted.

"These are not . . . YOUR . . . murders," Addison shouted back. "These are . . . MY . . . murders, you're still my prime suspect, and I've got three FBI agents behind me with pistols aimed at your head that say I'm right and you're wrong."

That was the last word Jennifer and Lorraine heard from Lieutenant Dickey.

"I don't think the lieutenant is too happy about being a prime suspect in a murder investigation," Jennifer commented.

"I almost feel sorry for him," Lorraine replied. "Maybe we shouldn't have told Addison that he resembled the man they were chasing."

"I don't feel sorry for him," Jennifer responded. "Have you forgotten what he said about us in there?"

"About us being possible accessories to murder?"

"That's right. Even if he isn't guilty, he deserves to be thrown into jail for fifty years."

"Who deserves to be thrown into jail for fifty years?" Sergeant Chambers said as he walked down the hallway toward them.

"Lieutenant Dickey," Lorraine answered. "Agent Addison of the FBI is questioning him about a possible involvement in two more deaths that just took place in the science lab."

"Lieutenant Dickey? What would make them think Dickey could be involved?"

The two women were quiet for several seconds. Finally Lorraine broke the silence.

". . . us."

"You?"

"We just happened to mention that he looked a little like a suspect the FBI agents saw leaving the building just before they arrived."

"Well, it wasn't Lieutenant Dickey," Chambers said. "Not unless he can be in two places at the same time. The lieutenant has been with me, and he hasn't been out of my sight for the past hour, until he came in here a few minutes ago."

"Oh my gosh," Lorraine sputtered. "We'd better go back in there and tell them."

"You two had better get out of here," Chambers ordered. "Let Dickey cool down a little before he sees you again, or he might just throw you back in jail. I'll let the FBI know he was with me."

"That's a shame," Lorraine said as they watched Sergeant Chambers entering the laboratory, and the door closing behind him. "A real shame."

"What's a real shame?" Jennifer asked.

"Dickey not going to jail for fifty years. I was kind of looking forward to that."

"Yeah, I know what you mean. Sometimes I forget what he is."

"A pervert?"

"A dirty rotten low life degenerate pervert. I don't suppose you've noticed that he threatens to have us arrested as accomplices to murder every time he sees us, not to mention your intimate moment with him and being thrown into jail for prostitution and assault the first time we met."

"We did assault him."

"He deserved to be assaulted. He's an unscrupulous cop who tries to make time with women when he's supposed to be working. And not just with you. Remember the way he came on to Mrs. Winslow? If we hadn't been standing there the first night they met, they would have copulated right on the spot."

"Copulated?"

"Had sexual intercourse. Made love."

"I know what copulating is. And I wouldn't call what he wanted to do to her, love."

"Well, I wouldn't be surprised if he was following us, so we'd lead him to her, so he could have another shot at copulating. If he hasn't been doing it already."

"What did you just say?"

"I said if he isn't copulating her already. I wouldn't be surprised if he's been doing it all along."

"Maybe that's it. Maybe that's the way to find Mrs. Winslow, and maybe even Professor Winslow."

"By copulating?"

"No, silly. By following Lieutenant Dickey. We keep saying we're going to do it, but we never have. If they really are fooling around, he should lead us right to her, and the professor. Instead of Dickey following us, why don't we follow him for a while?"

"That will be a switch, the hookers following the police detective. But it will be nice for a change."

Jennifer drove from the parking lot to a point where they could watch for the lieutenant when he left the science department. "Chambers will probably be with him," she said, "so if he's going to see Mrs. Winslow, he won't be doing it right away."

"Unless . . . ."

"Unless what?"

"Unless they have another love triangle going."

"Sergeant Chambers would never be involved in something like that."

Lorraine pondered Jennifer's words for a moment. "But what if Sergeant Chambers and Lieutenant Dickey are really international spies themselves, and they're working in cahoots with Mrs. Winslow, and Professor Winslow, and J.D. Hursh, and Jack O'Dell, and . . . ?"

Jennifer finished Lorraine's thought. "And the Westland Police Department, and the FBI, and the federal government. Where do you get these ideas?"

"It's my nature. I'm a prosecuting attorney, remember."

"I'm surprised you don't have the whole city in jail."

"It would eliminate some suspects. You know it's just my way of sorting out who's involved and who isn't."

"Do you happen to have my name in there?"

"Yes, but only as my best friend, and I would never eliminate you, at least until I get a puppy or a kitten or something."

Jennifer smiled crookedly. "Thank you. I really appreciate that."

They continued to watch the science building until there was movement at the door and Lieutenant Dickey came out. Sergeant Chambers was not with him.

"Chambers told us they came together," Lorraine said. "Maybe he went out another way. Should we wait for him or should we follow the lieutenant?"

"He's probably still trying to convince Addison that Dickey didn't commit the murders," Jennifer replied. "It doesn't matter. Dickey's the one we're interested in."

They watched the lieutenant as he crossed the parking lot and climbed into his Chevrolet. He waited a few minutes and then headed for the exit. When he had turned onto the driveway that led out of the campus, Jennifer started her car and followed.

Dickey left the university and headed north. He drove for several miles before turning onto another main thoroughfare. After several more blocks, he entered a less traveled side street, then the parking lot of an apartment complex.

They watched him walk from the lot toward the building. When they were sure he wouldn't spot them, they got out and followed. By the time they reached the area where he had entered the complex, he had disappeared.

"Now where did he go?" Jennifer muttered.

"I would say we have about a hundred choices," Lorraine answered, counting the doorways. "Unless of course, he slipped out another way."

Jennifer looked around the complex, searching for the unit that Dickey might have gone into. "If he did, it means he knows he was being followed. And it won't make any difference, so we might as well wait here and see if he really did go into one of the apartments."

"Speaking of Dickey, do you think he's meeting Mrs. Winslow?"

"Yes, unless he has another woman we don't know about."

"It wouldn't surprise me if he's having an affair with Mrs. Winslow, and attempting to have an affair with every other woman in the city."

Their conversation was interrupted by movement in a doorway on the second floor. Lieutenant Dickey exited an apartment. He was followed closely by Mrs. Winslow. They were carrying suitcases.

"I knew it," Lorraine said. "Her husband's body isn't even cold yet, and already they're fooling around."

"If they are, they must have his permission," Jennifer replied.

A third and fourth person had followed Dickey and Mrs. Winslow out of the apartment. They were also carrying suitcases.

"Professor Winslow," Lorraine exclaimed.

Jennifer nodded. "So much for Agent Addison declaring him dead."

TWENTY-ONE

"If Professor Winslow is dead, he sure has a strange way of showing it," Jennifer said.

"Do you recognize the other guy?" Lorraine asked.

"Bill Aroyo, one of Jack's henchmen who stopped us at the ranch, and who bought the green Pontiac the Winslows have been driving."

"Should we confront them?"

"I don't think so. Dickey is armed and probably not in a good mood, and he isn't going to like us very much since we turned him in to the FBI. And if the Winslows are into stealing secrets with him, they're going to be just as mean. We'd better find out where they're going and then call for help."

They arrived at the street in time to see the four people approaching the lieutenant's Chevrolet. Dickey threw his suitcase into the trunk along with the other suitcases and then slid behind the steering wheel. He drove out of the parking lot and continued north in the direction of the Hursh ranch.

Jennifer called the Westland Police Department, gave them a description of her Porsche and Dickey's Chevrolet, and let the dispatcher know that the lieutenant was with Mrs. Winslow and Professor Winslow, as well as Bill Aroyo.

When she told the dispatcher where they were headed, he asked her to wait while he passed along the information. He returned in a minute and informed her that the FBI and the local police already had the area under surveillance and that the Winslows would be apprehended at the entrance to the ranch. He cautioned her against getting too close and not to do anything on their own.

Jennifer swung the Porsche around and raced in the direction the other car had taken. In a short time the Chevrolet was in sight and she relaxed her foot on the accelerator to increase the distance between them.

"They're heading toward the ranch all right," she said. "And then they'll probably be leaving town. Why else would they have suitcases?"

"Probably," Lorraine agreed. "Our problem is going to be if the police and the FBI aren't at the entrance. If that happens, how do we get past Jack O'Dell? And what if Jack is in cahoots with Dickey and the Winslows? We got away from him once, but if he's involved, we might not get away again."

Jennifer remembered the many dips and hills in the road from their previous visit to the ranch, and she occasionally had to speed up to keep Dickey's vehicle in view. As they crested the last hill before the ranch entrance, she was looking forward to witnessing the lieutenant and the Winslows being apprehended.

Unfortunately, the police and the FBI had not arrived.

And Lieutenant Dickey's Chevrolet was nowhere to be seen.

"Not again," she muttered.

The drive to the road that led into the ranch showed no signs of Dickey or the Winslows. Jennifer attempted to call the dispatcher, but her cell phone displayed the usual no service message because of the mountainous terrain.

"I suppose we could drive up the ranch road and be caught by Jack and his merry band of thugs again," Lorraine offered. "Unless we consider what happened to us the last time we disobeyed orders to wait for the police."

"I'm considering it," Jennifer replied. "All right, it's been considered. Now let's find out where the hell they went."

Lorraine surveyed the surrounding terrain. "They couldn't have reached this entrance," she replied. "It must be over a mile from the top of that hill to here. There has to be another route into the ranch that we haven't seen."

"There's only one way to find out," Jennifer said as she shifted the car into reverse. She backed onto the main road and drove in the direction they had just traveled. When they reached the top of the hill where they had lost sight of the Chevrolet, she turned around again.

"What about there?" Lorraine suggested, pointing to a flat area by the side of the road at the base of the hill. "That looks like it could be wide enough for a car to double back."

Jennifer stared apprehensively at the narrow path, then deciding there was no other choice, made a wide turn and swung the Porsche off the pavement.

"I hope there are no rocks on the way down," she exclaimed as she followed a steep slope in the opposite direction along the side of the hill toward a ravine.

There were rocks. The Porsche skidded over them as they came perilously close to the edge, and more than once she had to jerk the steering wheel sharply to avoid going over the side. Finally, with one final lunge, the car veered and bounced to a stop on a graveled river bed under a bridge.

"Well, I don't think there's any question about which direction we're going to be going," she remarked, "since this is the way we happen to be heading, and I don't see any place to turn around in this ditch."

"I'm glad you see it that way," Lorraine replied, "because this is obviously the direction they went."

"And how do you know that?"

"Do you see any other roads around here?"

"No."

"And because I see tire tracks," Lorraine added, "and they're going this way. We were closer to them the other night than we thought. They must have hidden in a side road until we passed and then doubled back to here."

"It looks that way," Jennifer agreed, "although I think we'd be better off with a horse and a pack mule."

The Porsche bumped along the rocky river bottom until the tire tracks climbed an embankment and curved away into the desert. Jennifer guided the car up the embankment and between the cactus and desert plants as she swerved around boulders and dead foliage that protruded from the makeshift road.

They followed it until it cut into a canyon at the base of a mountain. After traveling into the canyon for a mile, the tire tracks vanished abruptly on the rocky terrain.

"Maybe they doubled back somewhere," Lorraine said. "They did it at the road coming in. Perhaps they did it again."

Jennifer nodded in agreement, then swung the car around and headed back to the opening of the canyon. She stopped at the entrance to another smaller canyon they had not seen when they were going in the other direction.

"We might as well have a look," she said, turning into the narrow entrance. "Dead end," she muttered when it appeared to go nowhere. "And not even a place to turn around."

"Perhaps we could turn around in there."

Jennifer stared past Lorraine's pointed finger to an opening in the rocks. Off to one side was a cave that had not been visible before. Tire tracks could be seen leading into it.

"No wonder we couldn't see where the road went," Lorraine said. "And since this part of the ranch is probably deserted, no one would suspect that anyone was ever here."

"If they are here, it might not be for long," Jennifer replied. "The Winslows and Dickey are probably getting ready to make a run for it. And the FBI and the police haven't arrived, which means if we don't do something, they'll get away for sure."

"What you really mean is, we're all there is, and you want us to find them and stop them."

Jennifer shook her head. "We're not going to find them. Those people are killers, and probably armed to the teeth. But we can try to slow them down and then go for help."

"Sounds good to me," Lorraine agreed. "How do you plan to do it?"

"By flattening their tires."

"What tires?"

"Those tires over there."

Jennifer pointed farther into the cave to where Lieutenant Dickey's Chevrolet was parked beside the Winslow's Pontiac.

They climbed out of the Porsche and cautiously made their way to the cars, keeping as close to the side of the cave as possible. When they reached Dickey's car, they used pebbles to press the tire valves and let air out. They did the same to the tires on the Winslow's Pontiac.

"That should slow them down, at least for a little while," Jennifer said. "Now let's get out of here and find the police."

"I think we've already found them," Lorraine answered from the other side of the Pontiac.

Jennifer straightened up and looked in the direction that Lorraine was facing. Standing a few feet away, with his thirty-eight revolver pointed straight at them, was Sergeant Chambers.

"I hope this means that help has arrived," Lorraine said optimistically as she looked into the barrel of Chamber's gun.

"Hello Sergeant," Jennifer said. The smile she had greeted him with disappeared when she noticed he had not lowered the weapon.

"Hello ladies," he answered. "I don't suppose I have to ask what brings you out here."

"I'm hoping the same reason you're here," Lorraine replied. She looked a little more apprehensive. "Did you get the messages Jennifer left with the police department dispatcher?"

"I got them."

Lorraine looked beyond him to the entrance of the cave. "So where are the other police officers and the FBI?"

"I'm afraid they won't be coming."

"And may I ask why not?"

"It seems that I asked the dispatcher to give the messages to me, and I forgot to relay them."

Lorraine was quiet for a moment. "Do you think I might be optimistic enough to suggest that you've come out here to help us?"

"I'm afraid not."

"Do you think I might be pessimistic enough to suggest that you're in cahoots with Dickey and the Winslows?" Jennifer asked.

"You might suggest that," the sergeant responded with a twisted grin. "Now, I would appreciate it if you would very slowly reach into your purses and take out those little guns you like to play with." He pointed off to one side of the cave. "And throw them over there."

"Remind me to listen to you the next time you suspect everybody," Jennifer said to Lorraine as she watched their guns disappear into the shadows. "I'm beginning to think the whole damned Westland Police Department is involved."

"Not quite," Chambers replied. "Why don't we just go for a little walk and you can meet Lieutenant Dickey again. I'm sure he wants to see you. Over that way please."

Jennifer and Lorraine did as they were told and walked away from the entrance. As they passed the opening, they could see the car that Chambers had driven to the ranch. It was a blue Chevrolet, the same as Dickey's.

"I see that Lieutenant Dickey has a likeness for the same make and color of car that Sergeant Chambers drives," Lorraine remarked.

"Or perhaps Sergeant Chambers has a likeness for the same make and color of car that Lieutenant Dickey drives," Jennifer added.

"Down there," Chambers ordered, pointing to some wooden steps, damaged from age and wear, that led deeper into the cave.

They made their way down the steps and walked along a ditch until they came to a tunnel. At the other end, they could see daylight. In a few minutes, they found themselves outside at the bottom of a ravine. Above, on the other side, was what appeared to be a deserted building.

They walked across the ravine and entered a tunnel on the other side. A hundred feet ahead, light filtered down from above. There, they came to another set of worn stairs.

They stumbled up the stairs and walked along a semidarkened hallway until they arrived at what appeared to be a partially finished laboratory.

Professor Winslow, Lieutenant Dickey, and Mrs. Winslow were sitting at a table in the middle of the room. At the other side of the room, leaning against a wall, was Bill Aroyo. His jacket was open and the handle of a gun protruded from under his arm.

"How's the interrogation going?" Chambers asked.

"I just gave him some truth serum," Mrs. Winslow answered. "We're about to begin. Well, do you feel like talking?" she said.

Jennifer and Lorraine watched Professor Winslow, waiting for a response.

"I certainly do," Dickey answered.

TWENTY-TWO

Surprised, Jennifer and Lorraine's attention moved from the professor to the lieutenant.

"And you will tell us the truth, the whole truth, and nothing but the truth, won't you," Mrs. Winslow said.

"I certainly will," Dickey responded again.

"I brought two of Lieutenant Dickey's friends with me," Chambers informed her. "I'm sure they'd like to hear what the lieutenant has to say."

Lorraine looked at Lieutenant Dickey, and then at Chambers. "They've given him truth serum?"

"That's right."

"Why?"

"Perhaps Lieutenant Dickey would like to tell you." Chambers placed his gun barrel under Dickey's chin and lifted his head up. "Tell them why we gave you truth serum."

"Because you want to find out how much I know about the secret experiments and scientific discoveries you've been selling to enemy governments," Dickey said.

Lorraine looked at Jennifer. "I have a feeling that Lieutenant Dickey might not be exactly what we thought he was."

Jennifer nodded back. "And I have a feeling that Sergeant Chambers might be exactly what we thought he wasn't."

"What about him?" Lorraine asked, gesturing toward Professor Winslow.

"I'm afraid I'm in the same position you're in," the professor answered. "They've held me prisoner ever since they found me."

"In a motel room by the university?"

Winslow nodded. "I went to the motel because my home was being watched. My wife saw me there the night she walked to our house with your husband. She came to get me, and when we left the motel, I thought we were getting away from Lieutenant Dickey. It wasn't until later that we discovered we were running from Sergeant Chambers."

"And of course when he did find out, it was just a little too late," Chambers said. He turned his attention back to Dickey. "What else do you know?"

"I know that you're a spy, and a thief, and a murderer, and you've been filling scientists full of truth serum to get their knowledge, and then you kill them."

"What made you suspicious of me?"

"You kept disappearing from your job and I kept wondering why. And then when I was in England on a seminar, I spotted you."

"You were in Europe at the same time Lieutenant Dickey was there?" Lorraine said to Chambers.

"Yes, except Lieutenant Dickey was there on official police business," Chambers replied. "I found my own way to get across."

"I knew you weren't supposed to be there, so I followed you," Dickey said. "You met Mrs. Winslow and had sex with her. Then you gave her some money and she gave you an envelope."

"Did you know what was in the envelope?" Jennifer asked.

"No. But I knew the amount of money he gave her had to be worth more than just sex."

"What else?" Chambers asked.

"I know that you've been impersonating me."

"When did you first suspect that?"

"I wondered if someone was impersonating me when these two . . . ladies . . . kept saying they saw me in places where I hadn't been. I figured it might be you when they said the Winslows followed me to your apartment, when I knew I hadn't been there."

"When did you know for sure?"

"For sure?"

"Yes, for sure, you idiot. When did you know for sure that I was impersonating you?"

"Today, in the laboratory, when you told Agent Addison of the FBI that I was with you when Dean MacRae was murdered. Since I wasn't with you, I suspected you must have known something about what happened there, and needed an alibi."

"Why would you say you were with the lieutenant if you were trying to get the dean's murder pinned on him?" Jennifer asked Chambers.

Dickey answered. "When the sergeant said he was with me, he was really in the lab, trying to extract information from Dean MacRae, and then murdering him and attempting to murder you."

Lorraine glared at Chambers. "You were one of the men who killed Dean MacRae?"

"I'm afraid so," Chambers confessed. There was no remorse in his voice.

"But the FBI agents said the man who ran away after Dean MacRae was killed, looked like Lieutenant Dickey."

"Correction. They said he had a bandage on his head. You were the ones who said the description fit Lieutenant Dickey."

"But you don't look like Lieutenant Dickey."

"I was able to look enough like him, especially from a distance. You don't spend twenty years in undercover work like I did without learning something about disguises."

Chambers pulled a fake mustache from a pocket and held it over his lip, then showed them a hairpiece and a white bandage. "You two made it even easier for me when you had your fight with him."

"Why did you have to kill Dean MacRae?"

Dickey answered for Chambers again. "For the same reason he kills everyone else. Because the dean was no longer of any use to him, and also because he might identify him. You were going to be next if you hadn't caused the explosion in the lab."

"When Agent Addison was finished interrogating the lieutenant in the lab, why didn't you leave when he did?" Lorraine asked Chambers.

"I had other business," he answered.

Dickey provided the information. "Mrs. Winslow was waiting for him in his car. They were going to her apartment to pick up Professor Winslow so that the sergeant could get the rest of the formula. Aroyo was holding him there."

"Her apartment?"

"She has her own place. She uses it to entertain."

"And I suppose you have been entertained there?"

"I've been there."

"Why did you go there today?"

Sergeant Chambers answered. "While you were following the lieutenant from the university to the apartment, he was following me and Mrs. Winslow. I was going to get rid of him eventually anyway because he knows too much, but when he walked into our hands, I decided to hang onto him."

"How did you know we were there?" Jennifer asked.

"When the others left, I waited inside to see if anyone else was around. That's when I spotted you two. When I followed you and saw you making your phone call, I figured you were calling the police. So I got in touch with the dispatcher and told him to relay all messages through me."

Chambers returned his attention to Dickey. "What else do you know?"

"I know that you killed Professor Reid and Professor Bentley, and Professor Smythe and Helmitten, and probably some other professors."

"If Sergeant Chambers killed Professor Reid and Professor Bentley, then how did Professor Winslow's fingerprints get on the hypodermic needles?" Lorraine asked.

"There were no fingerprints," Chambers replied. "Lieutenant Dickey was kind enough to leave me in charge of the investigation while he went off to play with Mrs. Winslow, and when the forensic team gave me their results, it was just a matter of going into the department's computer data files and adding the professors prints. Something else I learned during my years in undercover work."

"Why?"

"To give him time," Dickey said. "Using Professor Winslow's prints threw suspicion onto the professor and away from the sergeant who was the real murderer. It also let him use the police department to help him find the professor."

"What about the murder victim the Westland Police Department found out in the desert, that the FBI thought was Professor Winslow?"

"Same thing. After Sergeant Chambers knew where Professor Winslow was, he didn't need the police to look for him anymore, so he had Bill Aroyo produce an unrecognizable body, and gave them the professor's prints."

"The first night we met Mrs. Winslow, why did she go to the police station to report her husband missing if she already knew where he was?" Lorraine asked.

"She didn't know then, where her husband was," Dickey replied, "and since Sergeant Chambers also didn't know, he sent her to the police station to report a missing person."

"Why did Mrs. Winslow hire Jennifer?"

"To find her husband for the sergeant. But she also had another reason. She wanted Jennifer to find whoever it was she thought was trying to kill her."

"Her? I thought they were trying to kill the professor?"

"They were trying to kidnap the professor for his formula, and then they were going to kill him. But she also suspected that someone was attempting to kill her. That's why she was so frightened of me when she saw me at the police station. She had seen Sergeant Chambers hanging around her house disguised as me and driving the blue Chev, so when she saw me at the station, she was afraid."

Dickey looked at Mrs. Winslow. "You didn't know then that you were safe for the time being, or at least until the sergeant decided he had no more use for you."

"What?" Mrs. Winslow exclaimed. She stared at Sergeant Chambers. "Why?"

"Don't listen to him," Chambers responded. He glanced at Bill Aroyo who had suddenly become more aware of Mrs. Winslow.

"Why?" Mrs. Winslow asked again.

"Maybe he didn't want to worry you," Lieutenant Dickey interjected.

"I'm not going to kill you," Chambers answered. "So quit worrying."

"Who was watching us leave the parking lot at the police station the first night we met Mrs. Winslow," Lorraine asked, "and who was following the Winslows when we saw them leaving the Hursh Ranch?"

"That was the sergeant," Dickey answered. "Most of the time when you saw the blue Chev, he was driving it, disguised as me. He took it from the police compound and was keeping an eye on the Winslows so they didn't try to escape. The only times you saw me were when I was investigating the break-in at the College of Science, and your murders, and when you were soliciting me on the park bench at the university."

"You really thought I was a hooker?"

"A very nice hooker."

Lorraine was quiet while she considered the compliment.

Dickey grinned. "I was waiting for you to invite me somewhere to share an intimate . . . ."

"Why?"

"So I could arrest you for soliciting."

Jennifer interrupted. "Why wasn't Mrs. Winslow afraid of you at the university? When you left there, she appeared to be climbing all over you."

"She wasn't climbing all over me," Dickey replied. "She was afraid of me. She was checking my bandage and trying to figure out if it was me or someone impersonating me."

"So at that point, Mrs. Winslow wasn't afraid of the sergeant, who she didn't know was impersonating you, but she was afraid of you, who just wanted to have sex with her."

"I didn't have sex with Mrs. Winslow."

"What!!!! Really!!!! Why not????"

"I'm a cop. I was investigating her."

"Did you want to have sex with her?"

"Who wouldn't?"

"Did Mrs. Winslow want to have sex with you?"

"She wanted to have sex with everybody." Dickey nodded his head toward Lorraine. "Especially her husband."

"At the motel, did the Winslows know it wasn't you?"

"No. They couldn't be sure in the darkness. If it was me, the professor was sure he would be going to jail. If it was the imposter, he thought he would be kidnapped or killed. That's why they were considering shooting whoever it was they followed to Sergeant Chamber's apartment, until you and some passerbys interrupted them."

"Didn't the professor have to worry about Sergeant Chambers killing him?"

"No, not yet. He didn't know then that Sergeant Chambers was the imposter. Also, killing the professor would have ruined the sergeant's plans. He needed him alive, at least until he got the formula for the new truth serum. Of course, after that, he would no longer be of any use."

"How did Mrs. Winslow get rid of the Pontiac at her house?"

"Chambers. After you left him, he phoned and said you were coming. She distracted you by taking you to the kitchen at the other side of the house while Bill Ayoyo got rid of it. He took the professor with him."

"Why? If she was worried that someone was trying to kill them?"

"Not them. Just the professor. She still didn't know that Sergeant Chambers was eventually going to kill her too, so she handed the professor over to him."

Mrs. Winslow looked into Sergeant Chamber's eyes, searching for an answer.

"Quit worrying, I'm not going to kill you," he assured her once again. He glanced at Aroyo who was scratching his head and trying to figure out what was going on.

"What was Agent Hampson's role in all this?" Lorraine asked the lieutenant.

"He was sent by the FBI, supposedly to guard Mrs. Winslow, but also to get information from her."

"Did he?"

"Apparently not, although information appears to be about the only thing he didn't get from her. He was recuperating from Mrs. Winslow in the back bedroom while all this was going on, and didn't even know the professor was there."

"Who broke into the Winslows' house and tried to kill Hampson?"

"That was the sergeant and the terrorist that you killed in the science lab. They attempted to eliminate him because they thought he might have succeeded in getting some information, but when they heard him call the FBI they had to get away."

"What about Mrs. Winslow?"

"She went along willingly. She still didn't know what her eventual fate would be, and apparently still doesn't. But that's the way it is with people. They never know what their fate will be until it's too late."

Dickey looked at Mrs. Winslow.

Mrs. Winslow looked at Chambers. Worry lines were beginning to form on her face.

"Quit worrying," Chambers assured her one more time. "Your only fate is for you and me to escape to a tropical island and spend the rest of our lives in luxury."

Mrs. Winslow and Chambers both glanced at Bill Aroyo, whose face was beginning to fold into worry lines of its own.

"You'll find out what your fate is when you see Jack," Dickey informed Mrs. Winslow.

"Jack? What part does Jack play in all this?" Lorraine asked.

"I've suspected his involvement for quite a while," Dickey answered, "ever since I saw him talking to Sergeant Chambers in England."

"Jack can tell them himself when he gets here," Chambers said. "I'm sure he's looking forward to seeing them again. I'm also sure he'll have some questions about what they've learned about him."

"That's why the sergeant gave me the truth serum," Dickey said. "He wants to find out if I told the FBI everything I've discovered about them, and the secrets they've been stealing and selling."

"Well, did you?" Chambers demanded.

"No."

"You told them absolutely nothing?"

"Absolutely nothing."

"Why not?" Lorraine asked.

"With my record for harassing people, I figured nobody would believe me. I wanted to get an air tight case before I presented it."

"I decided to impersonate you for the same reason," Chambers said. "Nobody likes you, nobody would believe you, and nobody is going to miss you when you disappear out in the desert. Are you sure you didn't give anyone else this information?"

"I'm sure."

"You know what this means, don't you?"

"The truth?"

"Yes, you idiot, the truth."

"It means you think you can kill me without worrying that I told anyone about you."

Chambers waved the barrel of his gun at Jennifer and Lorraine. "And them?"

"It means you think you can kill them too."

"I think I liked it better when everybody was lying to us," Jennifer muttered.

Chambers looked suspiciously at Dickey. "Why do you keep saying . . . I think . . . I can kill you and them? You just said that you didn't tell anybody what you knew about me."

"I didn't."

"Then what the hell did you do?"

"I wrote it down."

"Shit." The muscles in Sergeant Chamber's face tightened and he rubbed the back of his neck nervously with his hand. "Where?"

"On a piece of paper."

"I know that, you imbecile. I mean where did you put the paper you wrote it on?"

"At the police station."

Chamber's teeth were gritting. "Exactly where at the police station did you put it?"

Dickey took a deep breath. "In my desk, in the bottom left hand drawer, at the back, under the files, in a large brown envelope . . . ."

"You couldn't have left the information there about Dean MacRae's murder because you didn't go back to the station after you left the university. You said you followed me."

"That's right. I just wrote down everything else."

"Like what?"

"Like you buying secret information from Mrs. Winslow when you were in Europe, that she got from Professor Smythe and Professor Helmitten during sex. I have pictures of you buying it. I also have pictures of you having sex with her."

"What the hell for?"

Dickey smiled. "That was for me. I like to look at them every once in awhile."

Chambers glared at him. "Your nosiness is going to cost you your life. What do you think about that?"

"I'm not very happy about it," Dickey replied.

Chambers pointed a thumb in the direction of Jennifer and Lorraine. "It's also going to cost your two lady friends here their lives."

Dickey smiled again. "I think I feel happier now."

TWENTY-THREE

"What did you do with the photographs you took of Mrs. Winslow and me?" Chambers asked Lieutenant Dickey.

Dickey took another deep breath. "They are at the precinct, with the letter, in the desk, in the bottom left hand drawer, at the back, under the files, in a large brown envelope . . . ."

"I know where the envelope is, you asshole," Chambers shouted. "Now, is there anything else that you think might interest me, that you think I should know, that you think might somehow even remotely affect me?"

"No. Except . . . ."

"Yes?" Chambers waited for a reply.

Dickey smiled crookedly. "I think you're an asshole too."

"I'm going back to town," Chambers said to Mrs. Winslow. "If I can get that envelope with the pictures and Dickey's notes, maybe we can stay in the country a while longer. Otherwise we'll have to get the hell out."

Mrs. Winslow still looked fearful. "Why don't we get out anyway, while we can . . . ?"

Chambers cut her off. "Because there's still more we can obtain here, and more we can sell. You can suddenly show up and say you were hiding in fear for your life, and your husband is supposed to be dead, so nobody is going to miss him. It will make things a bit messier, but the lieutenant and his two lady friends will just have to disappear out in the desert with him."

"I still don't like it," Mrs. Winslow complained.

"I don't care what you like," Chambers snapped. "You will do as you're told."

"Or you'll end up like Dean MacRae and Professor Reid and Professor Bentley and your two husbands in Europe," Lorraine informed her.

"And the way your present husband is going to end up," Jennifer said.

"And the way you're going to end up," Lieutenant Dickey added.

"Shut up," Chambers barked. He gestured toward a storage room at one side of the laboratory. "Get in there," he said to Jennifer and Lorraine. "You too," he ordered Dickey and the professor.

When he was satisfied that his four prisoners were securely locked away, Chambers headed for the hallway and the stairs to the cave where his car was parked. "We'll find out what they know when I get back," he said to Mrs. Winslow.

He turned to Aroyo who was still leaning against the wall. "But it's not necessary to keep them alive. If anybody tries to get away, or even makes a wrong move, shoot them. And I mean *anybody*."

Aroyo's eyes drifted from the storage room to Mrs. Winslow and back to the storage room. The worried expression he had on his face was mixed with some confusion.

It was quiet in the laboratory and the storage room for a few seconds after Chambers had gone. The silence was broken by Lieutenant Dickey.

"I think you're beautiful," he said to Lorraine.

"Thank you, I suppose," Lorraine replied.

"I think you're the most beautiful and sexy creature I've ever met."

"I didn't know truth serum could be so sickening," Jennifer muttered.

Dickey gave Jennifer half a sneer. "I don't like you."

He turned his attention back to Lorraine. "You, I like a little. I'm almost sorry I didn't get to know you a little better. We might have . . . ."

"Be serious," Jennifer scoffed. "You're a pervert, and you're locked in a cupboard, and Chambers is going to kill you in about two hours, if the truth serum doesn't kill you first."

"The truth serum won't kill him," Professor Winslow answered. "This is my serum."

Dickey gave Jennifer a triumphant grin. "See, the truth serum won't kill us. They'll have to shoot us, or find some other way to get rid of us."

"Is that supposed to make us feel better?"

"It means we have two hours to come up with something," Lorraine whispered.

"Shut up in there," Bill Aroyo ordered.

Jennifer held a finger in the air and pointed it at Dickey who was ogling Lorraine. "I have an idea. Do you think Mrs. Winslow could be persuaded to have sex?"

"Pfft, of course," Dickey replied with a positive snort. "When I took her home, she . . . ."

Jennifer stopped him. "I don't mean you. Do you think she could be persuaded to have sex with Bill Aroyo?"

Dickey wasn't given a chance to answer.

In a voice that was loud enough for Aroyo and Mrs. Winslow to hear, Jennifer whispered, "You know, I kind of wish that Bill Aroyo and I . . . you know . . . that Bill and I could have met in some other time and place . . . I think we might have . . . I think we could have . . . I think that he and I . . . ."

"He is one very handsome and sexy cowboy," Lorraine answered, also in a whisper loud enough for Aroyo and Mrs. Winslow to hear. "If you don't want him, maybe he and I . . . maybe he and I could . . . ."

"The man is ugly as a pig," Dickey chimed in.

"Shut up," the two women hissed at once.

"I wonder what he has under those tight blue jeans of his," Jennifer wondered out loud.

Lorraine exhaled as sensually as she could. "Do you think that all that could be a . . . do you think that all that could possibly be a . . . his . . . ?"

Jennifer finished the statement. "It's either that or he has a heck of a big gun in there."

Through the small window in the door, they could see Mrs. Winslow running her tongue over her lips. She gazed at Aroyo for a few seconds and then slowly swayed over to where he was standing. She put her arms around his arm and pressed her body against his as she whispered into his ear.

The cowboy nodded as she spoke. By the time they had finished their conversation, he was also licking his lips.

He motioned toward the storage room. "What about them?"

"They won't be going anywhere," Mrs. Winslow replied.

She crossed the floor and checked the door to make sure it was locked. Satisfied that the prisoners could not get loose, she walked back across the room to Aroyo, took him by an arm, and led him into the hallway.

"So much for your plan to get rid of them," Lorraine said to Jennifer. "It was a plan, wasn't it?"

"It was a plan."

"I'm hoping you have another plan to get us out of here."

"I have something a lot better than another plan, thanks to Professor Winslow who slipped me a key, and a lock that can be opened from either side."

Jennifer had already begun to insert the key into the lock and was gently shifting it back and forth. It moved with a click and she slowly pushed the door open.

"I think we'd better leave the lieutenant right where he is, for his safety, and ours," Lorraine suggested, "at least for now. She turned to Dickey. "Can we trust you to stay in there?"

"No," Dickey replied.

"Why not?"

"Because, after I get out of here, I'm going to have you both arrested again . . . ."

"You're certain . . . ?"

"Would I lie to you?"

Lorraine locked the door again.

"Make sure he stays in there," she instructed Professor Winslow.

They cautiously made their way out of the laboratory and down the hallway. Through a partly opened door, they could make out what appeared to be living quarters. Inside, Mrs. Winslow and Aroyo had begun to remove their clothes. Mrs. Winslow was caressing Aroyo's chest.

Aroyo stopped her. "We'd better go back to the lab and check the prisoners one more time, before we . . . ."

Mrs. Winslow continued to play with his chest. "There isn't any hurry. They're going to stay locked up."

"I'll tell you what our hurry is," he reminded her. "If Chambers comes back and discovers us in here instead of out there watching them, we'll be in more trouble than we care to get into. And if they escape, we might find ourselves dead in the desert with them."

"Oh, all right," she relented. She kissed the tip of her finger and touched it to his lips. "We'll make sure they're not going anywhere, and then . . . ."

"Can you take care of Mrs. Winslow?" Jennifer whispered to Lorraine outside the door.

"You bet I can," Lorraine snarled.

"Then I'll take care of Aroyo."

"How?"

"The same way I took care of Dickey the first night we met him."

Jennifer held up her purse which she had picked up on the way out of the room. She was swinging it back and forth by the straps.

Lorraine was about to remind her that she no longer had her gun in the handbag, when they heard the couple inside moving toward the door. They flattened themselves against the wall on either side and waited. Mrs. Winslow came out first. The cowboy was close behind.

Lorraine grabbed Mrs. Winslow's arm, spun her around, and drove a fist into her jaw. At the same time, Jennifer swung her purse and slammed it against Aroyo's forehead.

The purse made a loud thud as it connected, very much like the leather and metal and bone when she struck Lieutenant Dickey a few days earlier, except it wasn't metal. It had a different sound.

The forward momentum the cowboy had attained when he came out through the doorway caused his feet to fly ahead and into the air. His body lifted off the floor, seemed to hang there for a moment, and then he dropped. He didn't move after that.

Jennifer quickly checked to make sure he was unconscious, then she looked at Lorraine who was sitting on top of Mrs. Winslow, her fist poised and ready to strike again if she moved.

"What the hell did you hit him with?" Lorraine asked in astonishment. "You can't have your gun. Chambers took it."

Jennifer grinned proudly. "No. But I do have my purse . . . and this." She upended her handbag and shook out a large rock. It made a noisy thunk as it hit the floor. "I picked it up on the stairs when Sergeant Chambers was taking us up here. Lieutenant Dickey gave me the idea."

"I didn't hear Dickey mention a rock."

"In a way he did. When he had us arrested for assault and prostitution, he said we hit him with a brick. I figured if it was good enough for him, it would be good enough for this guy."

Lorraine nodded her approval. "I just hope you didn't kill him."

Jennifer retrieved the unconscious cowboy's gun and then nudged him with her foot. When he stirred awake, they ordered him and Mrs. Winslow back into the laboratory.

Professor Winslow offered to watch for signs of Sergeant Chambers returning. When he had taken his position, and Jennifer and Lorraine were sure that Chambers was not about to come back, they unlocked the door to the storage room where Lieutenant Dickey was patiently waiting.

"Do you think it's safe to turn him loose?" Lorraine asked.

"What about it?" Jennifer said to Dickey. "Is it safe to let you out of there?"

"No."

"Why not?"

"I told you, I'm going to have you arrested again. There is a still little matter of you interfering with my police investigation . . . ."

"We didn't interfere all that much . . . ."

"And breaking into the Winslows' residence."

"Oh . . . ."

"Could we get out of here before Chambers comes

back," Lorraine said. "He might have some other friends we don't know about."

"What about it?" Jennifer asked Dickey. "Does Sergeant Chambers have some other friends we don't know about?"

"Yes."

"Who?"

"His bowling team."

"Let me put it another way," Jennifer moaned. "Does Sergeant Chambers have any other business associates who happen to kill people and are involved in international spy organizations, that steal secrets and sell them to enemy governments?"

"Yes."

"Who, you asshole?"

"You're beginning to sound like the sergeant," Lorraine said. "Let me try." She moved closer to Dickey. "What is the name of the person or persons that could be acquaintances of Sergeant Chambers, that could also be involved in spying and selling secrets to enemy governments, that we might need to worry about?"

"Jack."

"Jack O'Dell," Jennifer exclaimed. "I knew he was involved."

"Jack Hursh."

"What??!!"

"Jack Hursh," Dickey repeated. "The first initial in J.D. Hursh's name stands for Jack."

"J.D. Hursh? The owner of this ranch?"

"Yep," the lieutenant replied with a sense of pride and accomplishment that the professor's truth serum had given him. "Sergeant Chamber's acquaintance who is involved in spying and selling secrets to the enemy is J.D. Hursh, the owner of this ranch."

"How do you know that?"

"I followed Mrs. Winslow in Europe one time after Chambers had sex with her. When they were finished, he gave her a package. I didn't know for sure what was in it, but I followed her anyway. Then she met J.D. Hursh, although I didn't know who he was at the time. She gave him the package and he gave her another package. I discovered later that the first package contained a secret experiment they were selling, and the second package contained the sergeant's payment and instructions for dealing with his next victim."

"How did you know they were involved in spying and selling secrets, and not just giving each other gifts or something?" Jennifer asked.

"Because when I got back here, I checked around like you did, except I was able to check further. I discovered that Sergeant Chambers had been in Europe when both murders were committed. I also discovered that J.D. Hursh made frequent flights to Europe in his private plane, and before at least two of his trips he met with Chambers. I suspected each flight probably carried some top secrets with it, and

Chambers too, when there was information to be obtained from science professors and murders to be taken care of."

"You suspected right."

The voice came from the other side of the room, away from where the professor had been watching for Sergeant Chambers to return.

It belonged to J.D. Hursh.

TWENTY-FOUR

Hursh looked at the disheveled clothes of Mrs. Winslow and the open shirt of Bill Aroyo. "What happened here?" he asked.

Mrs. Winslow pointed to Jennifer and Lorraine. "They jumped us when we weren't looking. There wasn't anything I could do."

"I can imagine," Hursh replied. "Chambers told me the position everyone was in when he left. The situation appears to have changed."

"They got loose somehow. I don't know how," Mrs. Winslow continued. "Please believe me."

Hursh ignored her and instead motioned with his gun toward Jennifer and Lorraine. "Get over there beside the professor," he ordered. Then he returned his attention to Mrs. Winslow.

"I'm afraid you've become a bit of a liability," he

advised her. "You give your body away a little too easily. I also have to wonder if you give information to the wrong people just as easily."

"I wouldn't, J.D.," she pleaded again. "Sergeant Chambers and I are the only ones who know about you, and we would never talk."

"I know about you," Lieutenant Dickey offered. He nodded his head at Jennifer and Lorraine. "And so do they. We'll all talk."

Jennifer grimaced. "I wish we had left him in the storage room."

"How long does your truth serum last?" Lorraine asked the professor.

"It depends on the person," he replied. "With most people, it usually wears off in an hour or so."

"It won't take that long for you to give me the formula for your truth serum," Hursh said. "Get over here and sit down." He turned to Dickey. "Where's the serum they used on you?"

"There on the table," Dickey replied as he helpfully pointed to a glass vial.

"How much did they give you?"

"Half?"

"Half the vial?"

"Half a teaspoon."

"That's all?"

"That's all it takes," Professor Winslow answered.

"Would you like to give yourself the serum or would you prefer I give it to you?" Hursh asked.

Professor Winslow didn't comment. He picked up the vial, poured some serum into a spoon, put it to his lips, and swallowed.

"How long does it take to work?" Hursh asked.

"A few seconds," the professor responded.

"Is it working now?"

"It's beginning to work."

"Is it possible for you to lie to me?"

"No."

Hursh reached inside his coat and pulled out a piece of paper and a pen. "Then start writing, Professor," he ordered. "I want you to write down every ingredient and the amount of it that went into making your truth serum."

"And don't leave anything out," he added, "because I already know most of what's in there. Do you understand?"

"I understand," the professor answered as he began to write. "I won't leave anything out."

After Professor Winslow had written for several minutes and put down the pen, Hursh picked up the paper and read it.

"What's this?" he asked, pointing to one of the ingredients.

"Nitrodyhydrocinoxide."

"What is it?" he asked.

"It's an industrial chemical that Dean MacRae discovered."

"What does it do?"

"It stimulates your body so you want to talk, and it lowers your inhibitions, all at the same time. The formula won't work without it. But you have to be careful using it, because . . . ."

"What are the ingredients of this chemical?"

"I don't know. Only Dean MacRae knew."

Hursh placed the barrel of the gun against the side of the professor's head. "What are the ingredients?" he demanded again.

"I don't know. Only Dean MacRae knew."

"Where did MacRae keep this chemical?"

"In the lab where we worked."

"Is it still there?"

"No. Sergeant Chambers told my wife that those two ladies destroyed it."

A note of optimism crossed the faces of Jennifer and Lorraine. It quickly changed when Hursh pointed his gun at them.

"But I have another bottle," Winslow added.

Hursh returned his attention to the professor. "Where is it?"

The professor gestured toward a cabinet in a corner of the room. "In there."

Hursh walked to the cabinet, removed a small bottle, and returned.

"Is this it?"

The professor nodded.

"Is there any more?"

"No."

"This is all there is?"

"That's all there is."

Hursh set the bottle on the table in front of him. "Could you test this and tell me what the ingredients are?"

"Probably."

"Could anyone else, if they knew what they were doing?"

"Yes."

"So I don't need you anymore."

"No."

Hursh waved his gun around the room at the others. "Or them?"

"I suppose not."

"Good."

Hursh picked up the vial of truth serum and the bottle of nitrodyhydrocinoxide. He slipped one into each pocket of his coat.

"Let's go," he ordered. "You people have a date with Sergeant Chambers. He's waiting for you in a ravine a short distance from here."

He smiled at Mrs. Winslow. "Especially you."

"Why didn't he come with you?" Mrs. Winslow asked.

"Because he's dead," Lieutenant Dickey informed her before Hursh could answer.

"Hmm," Hursh said as he looked at Dickey with amused admiration. "I didn't know that truth serum could also allow you to see through walls."

"I don't need truth serum to tell me that scum kill their own when they're no longer of any use to them," Dickey answered.

"So the truth serum has worn off?"

"No, it hasn't worn off," Dickey replied. "I just recognize scum when I see it."

"We'll see if you recognize a rock slide when you see it," Hursh said with a smirk. "Let's go for that walk."

He pointed to a doorway that led to the outside of the building and ordered everyone out. "You too," he said to Mrs. Winslow when she began to plead once again for him to let her go.

They left the building and followed a narrow path that wound through the rocks until it ended abruptly at the edge of a cliff above the ravine. At the bottom, a hundred feet below, they could see the body of Sergeant Chambers.

Lorraine had stopped to take off a shoe and pour some sand from it. "Why did you kill him?" she asked as she straightened up.

"Because he knew me," Hursh answered. "After the sergeant killed Professor Reid and Professor Bentley, he and Aroyo and Mrs. Winslow and the professor were the only people who could tie me to the thefts and the murders. Of course, that was before you two came along."

"Professor Bentley worked for you?"

"You might say that. Bentley was instructed to get

the formula from Professor Winslow and Professor Reid. He wasn't very good at it. He tried learning the formula by working with them, but didn't get anything. So he developed a sexual relationship with Professor Reid."

"Bentley wasn't any good at that either," Hursh said, "so Sergeant Chambers used the old truth serum on Reid. Unfortunately the serum killed her before he got all the information. Bentley made a break for it, but the sergeant caught him in his office and gave him some serum to see if he knew anything that would help. He didn't, and by now his usefulness was over, so he was given a bullet."

"You know," he said, "I'm sorry you got involved in this. I really liked you. I wish there was some way I could let you go, but of course there isn't."

"I don't suppose it would do us any good to suggest we could put in a word for you if you let us go, would it?" Jennifer asked.

Lieutenant Dickey interrupted. "It might make the difference between serving life in jail or only getting ninety-nine years."

Professor Winslow decided to help. "And we could testify that you're just a mass murderer and an enemy agent who is stealing secrets and undermining the security of the country."

"We could all testify," Lieutenant Dickey added. He pointed to Jennifer and Lorraine. "Even they could testify."

"I'm beginning to like that truth serum less and less," Lorraine remarked.

Hursh's expression suddenly changed. Before, except for holding the gun on them, and reminding them of their fate, he had acted almost friendly. But now his face was growing cold and taut.

"Get over there," he growled, grabbing Dickey by the collar of his coat and pushing until the lieutenant was teetering on the brink of the ravine. He was about to shoot him in the back and shove him over when a voice from a distant hill top caused him to stop.

"Mr. Hursh!"

Hursh released his grip and turned to search the hills above for the source of the sound.

"Don't do it Mr. Hursh!"

Hursh spun around in the other direction, trying to determine where the voice was coming from.

The distraction gave Lorraine enough time to throw the handful of sand she had picked up when she stopped to empty her shoe. It struck Hursh in the face and for an instant he was blinded.

Hursh stumbled, then regained his equilibrium and stepped in the direction where he thought they were standing. His foot caught a rock at the edge of the cliff and he tripped. For a moment, he balanced in the air, then he lost his footing and tumbled into the gorge. He slid down the steep embankment and came to rest beside the body of Sergeant Chambers.

He staggered to his feet and wiped the sand from his

face and eyes until he could partially see again, then looked around for his gun. He picked it up and began to claw his way back up the side of the cliff.

He had only gone a few steps when a long, slow, popping, rumbling sound began to rise from the floor of the canyon. The pops gradually grew louder and closer together until they filled the gulch with echos.

He looked around in confusion for the source of the noise. When he realized it was coming from the bottle of nitrodyhydrocinoxide in his own coat pocket, he frantically tried to pull it out.

Unable to extract the container, he dropped the gun and began to peel off his coat. The popping continued to echo from one side of the gorge to the other, then just as he had removed his arms from the jacket and was about to throw it away, the chemical gave one long last final pop and exploded.

There was silence for a moment after the blast, then another sound, not at all like the popping, could be heard. It rumbled beneath the earth as the edges of the ravine shook and slowly began to pour their sand and rocks down on top of him.

A cloud of dust rose out of the ravine and drifted above the group of people standing at the edge. Lorraine and Jennifer held Lieutenant Dickey and waited, hoping that the rest of the canyon wall would not give way. When the earth finally stopped shaking, they cautiously approached the rim and looked over.

There was no sign of either Hursh or Chambers at the bottom. They had been completely buried by the tons of rock and earth that slid down on top of them. The only evidence that there had even been a slide was the dust which had not yet settled, and a cloud of bluish white fizz that rose out of the rocks.

They moved away from the edge and searched the hills above for the source of the voice that had called out J.D. Hursh's name. A cowboy, his rifle cradled in his arms, sat astride a horse on an embankment overlooking the ravine.

"Jack?" Jennifer exclaimed.

Jack O'Dell nudged his horse with his heels. He guided it down the hill, stopped for a moment at the edge of the ravine where Hursh had disappeared, then rode toward them.

"That could be us down there if it hadn't been for you," Lorraine said. "Thank you Jack. You saved our lives."

Jennifer looked suspiciously at the cowboy. "You did . . . save our lives . . . didn't you?"

Jack grimaced. "Don't remind me."

"How did you know we were here?" Lorraine asked.

"After I talked to you the other night, I decided to have a look around," Jack answered. "I saw some old laboratory equipment outside one of these buildings. They hadn't been used since World War Two, and most of the equipment had been removed. Someone made the mistake of bringing in new equipment and then discarding the old equipment where it could be seen."

As Jack spoke, a helicopter appeared on the horizon. "I took the liberty of calling your boyfriend at the FBI to let him know we were here," he explained as it landed.

Agent Addison was among the people on board. "Are you all right?" he called out to them as he approached.

"We're all right," Lorraine answered. She turned her attention to Jack. "How did you know that Jennifer had gone out with Agent Addison?"

Addison answered before Jack could. "We've been investigating since we heard about the murders in Europe and then here. We suspected it involved the Winslows, but we didn't know how. We also didn't know the lab was here on the ranch until you two snooped around and Jack talked to you."

Addison hesitated, then continued. "When Agent O'Dell saw the discarded equipment, he investigated and let me know what he had found."

Lorraine and Jennifer looked open mouthed at Jack.

"Did you say . . . Agent . . . O'Dell?" Jennifer stammered. "You mean that you . . . he . . . ?"

"Yep," Addison responded with a wide grin. "Meet Agent Jack O'Dell of the Federal Bureau of Investigation."

"Temporary agent," Jack corrected him. "I think I'm about ready to go back to being just a cowboy."

"How did you come to suspect that J.D. Hursh was involved?" Lorraine asked. She motioned toward Jack. "And how did he get involved?"

"We found some top secret materials in a routine inspection of a shipment that was being loaded on one of Hursh's airplanes," Addison replied, "so we figured it had to come from someplace on the ranch. Anyway, we asked Jack to help us."

"We suspected it might be one of the workers at the experimental lab, the one you stumbled into when we were chasing you," Jack said. "We didn't know it was Mr. Hursh, until today. We also didn't know about Aroyo, or Sergeant Chambers."

"How does Lieutenant Dickey fit into all this?" Jennifer asked.

Addison answered. "We're not certain. We really think he's just a somewhat overzealous cop who was trying to do his job. We were hoping you could help us out on that one."

Lorraine looked at Dickey. "If you did decide he was involved, what would happen to him?"

Addison rubbed his chin. "Oh, I'd say he'd get about fifty years in the slammer."

"Fifty years?" Jennifer said.

"Did you say . . . fifty years?" Lorraine repeated.

"At least."

"Really?"

Jennifer took over, partly to preserve Lorraine's reputation, and partly because she had more experience sitting in a jail cell.

"Well," she said, "we did see a man resembling Lieutenant Dickey's description who was hanging around the science building. And we saw someone resembling the lieutenant out here at the ranch, at least twice, and at the professor's house, and at his motel room. And the professor was afraid of him, and he always seemed to be nearby every time a murder was committed. And your men did see someone who looked like him running away from the science lab. And he was with Mrs. Winslow and Bill Aroyo today, and they were carrying suitcases, and we thought they were on the run and leaving town."

"I was not on the run," Dickey declared, "and they damn well know it. I was a prisoner here, and they didn't see me out here, they saw . . . ."

"Perhaps if we were to ask Mrs. Winslow?" Jennifer suggested, "I'm sure she could clarify what the lieutenant's role is in all this."

"This whole thing was Lieutenant Dickey's idea," Mrs. Winslow said. "I was just an innocent bystander until he forced me to go with him. He threatened me. He took advantage of me. He tried to have sex with me. He . . . ."

"You wouldn't lie to us, would you?" Jennifer said.

"Of course not," Mrs. Winslow replied. "For twenty years, the lieutenant and I . . . ."

"I think we'd better take them both in for questioning," Addison decided. "At least until we get to the bottom of this." He grabbed the still complaining lieutenant by the arm and led him away. Other agents escorted Mrs. Winslow and Aroyo.

"I wish we could have given some of your new truth serum to your wife," Jennifer said to Professor Winslow. "I'd like to hear the truth from her, just once."

"It wouldn't do you any good," the professor answered. "I already gave her some during one of my experiments. She still lied her head off."

"You mean it doesn't work on everybody?"

"Almost everybody. Except liars. If you're the type of person who tends to tell the truth, then you'll continue to tell the truth under the serum, about everything, even things you wouldn't normally talk about. But If you're a compulsive liar, like my wife, then you'll continue to lie. It was just one of the little bugs I wasn't able to work out."

"I don't think we have to worry about national security then," Lorraine commented. "The serum would never work on politicians. So it did have some faults."

"Yes. I was attempting to solve them, but now with Dean MacRae's nitrodyhydrocinoxide gone, I guess I'll never know for sure if I could have done it."

Jack placed a foot in a stirrup and swung himself onto his horse. "I'm curious," he said, "how come you let them take the lieutenant away, when you knew he was innocent?"

"Because he's a dirty rotten low life," Jennifer answered. "And he had us thrown in jail. Why didn't you say something?"

"Same reason," Jack said. "I've met your lieutenant before. And I've also had the pleasure of spending a night in one of his jail cells."

TWENTY-FIVE

It was six-thirty in the morning.

"Why does your best friend also have to be a private investigator?" George asked Lorraine through bleary eyes as he opened the door for Jennifer. "Why couldn't you have picked a high school teacher or a secretary or somebody like that? Somebody who keeps normal hours."

"Because they aren't as much fun," Jennifer said. She took a look down her blouse as she spoke. "I have some news for you about the new owner of J.D. Hursh's business empire."

"You might as well come on in," George invited. "You can tell Lorraine all about it while I make some coffee. What are you doing getting up at this hour anyway?"

"I didn't just get up," Jennifer replied. "I've been

out celebrating my date's inheritance. We just came back from Vancouver. We flew there on his private jet."

"Agent Addison inherited a private jet?" Lorraine exclaimed.

Jennifer shook her head. "Not Agent Addison." She moved to the window and pulled back the curtain so that Lorraine could see outside. Leaning against a pickup truck was Jack O'Dell.

"Your date is Jack O'Dell?"

"Yep."

"Jack O'Dell inherited a jet?"

"He inherited more than that," Jennifer said. "He got three jets, fourteen ships, a few ranches, some manufacturing plants, stocks and bonds, plus a whole bunch of other stuff."

"Jack O'Dell inherited J.D. Hursh's estate?"

"He got the whole thing. Apparently Hursh didn't have any relatives, so he left everything to Jack. And here's the nice part. It's all paid for, thanks to the international crime syndicate that Hursh was involved with. They had paid it off as part of their deal with J.D."

"How come you went out with him?" Lorraine asked. "Because he's rich now, right? You went out with him just because he owns three jet planes?"

"Of course not. I would have gone out with him even if he owned only one jet plane."

"I thought you hated him."

"I did."

"Then how come you went out with him?"

"He asked me. And you were right. He said I remind him of one of his old movie hero's sidekick's horse. I think it must be the cowboy in him."

"What does Jack know about the professor and the truth serum?"

"Everything, now. Well, we sort of figured it out together."

"That's why you went out with him, isn't it. To get information."

"That, and dinner."

"Did he tell you how Sergeant Chambers got involved with Hursh?"

"Apparently they've been working together for years, although the FBI didn't know it was them. They just suspected it was someone from the Westland area. When Chambers was working undercover, he discovered Hursh was delivering secrets to foreign governments in his private jet, and instead of turning him in, he went to work for him and began to carry out assignments."

"What was Hursh's motive? He was a rich man, so he didn't need the money. And he was supposedly very patriotic."

"As it turns out, Hursh wasn't rich, or patriotic. His father was, but he wasn't. When J.D. inherited all of his father's wealth, he almost immediately began to lose it because of gambling debts and bad business decisions. He wasn't used to working. He was a philanderer and he didn't want the responsibilities of the businesses, but he did want the money."

"So he turned to selling secrets?"

"Eventually. He wasn't paying enough attention to his holdings and was in danger of losing most of them through bankruptcies and takeovers by competitors. So he made a deal with an international spy network that buys and sells secrets, much like crime families deal in drugs. They agreed to put up the money to pay off his creditors, and in return he agreed to go to work for them."

"By delivering top secret information?"

"Deliveries were one way. He traveled to countries in Western Europe quite often. He also visited other countries around the world. And when he didn't, his planes and ships frequently did. They were used to move stolen documents and chemical experiments. The FBI found hidden compartments that were used for that purpose. Of course, he didn't use his private plane just for smuggling. It also transported Chambers to carry out his assignments. They're still searching for his victims."

"What was Mrs. Winslow's role in all this?"

"A courier, delivering messages, documents, chemical discoveries, anything Hursh told her to. As far as everyone else was concerned, she just liked to sleep around. Actually she did sleep around. You could say she was one lady who really did enjoy her job."

"And Professor Winslow?"

"Just a scientist. He's lucky to be alive. Hursh found out he was on the verge of uncovering the new type of truth serum and wanted to get his hands on it. He planned all along to kill him once he had the serum."

"What's Lieutenant Dickey doing?"

"He's on leave from the police force while they try to figure out what to do with him."

"How long was he in jail?"

"Just overnight, although Agent Addison wouldn't have minded keeping him there longer. It seems he's also experienced Dickey's methods. Addison did one good thing though. He had a restraining order put out against the lieutenant."

"Why would Addison have to be protected from Lieutenant Dickey?"

"Not him. Us. Dickey kept threatening to arrest us and lock us up again. Finally, Addison convinced him that if we ended up in jail, he would be right in there alongside us."

"Yuk, not alongside us."

"You know what I mean. If Dickey even comes anywhere close to us, we just have to blow the whistle, and in he goes."

"Kind of makes me want to get close to him. How's Mrs. Winslow doing?"

"Fine," Jennifer said. "I saw her yesterday. She offered us another ten thousand dollars to prove her innocence and get her out of jail."

"Us?"

"You and me."

"You've got to be kidding."

"Does this mean you don't want to help me prove her innocence?"

"The woman is an accessory to murder, four or five times over, or more. How can you even think about getting her out of jail?"

"Of course you're right," Jennifer admitted. "I've already told her we wouldn't accept the money."

"Good."

Jennifer pulled a piece of paper from her purse.

"What's that?" Lorraine asked suspiciously.

"It's a check for twenty thousand dollars. Mrs. Winslow said she didn't blame us for not accepting ten."

"Are you going to do it?"

"Of course not. What kind of a person do you think I am."

"Let me see that." Lorraine took the check and examined it. Across it, in large letters, was printed, "Non Sufficient Funds."

"What about the other two checks she gave you?"

"They were non sufficient funds too. I wasn't fast enough getting to the bank."

"Where did her five hundred and eighty thousand dollars go?"

"Search me. She moved it to another bank, or out of the country. Even the police can't find it."

Lorraine smiled. "Oh well, you always have Jack's jet planes."

"You're right." Jennifer looked out the window once again at O'Dell, then began to walk toward the door.

"Wait a minute," George called out. "How many husbands did Mrs. Winslow have, and what happened to them?"

"At least two or three, besides the ones we know about. They were all murdered. According to her, she didn't know why. She thought she was just an unlucky widow. Of course, the way she lies, we might never know for sure exactly what her role was or how much she knew."

"Let me get this straight," George said. "Lieutenant Dickey and Professor Winslow and Jack O'Dell, who you thought might be guilty, were really innocent."

"Yes."

"And J.D. Hursh and Sergeant Chambers, who you thought were innocent, were really guilty."

"She thought they were innocent," Lorraine said, pointing her finger at Jennifer. "I thought they could be guilty."

"You thought everybody could be guilty," Jennifer reminded her.

"So did you." Lorraine pointed a finger at Jack. "Including him. Why are you really here?"

"We just came to let you know we were flying to Niagara Falls for the weekend," Jennifer said.

"You can't be getting married already."

"No, silly. We dropped by to ask if you wanted to come with us."

George looked at Lorraine and then at Jennifer. "No thanks. I figure with you in Niagara Falls, and Mrs. Winslow in jail, and Dickey with a restraining order against him, I should be able to spend some time with my wife."

They were interrupted by the telephone ringing. Lorraine answered it.

"Who would be calling at this hour?" George asked. "It can't be Jennifer, unless she's hired someone to bother us when she's not here."

"It was the prosecutor's office," Lorraine said. "They need me to come in early. Apparently I've been chosen to prosecute Mrs. Winslow, and I have to meet with her and her court appointed lawyer to take a deposition. Since she has no money, or so she says, they had to appoint a lawyer for her."

"I'd sure hate to be in his shoes," George remarked.

"You are sweety," Lorraine informed him. "You're the lawyer that's been chosen."

* * * * * * * *

acadiascale.com

**Acadia Scale Press books
may be purchased at
amazon.com
barnes&noble.com
Barnes & Noble Book Stores
Borders Book Stores
borders.com
and other book and gift stores.**

**Most stores will be happy to order books
if they do not have a copy in stock.
Stores may order through
INGRAM BOOK COMPANY
and other book distributors.**

www.ingramcontent.com/pod-product-compliance
Lightning Source LLC
Chambersburg PA
CBHW021456240626
47154CB00002B/391